HEAD OVER HEELS FOR THE HOLIDAYS

JENNIFER BERNARD

CHAPTER ONE

About four months before Christmas ...

ABOVE ALL THINGS, Maya Badger prided herself on keeping her cool. All of Lost Harbor would most likely agree that she had no trouble bringing order and authority to any situation, including drunken brawls and stray moose wandering into traffic. That was why she was the youngest police chief in Lost Harbor history.

But she'd never faced someone quite like the extremely fit man in the Lost Harbor holding cell with her. He wore a gray cable-knit sweater and jeans, along with work boots. He'd introduced himself as Rune Larsen, her father's new nurse. But he looked more like a ski champion or an extra in a Thor movie. He just had that physicality about him that screamed "athlete." Maybe that was why he looked vaguely familiar. Maybe she'd seen him in a movie or on TV competing in the Olympics.

He glanced around the tiny jail cell with eyes the color of a green lake on an overcast day. "Do you normally hold meetings in here?"

"No. We're short on space. You said you wanted to meet privately and right now, this is the best I got. So you're the travel nurse the agency assigned?"

"That's me. I just arrived in town."

"Welcome to Lost Harbor." She gestured around the holding cell. "Sorry for the lack of a fruit basket or whatever. But I sure am glad you're here. My dad's apparently running for Worst Patient of the Year."

He smiled slightly. Again that tug of recognition blinked at the edge of her mind. "I hear that a lot. No worries."

His voice was deep and somehow very reassuring. But when it came to her father, "no worries" didn't apply. "Sorry, but of course I'm going to worry. It started with heart surgery, but it cascaded from there because he refused to just rest. He got an infection, then he sprained his wrist. If you're going to work with him, I need to know you're taking it seriously."

His eyebrows lifted slightly. "Of course."

She wondered if this was how parents felt when they handed over their children to daycare. Fretful and nervous. "I mean, I didn't think I'd need a private nurse. I thought I could take care of him myself. But I'm the police chief around here and that means I have a lot of serious responsibility and—"

A knock sounded at the reinforced metal door. She opened it; Bob Hollister, one of her five sergeants, held up a flyer. "You want to approve this before I post it, Chief?"

Of all things to impress the hot nurse, a flyer of a missing yak would not have been her top choice.

The Tibetan yak belonged to Mrs. Holt, who was close friends with the mayor. Maya had caved to political pressure and opened a case on the missing yak. A reward was being offered. Flyers were being posted.

She glanced at the flyer, which featured several shots of the yak—two closeups from different angles, one of the yak chewing some grass, another of him posing in a field, even one with Mrs. Holt riding him in the winter parade.

"You can drop the photo with Mrs. Holt. The yak is missing; she's not out there riding it."

"Someone else might be." Hollister stroked his fringe of white beard, which made him look vaguely like Santa. "Got to cover all the bases."

"Did she send you that photo?"

"I got it from the archives. Winter parade two years ago."

She sighed. "Clear it with her. Make sure she's good with her face showing up all over town."

"Yes ma'am. Good thing I checked. That's why I interrupted whatever you're doing in here."

He glanced curiously at Rune Larsen—by her count, at least the third time he'd done so.

"Back to work, Sergeant."

"Yes, Chief." He whisked himself back to his desk, but left the door open. She saw that the other people in the office— another sergeant, a citizen filing a complaint, and a state trooper —were also peering into the holding cell.

Firmly, she closed the door and faced Rune again.

He looked highly amused. A crease dented his cheek, which was covered in a nicely trimmed layer of beard. Normally she wasn't crazy about facial hair on a guy, but she could make an exception in his case. He pulled it off.

She folded her arms across her chest.

"Obviously, I'm extremely busy with a lot of earthshaking duties. My dad needs more than I can do for him right now."

"Understandable."

"He doesn't like me fussing over him."

"Of course not. Too independent, right?"

"That's one way to put it. Stubborn works too."

Another knock. She let out a frustrated breath and opened the holding cell door. *"What?"*

This time it was Jessica, her best friend. She, too, shot a wildly curious glance in Rune's direction. "We're, uh, taking off now." She gestured at the tall man behind her—Ethan James, her new love and a private investigator. They'd taken over her office to fill out some paperwork, which was why she'd brought Rune Larsen in here. "Your office is free if you'd rather meet there."

"Thank you. You could have just texted me."

Jessica shrugged, offering a merry smile. "We wanted to say goodbye in person."

"Goodbye."

"Goodbye. And hello." Turning to Rune, she offered her hand. "I'm Jessica Dixon, owner of the Sweet Harbor Bakery and B&B. We have the absolute best walnut-cinnamon sticky buns in town, so stop by any time between seven and two-ish, depending on how busy we are."

"Jess," Maya said in a warning tone. "Little busy here."

"Of course. Sorry. Everyone has to eat, though, right? And sleep. Do you need a place to stay?" she asked Rune. "I mentioned the B&B part, right?"

"We have a place for now," he said in that deep, sexy voice.

We.

For some reason, that word disappointed Maya. That "we" meant he was married, or partnered up with someone.

Sometimes it seemed she was the only one who wasn't a "we." Especially now that Jess had hooked up with Ethan, the only "we" in her life was her and her father.

"Gotcha. Okay, I'll get out of your way. Call you later, Maya. Kate wants to get together for some dancing now that the peony harvest is over. Do you dance?" Once again, she directed that question at Rune.

He didn't get a chance to answer because Maya manhandled Jessica out the door and shut it behind her.

"I'm really sorry," she told Rune. "Just a little taste of my life right there. And it's still early."

"I hope with everything going on, you still make time for dancing."

She shot him a surprised look. Did he mean that in a medical-advice type of way? "It's not at the top of my list."

"I guess you're a lot busier now that you're grown up."

Now *that* was an odd thing to say. Her forehead creased as she looked at him.

And then looked again.

"Wait..." Why did he look so familiar? Who was he?

He smiled broadly for the first time, a full-on grin that set off another round of bells in her brain. She *did* know him from somewhere. But where?

He tugged his hair into unruly spikes so he looked like a mischievous kid.

Her jaw dropped open. "Jay? Jay-Jay from Hawaii?"

With a laugh, he smoothed his hair back down as best he could. "That took you a while. And here I thought you were a detective."

"Yes, but..." She blinked at him as if he might vanish like some kind of mirage. "What are you...I never expected...why didn't you... Oh my God, it really is you, Jay-Jay!"

He opened his arms wide and she didn't hesitate. She launched herself at him and flung her arms around her old friend.

Jay-Jay Breton. From Oahu. Her savior during the year her father had been stationed in Hawaii. She meant that literally; he'd saved her life in the ocean one day. He'd been spearfishing while she'd been sitting on a rock, feeling homesick. An extra-big rogue wave had knocked her off into the water. He'd abandoned his gear and swum to her rescue. She'd been so outraged by her dunking that she'd yelled at him about how much she hated Hawaii.

They'd fought about it, facing off on the sand after he towed her to shore. Then a crab had crawled up her leg and she'd shaken it off with a shriek. It had landed in his hair, which had struck them both as so funny that they'd burst out laughing and wound up in hysterics on the sand.

That was how they'd become friends. Jay-Jay was a sunshiny, scrappy kid with a knack for trouble. They were so different; he was friendly, she was reserved. He was reckless, she was responsible. He loved the ocean, she much preferred solid ground. But somehow it just worked and they were inseparable until she went back to Alaska.

He sure hadn't had the muscles that now surrounded her. Or at least they'd been much, much smaller.

The door to the cell flung open and a laugh of surprise rang out. "Chief Badger?"

She pulled herself away from Jay and whirled around to face Lucy Krakowski, who was a reporter from the local weekly newspaper.

Lucy wore the same look of wild curiosity Maya had seen three times now. "Sorry to interrupt, but I'm on a deadline and—"

"I know, I know, the police blotter. Doesn't anyone text or email anymore?" Maya couldn't help but grumble. She hadn't seen Jay-Jay in twenty years. They hadn't kept in touch after she came back to Alaska. She hadn't even known he was in the state.

"We can do this later," Jay said. "I'll give you my number."

"No. No. Stay where you are. Lucy, Sergeant Hollister can help you out. This is a very old *friend* of mine." She took care to emphasize the word so Lucy wouldn't go spreading anything false around town. She was about to say his name when she remembered that he'd used a different name at first.

When—and why—had Jay Breton become Rune Larsen?

Lucy turned to go, and Maya called after her, "We'll have a flyer for you soon too."

"The yak, I know." Lucy waved her hand. "Don't worry, we're doing a front-page spread on it. Janet Holt sure has some major pull around here. I'm off to interview her now, actually."

The door clanged shut again. Maya and Jay/Rune stared at each other.

"Looking forward to reading that," he said mildly.

They both started laughing at the same moment. Just the way they used to.

"Let's get out of here," Maya told him. "I'm gonna put out the 'gone fishing' sign and let them all fix their own problems."

"Does that happen a lot?"

"Nope. You know me and the ocean. We still haven't really warmed up to each other." She swung open the door, saw that everyone in the bullpen was watching with google eyes, and shut it again. "This place has lost its damn mind. They always want to know my business."

A slow wicked smile spread across Jay-Jay's face. "Should we really give them something to talk about?"

Oh lord. *Here comes trouble.* When had he gotten so freaking sexy? Twenty years sure changed a lot of things in a man.

"I think we've already got that covered. I have to look out for my reputation. I know my dad's going to want to see you. How about I drive you over there and we can catch up on the way?"

He nodded, but his face went serious again. "It's more than catching up. There's a situation I have to talk to you about. In private, not around your father. It's why I came to see you as soon as we got to town."

There was that "we" again. She scolded herself to stop getting carried away just because her old friend had grown into a stone-cold fox.

"I get it. But not here, too many interruptions." She put her hand to the door handle again, then hesitated. "So which is it, Rune or Jay-Jay?"

"Rune, if you can remember."

"Rune." She repeated it silently to herself. At least it suited him, but it would be weird calling him by a different name. Maybe it would help that he looked so damn different. "Rune Larsen, RN."

"LPN," he corrected. "Practical nurse. Also a paramedic, but I'll explain all that later."

"Let's go, then. We only have about twenty years of catching up to do."

He touched her on the shoulder, a gentle touch that made her remember how strong his arms had felt when they'd hugged. "I always knew you'd grow up to be something special."

Her face heated, and she braced herself to meet the collective stares of the department after she opened the door. "I bet you never thought I'd be a police officer though."

"I didn't have a clue *what* you'd be. Just that you'd knock it out of the park, whatever it was."

She narrowed her eyes at him. "You didn't say that when I fell off every paddleboard you tried to put me on."

"Anything land-based," he corrected with a grin.

"You'll find lots of other ocean lovers around here. It's a fishing town, though we tend to fish from boats instead of swimming around with spears."

His smile faded. "I won't be staying, Maya. I only take short-term assignments. Six months at most."

Right, he was a travel nurse. In Alaska, there was a big demand for travel health care workers, since so many villages weren't big enough to support a full-time dentist or physical therapist or ophthalmologist.

Important to remember that he was just passing through Lost Harbor.

Also that he was a "we."

"That must be hard on a relationship."

He looked at her blankly. "Excuse me?"

Had that come across as blatantly fishing for information? And was that allowed? They hadn't seen each other in so long. He could be married for all she knew. Her Jay-Jay—married. Such a strange thought.

Considering the possibility, she found she didn't like it much. She pushed down the door handle. "Whoever you're traveling with," she explained.

Just as the door swung open, he said, "Oh, you mean my sister."

Which meant that the entire department got a good look at her suddenly delighted grin.

CHAPTER TWO

Rune tried to ignore the gawking onlookers as he followed Maya through the police station. They must not be used to strangers around here. He sure wasn't doing anything to draw special attention. That was the last thing he wanted, as a matter of fact.

Maybe it was Maya who was sparking all this interest. Maybe she didn't have people from her past showing up very often.

"You're in charge, Hollister," she called to the roly-poly white-haired sergeant. "But don't put out that flyer until I see it again."

"Cross my heart."

Obviously her staff respected her, but that was no surprise. Even at age nine, Maya had commanded respect. She didn't get into scrapes like he did. In fact, he could always count on her to explain to the adults that they hadn't *intended* to get lost in the lava tube, or to forget to pay for the shave ice, or to lose his brand-new deep-water fins.

His mother—a flighty, surf-mad teenage mom raising him on her own—had loved Maya because she was twice as level-headed as either of them. If she knew Maya was going to be with him,

Mom didn't worry. They'd get together after school and hang out at the beach, or play cards, or sometimes do art together. They both liked to read. They laughed a lot. She'd complained about the weird Hawaiian food—poi and loco moco. Maya liked to dance, he remembered that. They used to make campfires on the beach and dance around them to music from her iPod.

Then she'd moved back to Alaska and that had been the end of that.

Now...wow.

He didn't quite have the words for how she looked now. In his memory, she'd had some baby fat and clear braces. Awkward wasn't really the right word, but shy might be. She was generally pretty reserved, until she let down her guard while dancing around a bonfire or something.

Twenty years later, that quiet manner of hers had transformed into something much more magnetic. She came across as the kind of person that you automatically looked toward in a crisis—the person you knew would think fast and be able to handle anything.

Also, she was stunningly beautiful, in his biased old-friend opinion. Her rich brown skin glowed with an extra sheen of dark gold. Her eyes were a few shades lighter, warm and sparkling. She moved with confident grace through the station—it was her domain, after all, and it showed.

Outside, she gestured toward a patch of birch woods behind the station. A signpost marked the start of a walking trail. "We can walk for a bit if you need some time to tell this story of yours before we see my dad."

He checked his watch. Cara was waiting back at the hotel they'd checked into—the Eagle's Nest Resort. He'd splurged so she could have some fun before school started up in a few days.

"Sounds good," he agreed. She tucked her hands into the pockets of the jacket she'd pulled on over her police uniform.

Even though it was late August, the chill of fall added a bite to the air, especially on an overcast day like today.

"So, your sister..." Maya screwed up her face, obviously searching for a name.

"Cara. She wasn't born yet when you were in Hawaii."

"Oh. Good." She smiled at him. "I can skip feeling guilty for not remembering her name. So she travels with you for your job?"

"Sort of. She's going to start at Lost Harbor High in a few days."

"Oh yeah? Junior, senior?"

"Senior."

Maya's eyebrows lifted. "Usually kids like to finish high school with their friends."

The trail wound through a stand of birch forest that stretched between two neighborhoods. On either side, he could see houses through the dappled woodlands. Nice backyard for a police station.

"Yes, but that's not an option." He hesitated, then decided there was no need to delay this explanation any longer. "The past five years or so, I've been working on the mainland as an EMT and paramedic. Two years ago, Cara came to visit me. I was living in Montana at the time, and she wanted to see the snow. The only time she'd seen snow was when we went to the Big Island one winter and it snowed on Mauna Kea. We drove up and filled the bed of our truck with snow, but it melted by the time we got back."

"That sounds like something Jay-Jay would do. We have snow here," she pointed out. "You could have reached out to your old friend."

"I didn't know if you'd even remember the rascally boy you had to keep out of trouble."

"You mean the one who saved my life?" She nudged him

with her elbow, making his muscles tighten in reaction. Even though it was a playful gesture, it still had an impact on him.

"So you finally admit it. It only took you twenty years."

She gave that rich, bubbly chuckle that he'd always loved inspiring. It sounded like sea water rushing over lava rocks.

"Anyway, go on. Cara came to visit you."

"Yes. She was fifteen. It was the end of summer and I was working. When I was on shift, she was on her own. She used to go to a coffee shop down the street. She's very social, very friendly, heart of gold, but a little bit naive. When this older man started talking to her, she was kind to him. He would come to the coffee shop and rant about politics and other stuff."

"I know that kind," Maya said. "Not entirely all there, is that what I'm getting?"

"Worse than that. He started following her around. He'd lurk outside my apartment all night long. He was obsessed, even though obviously there was never anything more than a conversation between them."

"You called the police, right?"

"We talked to them. There wasn't much they could do. They talked to him and warned him off, but he made up some story. He knew how to talk to police. I think he was former military. I sent her back to Hawaii early. She never even got to see the snow."

This was the part where it got truly scary.

Maya was listening closely. "Don't tell me he followed her back there."

"Oh yes. He turned up at my mom's house when she was at work. Grabbed Cara and put her in a car. She got away from him with the help of a bottle of body spray she had on her."

"That was quick thinking."

Rune nodded. He'd heard the story later, and been amazed at how a fifteen-year-old could keep her head like that.

"My mom, on the other hand, lost her shit. You know how

she is; she went straight for the white wine spritzers. Cara's father left a few years ago, so he wasn't much help either. We all agreed that she'd better come back to the mainland where I could watch out for her. But since he knew where I lived, I left my job and moved cities. My life changed overnight. I went from a fun-loving EMT to a full-time bodyguard. I finished my LPN certification. The two of us changed our names. Her birth name is Torrey, by the way, but she likes Cara better. She started going to school in St. Paul, Minnesota. Then he showed up again out of the blue."

"Some stalkers are very persistent and clever."

"I don't know his background. I don't even know his real name. All I know is that he told Cara his name is Chad. That's it, Chad. I do have a picture of him but it's blurry." He dug out his phone and pulled up the photo of the asshole.

Maya stared at it for a long moment, then sent it to her own phone and handed it back. "Chad. Such a white-bread name for a scary stalker."

"We don't know his real name. The ID he gave the police in Montana was fake."

"He's younger than I pictured."

"I'd guess he's in his mid-thirties. I believe he has military experience, like I said. He's able to blend in really well. Maybe he had undercover expertise too, I don't know. I've tried to find out more about him but he's a wily bastard."

"So you're afraid he might follow you here?"

"Yes. There's a good chance. After he found us in St. Paul, I signed up for the travel nurse agency. That way we have a chance to stay ahead of him. It takes him some time to locate us when we move. This is my fourth assignment since I signed up with the agency."

Out of habit, he scanned the bit of road he could see through the trees. For the last two years, he'd gotten used to scoping out every place he went as if he were in the secret service.

"How did you get assigned to Lost Harbor?"

"I chose it because of you. I don't always trust law enforcement to deal with the situation, but I trust you."

She quirked her eyebrows at him. "Based on fourth grade?"

"You were a pretty badass fourth-grader."

They reached a fork in the trail; one path headed up a hillside, the other paralleled its base.

"How'd you even know I was the police chief here? Are you stalking me?" She made a face at her own joke as soon as it left her mouth.

But he chuckled at it anyway. He'd always liked her dry, understated sense of humor. "I saw Lost Harbor on the list of locations the agency services. I remembered that's where you lived, and did a little digging. Your photo on the town website doesn't do you justice."

In the photo, she was staring directly into the camera without smiling—a stern, no-nonsense keeper of peace and bringer of order. There was no hint of the dance-crazy girl he remembered —the one who had once laughed so hard when he got a blueberry stuck up his nose that she'd peed her pants.

"That's my don't-mess-with-my-town Police Chief Badger look," she told him. "Never fails to get people's attention."

"It got mine."

She shot a curious glance up at him. "In a good way or a bad way?"

"A good way. I want to keep Cara safe. I might be a nurse—and a damn good one, don't worry—but for now my main job is protecting my sister. That's why we chose Lost Harbor. Not only is it very far away from...everywhere...but I have a personal connection with the police chief. Cara's very excited to meet you, by the way. I told her about our bonfire dances."

She sighed. "Like I said, I don't have much time for dancing lately. Between my job and my dad—"

He lifted one hand to stop her there. "Rune Larsen to the rescue. I can handle Mr. Badger, so long as he doesn't still think of me as that skinny little kid."

"He has eyes," she said dryly. "His heart surgery hasn't affected his vision. You are definitely not that kid anymore. So what else can you tell me about this dude? Stalker Chad?"

"I think he's more comfortable in larger towns. He can hide better there. I think he has skill with vehicles. Cara said he drove like a race car driver. He's also very good at blending in and disappearing into the background. He's savvy about avoiding cameras. I don't think he would hurt Cara, but I'm not sure. I've learned not to underestimate him. He's good at earning people's trust."

She frowned. "I don't like the sound of that. This is a pretty welcoming community. We're all the way at the end of the Misty Bay Peninsula. The road doesn't go any further. And for some reason that makes people relax, like nothing bad can happen here."

"You do have a very low crime rate," he pointed out. "But maybe that's because you have such an outstanding police chief."

"Flattery, Jay? Really?"

"Rune," he corrected. "It's my middle name. My mom chose it for good luck, so I'm hoping it helps."

She shook her head at her mistake. "Sorry. Rune. Now that I know *why* you changed your name, it's even more important. I'll remember, I promise. You're Rune from now on. Anyway, we do have crime here. I can show you a whole police blotter full of calls. And then there's the theft of Mrs. Holt's yak. Crime of the decade right there."

He laughed. "You're sure it didn't just wander off, right?"

"It's a possibility, especially since Mrs. Holt is convinced that her dead husband has somehow been reincarnated into the yak.

They used to fight a lot, so maybe the poor beast just had enough."

He snorted as they passed a gap in the trees, sunshine filtering through in a golden haze. He took a breath of the air—so pure it felt like liquid crystal—and a tiny bit of his habitual tension released.

"I think I'm going to like my time here."

"It'll be interesting, I can pretty much guarantee that."

Even more interesting now that he'd met the fascinating all-grown-up version of his long-lost friend.

CHAPTER THREE

When they returned to the shared police and firefighter compound, Maya spotted a crew of volunteer firefighters cleaning the ladder truck in the back lot. It sparkled in the sunshine like a neon-yellow play-toy.

"You should get to know these guys," she told Rune. "They're all first responders. And I'm sure they'll want to meet you."

Already the firefighters were glancing their way. Awesome—more fuel for the rumor mill. The firefighters were notorious gossipers, rivalling the legendary stitch-and-bitch group of crafters.

"Hi Chief," called Darius as he emerged from behind the engine.

"Hi Chief," she answered in their traditional greeting.

Honestly, being called "chief" never got old.

"That's our fire chief." She lowered her voice for Rune. "Darius Boone. It'd be smart to bring him up to speed on the situation with Cara too. When calls come in, you never know where they'll get routed."

"If you think it's best."

A guy respecting her advice; another thing that would never get old.

Maya beckoned to Darius, who loped over to them, washrag in hand.

"Darius, this is Rune Larsen. He's an old friend of mine. Rune, Chief Boone."

Maya caught the speculation in Darius' glance as he surveyed Rune. Why was everyone so surprised by Rune's presence? Just because she'd lived most of her life here in Lost Harbor didn't mean everyone knew everything about her.

"I'm a former EMT myself," said Rune as they shook hands.

"Is that how you know Maya?"

"No, Maya and I met when we were kids."

Darius' eyebrows lifted. "Huh. Are you from Lost Harbor?"

Maya interrupted this completely irrelevant conversation. "Can we keep on track here? Rune has a situation he needs to discuss with the law enforcement community. What does it matter where we met?"

"Is it a secret?" Darius asked. "Because that's really going to get tongues wagging around here."

"It's not a secret. It's just irrelevant. Can we stick to the facts? He's a friend, we met a long time ago, and now he's here and he's got a problem."

"Touchy." Darius looked like he was trying hard not to laugh. He turned to Rune. "Go ahead, fill me in."

As Rune recounted the same chain of events he'd told Maya, she watched him covertly, marveling over how much a person could change. If she'd seen him walking down the street, she would have noticed that he was a beautiful hunk of a man. And then she would have kept walking, assuming they had absolutely nothing in common.

And maybe she *didn't* know him anymore. Obviously his life

had changed a *lot* since the age of nine. So had hers. Police chief? Hello?

But as she watched him talk to Darius, she kept noticing little things that felt familiar. The shape of his mouth, for one. The way he bent his head at a certain stubborn angle. The scar on his chin had survived the journey to adulthood. So had his friendliness and his sense of humor.

That was what had drawn them together in the first place. That and the fact that they both felt like outsiders.

Jay-Jay—no, *Rune*—had been one of the kids who hung around the base but didn't really belong there. His mother worked in the commissary, and they'd lived in a little abandoned beachside shack until it got torn down by the county. And then there was his size—at that time, he was smaller than other kids their age. He liked to wear his hair long, to his shoulders. That had changed, but maybe that was because he was hiding his appearance from Stalker Chad.

Despite his size, he was a scrapper, and he was constantly getting into fights with bullies and other kids who were bigger than him. Sometimes she got dragged into it too, trying to defend him, which always got her in trouble with her dad.

Eventually, Harris had sat them down and laid down the law. "If you get Maya into any more fights, you can't come around here anymore. Got it?"

"But they keep saying shit about my mom."

"You think that's bad? You should hear what got slung at me all these years. Brush it off, kid. Or no more hanging out with Maya."

Rune had torn at his hair in that funny way he had, gone for a quick jog around the block—he always had to work off his energy—then come back and plopped back down at their kitchen table. "Okay, Mr. Badger."

"Okay, son. I'll be watching."

"Maya? You with us?" Darius was addressing her. She shook herself back to attention.

"Yeah. What's up?"

"Rune's going to volunteer for a few shifts with us. It's great to have another trained paramedic in town."

She glanced at the grownup Rune, with his strong build and long, powerful legs. He could have used all those muscles back in his skinny-kid days. With all his excess energy, it made sense that he'd chosen to work as a first responder. In Hawaii, that probably meant a lot of ocean rescues.

"Sounds good. We can always use help."

Darius snapped his fingers. "Hey, you should bring Rune to the party."

"What party?"

"Kate's calling it the 'Never Want to See Another Peony Party.' It's to celebrate the end of the harvest." He turned to Rune. "My girlfriend has been helping her grandmother at her peony farm. I've barely seen her for the past month. I know she'd love to meet any friend of Maya's."

Maya could see where this was headed already. All of her friends would be micro-analyzing Rune and trying to figure out what their relationship was. She had to put this to rest before it snowballed out of control.

"I probably won't be able to make it," she told Darius. "I'm very busy between the Lost Souls investigation and my dad's recovery, and some new cases that have come in."

"Sure, sure, I get it. You're probably burning the midnight oil trying to locate that missing yak."

She glared at him while Rune chuckled softly.

"You're invited whether or not Maya can make it," Darius told him. "If you're new in town, it's a good opportunity to meet some people. Now that the summer's just about over, people have time for their social lives again. From now until New Year's, it's one party after another."

Maya's heart sank at that reminder. Everyone else loved the holidays, but for the past five years—ever since her ex dumped her on Christmas Eve—they'd been nothing but depressing.

Rune glanced at Maya and must have read her ambivalence on her face. Without her having to say anything, he picked up on that cue. "I'll be busy getting settled in. I have to find a place, get my sister enrolled in school, meet the patients I'll be working with."

Darius didn't push it, which Maya appreciated. If Kate had issued the invitation, it would have been a whole different story. She would have approached it like the lawyer she was and interrogated poor Rune into accepting the invite.

"We need to get going," she told Rune. "My dad's nap is going to start soon. If there's one thing he's always on time for, it's that nap."

After a few more words with Darius, she led Rune to her beloved Chevy Silverado crew-cab truck. She'd bought it when she got the police chief job and loved it like a firstborn.

At this rate, it might be the only kind of firstborn she'd have.

Rune stopped to check a message that had come in on his phone. "Cara's getting bored in the hotel room. I'll pick her up and meet you at Harris' house."

She felt a twinge of disappointment that they wouldn't be driving together. Being with Rune brought back a time in her life that she'd completely forgotten about. Hawaii had been such an adventure. Going to a place where no one knew her had been wildly freeing. In Lost Harbor, everyone knew the Badgers. In Hawaii, she could be anyone she chose. She'd even told one kid that she was a Haitian princess.

Rune had done everything he could to spread that rumor, figuring it gave him an extra bit of clout.

But this wasn't Hawaii. This was Alaska, and she was just plain old Maya Badger, filling the unglamorous shoes of a police chief.

"You have the address?" she asked Rune.

"I already looked it up on GPS. I'll see you there."

They parted ways and she swung herself into her Chevy. Before she started the truck, she checked her phone, which had been beeping periodically during their walk.

Ten messages from various friends and acquaintances—all asking about Rune and inviting the two of them to some social event or other.

Once he realized what he was in for, he was going to request a transfer.

Or hell, maybe *she* should. Why was everyone in Lost Harbor so interested in her personal life?

She started up her truck and headed for her father's house.

Sad to say, she knew why people found her personal life so fascinating. Because she didn't *have* much of one as far as they knew. She had a strict policy of not dating anyone she might have to arrest someday. Which meant no one in Lost Harbor, which kind of limited her selection.

Since high school, all of her boyfriends had lived either in Anchorage or somewhere even farther away. Long distance was the only kind of relationship that worked for her. The only time she'd broken that rule was with Jerome Morris, and look how that had ended up. Dumped on Christmas Eve for another Lost Harbor girl. Utter humiliation.

Since then, she'd kept things simple. When she needed some fun, she headed to Anchorage, where she had a long-time "friends with benefits" arrangement with Tyler, a workaholic civil rights lawyer.

Maybe she should schedule another trip pretty soon. She

might need a distraction with Rune around, being so unexpect-edly hot.

She approached a group of teenagers walking down Main Street, goofing around, passing a joint back and forth.

She should stop and lecture them. Give them the stern glare that might make them think twice about flouting the law against underage smoking. Scare them with the threat of a night in the holding cell.

But she was on her personal time now, so she just slowed down as she passed and gave them all a wave.

The joint went flying onto the sidewalk as the teenagers turned innocent, nervous faces in her direction.

Wow. She hadn't even frowned at them. Apparently she had the youth in this town very well-trained.

Since she was the police chief, that was good, right? Then why did it feel so irritating? As if for most of the town, she had one mode: stern and authoritative. And only a select few saw her other sides. With Jay-Jay, in Hawaii, she used to run around bare-foot and dance around a bonfire and stargaze past her bedtime.

She made a note to text Tyler to see what kind of time he had in the next few weeks.

CHAPTER FOUR

Rune found Cara taking selfies on the balcony of the Eagle's Nest Resort and Spa. None of those selfies would ever see the light of day, since she was strictly banned from using social media.

But at least she'd have a very thorough family album to look back on some day.

She leaned an elbow on the railing and angled her hip as she snapped the photo. Beyond her, the mountains of Lost Souls Wilderness looked almost violet under a heavy cloud layer. On the far horizon a perfect cone of a mountain rose from the ocean; a volcano, part of the Ring of Fire that linked Alaska to the Pacific Rim. It gave him a sense of home, since he'd grown up on a volcanic island in the middle of the ocean.

Maya used to tell him stories about Lost Harbor, about the mountains and the glaciers and the bay that filled with fog. But the reality was so much more spectacular than he'd pictured. He didn't know if this place was remote enough to evade the stalker, but it felt like it was.

"Hello brother," Cara greeted him cheerfully. "I think I like this place. These photos are fricking amazing."

"Yeah, that's the most important thing to look for," he said dryly. "What kind of background a place offers for your selfies."

She made a face at him and straightened away from the balcony. Even though she was his little sister, he knew perfectly well that she was magnetic with her thick butter-blond hair and loving nature. It was irritating because it made his life more difficult. She wanted to make friends with everyone. Which was why they were in this mess to begin with.

"Are we going to meet Maya?" she asked eagerly.

He'd told her all about his long-ago friend. She loved his Maya stories, and had been delighted at the thought of living in Lost Harbor for six months.

"Yes, let's go. Not just Maya, but her father. He's my patient, so be cool."

"*You'd* better be cool, or Maya will know you used to have a crush on her." She stuck her tongue out at him as she danced past him, back into the suite.

"Cara," he warned. "You say anything like that and I'll toss you off that balcony."

"No one should be punished for telling the truth," she said virtuously, crossing her heart like some kind of mischievous nun.

"It's not the truth, and you definitely will be. I'll start by leaving you here. I'll tell Maya you weren't feeling well because you fell off the balcony."

She giggled and grabbed a neon-pink hoodie off the table next to the door.

He eyed it unhappily. "Really? Have you learned nothing about laying low in the past two years?"

A shadow came over her face. "Yes, I've learned that for six weeks, I can do whatever I want because it takes him time to find us. After that, I have to tone down what I wear for a month. Then I have to change the color of my hair. *Then* I have to avoid going outside until the day you come home and tell me it's time to move on."

His heart wrenched at the sad resignation in her voice. Why had he done anything to bring down her mood? He should be grateful for every moment that Cara was her normal joyous self.

"Fine," he said. "You can wear the hoodie. But you still have to behave yourself."

She brightened, like a sailboat regaining its equilibrium after a gust of wind. "No, you have to behave yourself or I'll show Maya your old diary."

He made her wait to exit the suite—that was one of the rules. He always went first to scope out the surroundings. With a jerk of his head, he indicated that the coast was clear. "You don't have my diary."

It wasn't a diary so much as a few drawings in an old sketch-book. But there was certainly some incriminating material there. Luckily, Cara had only seen it once.

"No, but I memorized it." She breezed past him. "I can recreate it."

"Better stick to selfies, kiddo."

Still bickering, as was their habit after two years of living mostly on the run, they made their way down to the boring Toyota they'd bought in Seattle, then ferried to Alaska. He missed the days when he could drive flashier cars.

"Can we drive past the high school?" Cara asked when they'd buckled themselves in.

"Don't you want to see the sights? The boardwalk, the harbor, all the fishing boats? This town is one of the most scenic locations in all of Alaska, or so they say."

Cara shrugged, ignoring the panorama unfurling out her window. Here at the tip of the boardwalk, the backdrop of snow-peaked mountains loomed like a majestic reminder that humans were short-timers here. "I just want to see the high school."

Since he knew that the prospect of being able to attend an entire semester at one school was overwhelmingly exciting to her after so much home-schooling, he nodded. "We can swing by there. But it wouldn't kill you to take in some scenery on the way."

They'd reached the harbor, where storefronts and restaurants were jumbled together on either side of the boardwalk. Some were perched on stilts sunk into the mudflats, some were covered in weathered shingles, others painted bright colors—purple and green and blue.

Cara looked out the window just in time to see a young fisherman, about her age, emerge from the top of a ramp that led to the harbor. He carried a cooler on one shoulder and wore nothing but a muscle-baring sleeveless shirt under his oilskins.

"Okay, fine, I'll look at the scenery," she said, eyeing the kid. "I wonder if he'll be going to my high school?"

Rune was only thirty, but in that moment he felt at least ten years older. On top of everything else, teenage hormones? Lord help him.

CHAPTER FIVE

Harris Badger lived in a tidy one-story home on the edge of Trumpeter Lake. From the house, a lawn sloped down to the shore, where a dock extended into the water. A cedar-shingled cabin—maybe a fish house—squatted at the top of the dock. Rune could imagine Harris sitting on the end of the dock, fishing on a sunny afternoon.

Everything on the property looked well-kept, despite the usual Alaska decor of old cars and piles of lumber.

Maya paced across the lawn near the front door, talking on her cell phone. She waved at them in greeting, then held up a finger to indicate she was almost done with her conversation.

She still wore her police chief uniform, but that didn't take away from the confident grace with which she moved. Her hair was flattened close to her head, with a few pins keeping stray strands under control.

A quick flash of insight told him she spent a lot of time keeping things under control generally.

He knew the feeling.

"Wow, she's really pretty," said Cara, sounding kind of awestruck. "And a little bit scary."

"That's right. She's terrifying. You'd better behave yourself."

He didn't find Maya terrifying at all, but he didn't mind spreading the legend.

"If she tells me to, I will," Cara vowed.

Yesss. He'd done the right thing, moving them here.

But then Maya ruined everything when she ended her call and aimed a radiant smile at his little sister. "You must be Cara. I'm Maya, old old *old* friend of your brother."

"I know who you are." Cara looked as starstruck as if she'd just met Beyonce. "Rune told me all about you."

"Uh oh. Don't believe a word of it," Maya said cheerfully. "Unless he mentioned that I'm a Haitian princess. That's completely true but I'm here incognito so don't tell anyone."

Rune laughed at the expression on Cara's face—as if she was perfectly willing to believe that Maya was royalty.

"Sorry to make you wait, there's a big investigation going on that's suddenly getting a lot more complicated."

"The yak?" Rune asked, dryly.

"No, not the damn yak. This is about Lost Souls Wilderness and some shit that's going on over there. I'm trying to get the FBI to pay attention, but to them it's like that wilderness is a no-man's-land. They want nothing to do with it. Anyway, you're not here for that. Dad's excited to see you." She ushered them toward the front entry, which had a boot brusher to one side and a welcome mat that said, "Enter in Friendship."

"I had to remind him who you are," she said in a lower voice, before opening the door. "The surgery took the juice out of him for a while. But he remembers now."

The interior of the house was just as orderly as the exterior. Framed family photos lined the walls. There was a wedding photo of Harris and Maya's mother—he knew that she'd died when Maya was only two. He spotted shots of Maya through the years, as well as some older relatives and a few family reunions. And then there were the stunning ocean shots that Harris must have taken in his Coast Guard days.

"Well look at you, fine fellow." Harris Badger emerged from the living room, wearing a track suit and a pair of house slippers. His hair was grizzled with gray and his face more lined, but his kind smile hadn't dimmed a bit. "That little fisher boy that kept coming around the house every time we looked up."

Rune smiled and reached out his hand. "That's me. I guess you still can't get rid of me. I'm Rune."

Harris shook his hand, frowning slightly, as if he knew that name wasn't right but wasn't going to dispute it.

"Rune. You can call me Harris. And who's this little thing?" He turned to Cara, who beamed back at him. Between the two of them, their smiles could set off a rocket ship.

"My sister Cara. She's going to Lost Harbor High this year."

"Well, good for you. Maya graduated at the top of her class, did you know that?"

Maya rolled her eyes slightly. "*Near* the top, Dad. And you don't have to boast about me to every single person you meet."

"Now you know that ain't true." Harris winked at the two of them. "I gotta boast. What else is going to heal this old heart?" He thumped his chest. "You two want to sit down for a bit?"

They followed him into the living room, where Maya helped him into a recliner upholstered in tan corduroy. He shooed her away, obviously eager to do everything himself.

"So you're going to be my nurse." Harris settled into his chair and touched his chest. "Didn't know I needed one but I gotta do what the police chief says. Can you believe little Maya's our police chief?"

"I'm not surprised, actually." Rune sat on the couch, and

Cara plopped down next to him. "She's kind of a natural when it comes to ordering people around."

He aimed a smile in her direction to show he was just teasing. She raised one eyebrow with a "you're dead" kind of look.

But Harris loved his little joke. He threw his head back with a peal of laughter. "Ain't that the truth. You should see how she pushes me around trying to say it's for my recovery. For my own good. I can decide for myself what's for my own good."

Now Maya raised both eyebrows at Rune. "See what I mean? He doesn't listen to me. He keeps saying I'm not a doctor so he doesn't have to."

Rune could definitely see the problem. Two independent and stubborn personalities like Harris and Maya were bound to clash. He had his work cut out for him. "We can talk later, you and me," he told the man. "Work out some ground rules."

"I have a say in it?"

"It won't work unless you do. My job is to help you get back on your feet and maybe even better than before."

"Can you make me look like you?" Harris gestured in the general direction of Rune's chest. "Much as an old man can?"

Rune grinned at him. "You can't fool me. You're a strong man. I remember the time I took you spearfishing, you picked it up fast. You could probably outlast me on a winter day on the ocean."

Harris gave a gleeful cackle and leaned forward to offer Rune a high five. That's what he needed—the beginnings of a bond. The fact that they'd known each other in the past made all the difference.

He looked at Maya and gave her a wink, letting her know that everything would be fine. She flashed him a thumbs up. Already she looked more relaxed, those lines of worry smoothing out.

Maya carried a lot of responsibilities on her shoulders, he could already tell. He found himself wanting to ease those burdens any way he could. What was that saying, that once you save someone's life, you're responsible for them? Something like that.

"Where y'all staying?" Harris asked.

"At the most beautiful hotel!" Cara said exuberantly. "It has a hot tub and a balcony."

"Just for a night or two. We're looking for something else," Rune explained. "Any tips on good neighborhoods?"

Maya answered before Harris. "Depends. Where do you stand on outhouses?"

"Outhouses?" Cara's eyes went round.

"Outdoor toilets," Maya explained. "You plop a little shack over a hole in the ground and there's your bathroom."

Cara sent a panicked glance at Rune. "*Outhouses?*"

"I read about them in the guidebook I picked up," Rune told her gravely. "It's a timeless Alaskan tradition. You said you wanted an adventure, didn't you?"

"They're definitely an adventure." Maya seemed to pick up on his line of teasing. "You can't call yourself an Alaskan until you've put on your boots and coat to battle your way through a blizzard just to take a dump."

"Blizzard?" Cara said faintly.

"We get a few every winter. I once assisted in the rescue of a gentleman who got trapped in his outhouse by a moose who decided to take a nap right outside the door. He couldn't get it open. Finally his wife came looking for him and called us. He just about froze out there."

"Froze?" Cara repeated.

"She was lucky it wasn't a bear—"

"Stop scaring the girl," Harris interrupted them. "We have plenty of houses around here with indoor plumbing. Even my fish house has a—you know something? You should just stay in my fish house. I converted it to a guest house a couple years ago.

It's got a bedroom and an extra loft. Bathroom, kitchenette. You could stay there for free."

Rune glanced over at Maya, who shrugged. "It's small, but it's got everything. Want to take a look at it?"

He wasn't at all sure it was a good idea, but didn't want to be rude. "Sure."

Harris started to get up, but Maya shooed him back down. "I got this. I swear, I need to hang a sign around my neck that says "sit down, I got this."

Grumbling, Harris relaxed back into his recliner and picked up a half-completed scarf with knitting needles sticking out from it. "Guess I'll get back to work then. Winter's coming. Got my Christmas list to fill."

Outside, Maya led the way to the shingled structure perched at the head of the dock. Cara ran ahead of them to check out the dock itself. When she reached the end, she flung her arms wide and yelled, "I'm the king of the world."

Goofball.

"Is he really prepping for winter already?" Rune asked Maya as they strolled more slowly down the slope. Her phone beeped. It beeped a lot.

"Better believe it. Some people have been chopping wood and smoking salmon all summer. Dad's fine, though. He talks tough but he has everything he needs. The way he talks, finishing all his Christmas gifts is a matter of survival."

The affectionate tone in her voice took all the sting from her words. Maya and her father were just as close as ever, except now she was taking care of him instead of him taking care of her.

"I always envied you, you know," he told her softly. "Your relationship with your father, I mean."

She nodded, obviously knowing exactly what he meant. He'd never known his father, who'd had a quick vacation fling with his mother and didn't leave a number. In some ways, Harris had provided the best male role model of his childhood—until a lifeguard had rescued him from an ocean current and he'd discovered EMT work.

"I want to keep it that way," Maya was saying. "My dad's a wise old man, except when it comes to taking care of himself. When he started arguing with me about how many pillows he wanted in his chair, I realized that someone else better take over. That's where you come in. I can tell already that he'll listen to you more than he does to me. Funny how I can get a three hundred pound inebriated fisherman to obey me, but when it comes to my own dad...I'm still a little girl, in his eyes."

He caught the wistfulness in her tone. "It's hard to blame him. You were a very cute little girl. Do you still have those purple bear barrettes you used to wear?"

She burst out laughing. "Damn, you remember those?"

"Yup, after all these years. Never going to forget those barrettes. That's how cute they were."

"I mean, I have them in photos, but nope. Those are long gone. Along with my braces and a few other embarrassing things."

To his mind, endearing was a better word than embarrassing. But she seemed uncomfortable with his compliments, so he didn't say so.

The guesthouse was perfect—light and airy, with a view of the lake that brought an immediate sense of serenity. A small bedroom in the back would suit Cara just fine. She'd get the privacy she craved, while he could sleep in the loft. Security-wise, he liked it because it would be impossible for anyone to lurk nearby without being spotted. Not a single bush or tree or even a large boulder within fifty yards. A stand of spruce trees provided a border at the edge of the property.

"This could work," he told Maya as he turned in a slow circle, checking out window placements and lines of sight. "But I don't want to put Harris in any danger."

"From the stalker, you mean? Has he ever hurt a bystander?"

"Not that I know about. He swung a bat at me once, when I tried to chase him away. But I worry that he might escalate. From what I've read, these guys can get very twisted."

Maya cocked her head, thinking it over. Hopefully taking it seriously. "My father's dealt with a lot in his life. He has a hunting rifle locked in a safe. Normally, he'd be an asset. But while he's recovering, I don't want him to have extra stress."

Rune nodded through his disappointment. "Enough said. We'll find something else."

"No, that's not what I'm saying. You said you usually have some time before the stalker finds you."

"Yes, a couple of months at least."

"Then let's hold off on explaining the situation. You guys move in, and if it suits you and it seems like it's working out, I'll tell him. It's better if he knows, I just want to get the timing right."

"Your call on the timing. If he decides he doesn't want the risk, we'll move out." Rune wanted to make sure that was clear. "We're used to moving."

Maya shook her head as she checked her phone again. "I gotta go. I'm sorry you two have been dealing with this creep. I wish we could put him behind bars instead of making you move around the country like you have been."

"I wish that too, except that would mean he actually harmed someone. That's what the police told me, that he has to commit a crime before they can do anything."

"Yeah, that's the way the laws are written. Did she ever try to get a restraining order?"

"We tried, but without his real name it's tough. We were able to in Hawaii, but since then we've had no luck. He's extremely savvy. I don't think even a court order would do much to stop him." He rubbed a hand across the back of his neck, the tendons tightening the way they always did when he talked about the stalker. It was unbelievable how one man had caused such an upheaval in his and Cara's lives.

"Best believe that if he comes here and makes one wrong move, I'll be on him like scales on a fish," Maya told him. "Might even gut him like one too. That's not in my official capacity," she added quickly. "Officially, all rules and regulations will be followed."

He smiled at her, with the sense that for the first time, he had a real ally in this ongoing battle. None of the other law enforcement people he'd worked with had brought him this much sense of hope.

Cara ran up from the dock and burst through the door, her face as bright as a light bulb. "Can we really live here?" she asked.

"I'm in if you are."

She danced around for a moment, then paused in mid-pirouette. "There's a toilet, right? Show me the toilet."

CHAPTER SIX

About three months until Christmas...

MAYA WAS LATE. Of course. Her friends were supposed to know that she was overloaded these days. So why did they keep texting her? Over the past twenty minutes, she'd gotten messages from Kate, Jess, and Toni, all reminding her that they were gathering at Sweet Harbor Bakery for a girls' night in.

Be there in a few, she texted Jess. *Can you get everyone off my back?*

I can buy you ten minutes.

Maya shook her head and turned her phone off.

One month ago, she never would have done that, in case her father needed her. But with Rune around, she didn't worry nearly as much. At least forty percent less, anyway.

Ten minutes. She could finish up in that amount of time. She turned back to Ethan James, who'd stopped in to deliver his report on his latest trip to Lost Souls Wilderness. He'd been hired by the brother of a plane crash victim to find any information he could about what had brought his sister's plane down fifteen years ago.

"Your girl is starting to get on my nerves, Ethan. Wrap it up quick, would you? I need something I can use to convince the Feds to come down here."

The tall private investigator, who was now engaged to Jess, leaned forward and planted his elbows on his knees. "There's a lot to report, but I don't know if it helps you. We located the idiot who shot up Jessica's float plane."

"Great news." That bit of the Lost Souls mess was the only part that fell within her jurisdiction in any way. "Did you learn anything from him?"

"No. He claimed he did it to keep Lost Souls Wilderness from getting overrun by tourists. I have all his information for you if you want to follow up. Which you should."

"You don't believe him?"

"Not for a hot second. It's absurd. The damn lake doesn't even have a name, let alone a churro stand."

"Churro?"

"It's an LA thing. Fried dough with sugar. Like a funnel cake. You really need to get out of Alaska, babe."

"Don't call the police chief 'babe,'" she said severely. "There's a fine for that. Moving on to the other plane crash, the one that killed Carole and Anthony Berenson. Good job on finding the crash site. I already called the coroner and the NTSB. They'll send someone out to take a look."

His quiet hazel eyes went grim. "There's not much in the way of remains. That was rough for Alastair, but it might bring him some peace. I took a lot of photos of the wreckage." He handed her a thumb drive. "It's been fifteen years, so there's not much to see."

"Anything to back up the theory that it was shot down?" In other words, something she could use to get the Feds involved.

"Not that I can tell, but the NTSB might find something."

She sighed in frustration. In many ways, Lost Souls Wilderness *was* a no-man's-land. In such rugged, inaccessible territory, how was anyone supposed to investigate anything? No wonder the Feds wanted nothing to do with it.

"Your client, the victim's brother. Alastair Dougal. What's his status?"

"He had to go back to New York. Finding the crash site helped bring him some closure, but he's still not satisfied. He's convinced it was a deliberate act and that means murder." He shrugged. "If so, the trail's cold. But I'm betting he'll be back as soon as he can."

"Well, maybe between the NTSB's report and the shooter you found, maybe I can make a case for the Feds."

"Good." He sobered, his hazel eyes concerned. "I never liked the idea of you chasing this one down. My theory is that it's either drug-related or a trafficking ring of some kind."

Great. Whatever was going on out there, Lost Harbor was uncomfortably close to it. She sighed. "Send me everything you've got. Thanks for filling me in, Ethan."

Ethan nodded and unfolded himself from the chair. "One more thing. We saw Kelsey Lewis at the Aurora Lodge. I asked if she was ready to see S.G.—Maggie, I should say. She said she's been thinking about it nonstop, but she still doesn't think it's safe. It'd be great for Maggie if she finally got to meet her mother."

"I'll talk to her. I'd love to see that happen too, but not if it puts her in danger."

"Agreed."

Maggie—formerly known as S.G.—had been kidnapped as a baby and raised by a trapper in Lost Souls Wilderness. Just a couple months ago, Ethan and Jessica had located her long-lost mother, Kelsey Lewis. Kelsey was the manager of the Aurora Lodge, which was an insanely pricey high-end resort in the heart of Lost Souls. It catered to wealthy adventure-seekers who didn't want to give up their luxuries. Instead of outhouses, it offered suites with two-person showers and private Jacuzzis.

Whatever was going on in Lost Souls, Kelsey clearly knew something about it, but so far she'd refused to talk. Clearly she was being threatened. For years, she'd received occasional photos of her missing daughter. The message: *say anything and we'll hurt her.* Even though Maggie was now safe in Lost Harbor, Kelsey still feared for her daughter's life. That was why she insisted it wasn't safe for her to see Maggie yet, no matter how much both of them longed to.

Maya certainly understood, though it made her job a lot harder. Damn the FBI and their reluctance to get involved.

Ethan's phone beeped. "It's Jessica. She says if I don't vacate your office in two minutes, I'll be cut off from sticky buns for a week. Sorry, gotta go, Chief."

"That's a dirty trick."

"For a good cause. You need a break, Maya. Your friends await you."

He gave her a salute and strolled out of her office. She sighed wistfully, just a teensy bit jealous of Jessica's blissful new relationship. Ethan and Jessica were adorable together. In their group of friends, Jessica had always been Team Romance. Kate was Team Sex—although now she was madly in love with Darius Boone, so consistency wasn't really her forte.

Maya, on the other hand, was Team See-Where-It-Goes. She was open to romance, and to sex, together and separately. Except that neither ever seemed to pan out in her case. The last time she'd been in love, she'd gotten her heart crushed.

On Christmas Eve, Jerome had come to her house to pick her up for a party. Except instead of a whisking her off to the Elks Lodge, he'd told her that he'd met someone else. Leanne McGee, who was barely out of high school.

"They're transferring me to DC," he'd told her, barely able to look at her. "Leanne's coming with me and we're going to get married."

"Wait...*what?*" So confused, so stunned, so tongue-tied.

"You know it wasn't working with us, babe. I need someone who's a hundred percent for me. That's never going to be you, not with your job."

The rest of it was still a blur. He'd crushed her heart under his boot heel like one of the gold ornaments on her Christmas tree.

The worst part was that he'd found someone else right under her nose without her noticing. So he'd humiliated her professionally as well as personally.

Ever since then, the holiday season had lost a lot of its joy.

She shook off the unwelcome Jerome memories and hurried into the station restroom to change out of her uniform. She kept several changes of clothes at the office because she worked late so often.

As she pulled on a pair of skinny jeans, she propped her phone on the sink and scrolled through the messages she'd missed during her meeting with Ethan.

Greg, 29, a lawyer from Anchorage: *Lost Harbor chicks are the bomb. Want to meet halfway with a six-pack of beer?*

Okay, no. What kind of lawyer talked like that anyway? She texted him back. *I don't think this is going to work out. Good luck.*

The next message came from Neal, 38, a biologist from Sitka. *There's a documentary on seal pups playing here next weekend. Like to make a first date of it?*

She copied her answer to Greg and pasted it into a text to Neal.

Next one: *Always wanted to date a black girl. Do you mind if I call you black, or should it be African American?*

Good thing she had her response already pasted and ready to copy.

Pulling on a fuzzy sweater in her favorite shade of goldenrod yellow, she thought about throwing her entire phone in the bay. What had possessed her to sign up for a dating app?

She blamed it on one thing: the holidays. She just couldn't face another holiday season on her own. This one would be harder than ever, with Jessica and Kate both happily paired up. Out of desperation, she'd decided to try the AK Hearts dating app. If there was any chance she could find someone to date for the next few months, it was worth a try.

There was another reason too: Rune.

He was on her mind a lot. She kept running into him at her father's house, or around town, or while jogging on Seafarer's Beach. Even though he was always his friendly self, the chemistry between them didn't feel "friendly." It felt tempting. Distracting. Her heart always jumped at the sight of him. She'd find herself completely focused on him, oblivious to everything else. But they were just old friends.

She needed someone to take her mind off him.

Speaking of Rune, a text from him flashed onto her screen. She grabbed up her phone and scanned it quickly. There was always the chance that it was about her father.

But if she was honest with herself, that wasn't why she gobbled up his texts. It was because they made her feel good.

Howz girls night? he'd texted. *C and I are watching a Community marathon. We have popcorn. Sugar and cayenne, just how you like it.*

God, that sounded fun. Maybe even more fun than girls' night, which she wouldn't have imagined saying a few months ago. But Rune...spending time with Rune was like...she didn't really have a good comparison. Maybe like gorging yourself on calorie-free cheesecake? Sinfully enjoyable and yet guilt-free?

Being around Rune made her...what was the word? Oh yeah. *Happy.* He never made her feel bad about getting called away for work. Even when she was at her most exhausted and grumpy from some shit that had gone down at the station, he always looked at her as if she was beautiful. Was it because their old friendship had clicked into place just like before?

Community marathon and popcorn with his little sister. Ultimate friend activity.

But it sure did sound relaxing, especially compared to the barrage of ridiculous messages she'd gotten since she'd signed up for that app.

She answered his text. *Still haven't made it to girls night. Maybe another night?*

Ok. I'll tell Cara to stop crying because her Auntie Maya never comes over.

Auntie Maya? No. Just no.

LOL. I knew that would get you. Better come kick my ass.

She smiled, then moved her thumb over to the dating app, ready to delete it.

Then she remembered that the first meeting of the Winter Parade committee was coming up next week.

As police chief, she had to ride in the winter parade in a cruiser decorated with tinsel, with a plastic snowman wearing a Lost Harbor police jacket mounted on the roof. After that, she'd be serving hot chocolate at the Lost Harbor Home for Seniors. And then came the station holiday party.

She'd be doing all of that alone unless she found herself a damn date. *Three months to go.* She could do it. Or lose her mind trying.

CHAPTER SEVEN

"So how's the date hunt going?" Kate asked her as soon as she was settled in with a glass of wine in the corner of the glassed-in terrace at Sweet Harbor Bakery. She was wearing her purple suede half-boots, which she propped on the next table over in that casual, jaunty way of hers. It was probably driving Jess crazy, but she was too tenderhearted to say so.

"Ask me after I finish this wine," Maya grumbled in answer. "And by 'this wine,' I mean that bottle." She gestured toward the full bottle of red in the middle of the round table.

"Going well, then." Jess lifted her glass in a toast. "Here's to Maya finding her soul mate. Whoever he is, I can't wait to meet him."

"I'm not going for soul mate." Maya had to correct that misunderstanding. "I'm going for 'Let's hang out for the holidays.'"

"That's about as unromantic as it gets," Jess complained, lifting her mane of curly auburn hair off her neck. Maya used to envy Jess her hair, until she'd found out that when she didn't comb it, knots would develop that she had to snip out with scissors. "I think you should aim for 'head over heels for the holidays.'"

"Well, this isn't a rom com, Jess. You know me. I'm realistic AF. I like to be honest with myself—and everyone else," she added.

Toni poured herself another glass of wine with a gesture straight out of a movie about rival New York sommeliers. She was a bartender, after all. "Be honest with us, then. How many guys have you already shot down since you joined that app?"

Maya counted on her fingers. "Ten." Then, for the sake of full disclosure, she added, "Today."

The girls all burst out laughing. "And how many days have you been on it?" Kate asked. "About a week?"

"I'm gonna say about a year, cause that's how it feels. But yeah, six days, I think. The free trial's almost over and I'm thinking I want my money back."

"Why don't you just let us set you up?" Jess asked longingly. "You can't rely on an algorithm."

"Jess, be real. You know my rules. I can't date anyone I might have to arrest. Who do you think you're going to set me up with? I already know everyone."

"You *think* you know everyone. But maybe you don't know them as well as you think you do. People have hidden depths. They have other sides you don't even know about. Also, you know the people who have committed crimes, where as I know the people who have a sweet tooth. I have several excellent choices in mind, especially if you're able to open your mind a little bit."

Maya rolled her eyes. "If you're talking about your new twenty-one-year-old server with the yin-yang tattoo on his neck, forget about it."

Jess' face fell. "Ignore the tattoo. Look deep into his eyes. He's an old soul."

"Smoking a lot of weed and quoting Rumi doesn't make someone an old soul. More wine, please."

Toni filled her glass with another elaborate swoop of the bottle. "An interesting guy came through the Olde Salt the other night."

Maya could only imagine. Working at the town's historic old saloon brought all kinds of "interesting" people onto Toni's radar. "Really. Is it his arrest record or the variety of addictions that makes him interesting?"

"For once, neither." Toni grinned, unembarrassed by the rowdy crew she ran herd over at the bar. "He's Scottish and very well-dressed. I think he has money. He left me a massive tip, which is why I remember him. Also, that accent. And his eyes were this lovely green color, almost like melon liqueur—"

"Alastair Dougal?" Jess exclaimed. "We met him in Lost Souls. He's very nice, but no no no. He's all wrong for Maya."

Maya bristled. "Why is he all wrong for me? I like well-dressed men with accents."

"Because..." Jess shook her head with complete conviction. She relied a lot on her intuition, and Maya occasionally did too. She had a way of sensing things about people that had helped Maya crack a case or two. "He's too...no. It wouldn't work at all. He's got some things to work out and Maya doesn't have time for that."

Toni cocked her head thoughtfully. "Yeah, you might be right about that. He had the wounded hero vibe about him. I never got the lowdown, though. The bar was too busy."

"Ethan just told me that Alastair went back to New York." Maya ended that line of discussion with facts. "So we can all cross him off the list."

"Good," Kate declared. "Because Darius has a guy coming in to train the crew on infectious disease protocol and let me tell you —I saw his website and he is—" she whistled. "Infectiously sexy."

"Oh no." Maya shook her head as the others booed along with her. "Not good, Kate. Not good. Wipe that from my brain, please."

Kate smiled unrepentantly. "Want to see for yourself?"

"Pass." How long could an infectious disease training take? He'd be gone in a week or two. He didn't solve her problem at all. She needed someone who'd be here at least until January.

Maya sipped her wine, feeling a sense of despondency set in. She'd be best off just accepting reality and bracing for another long single slog through Lost Harbor's holiday season.

Jessica gave her a soothing touch on the arm. "Did you ever think that maybe you're trying to solve the wrong problem?" she said softly.

"How do you mean?"

"Having a partner for the holidays is good and all, but wouldn't it be better if it was someone you were in love with?"

"Maybe." Maya dabbed some droplets of wine that had spilled on the table. "But I don't think..."

"What?" Jessica prompted when she fell silent. The entire table of friends went quiet, waiting for her to finish her sentence. It was the kind of moment in which she usually deflected and found a way to shift the focus somewhere else. Her business was her business. She solved her own problems.

Except when she didn't.

Take Rune, for example. Hiring Rune to help with her dad was quite possibly the best thing she'd ever done. With his rock-like strength and dry sense of humor, he was magic with Harris.

Yesterday, Harris had slipped while getting out of bed. He'd found himself on the floor, unable to pull himself up. Luckily his phone was within reach, so he'd called Maya. But she was in a meeting with the town council, so she'd called Rune.

"On it," he'd said, calm as could be.

Harris told her later that Rune had picked him up as if he

weighed no more than a bag of yarn. By the time she escaped the meeting and rushed to her dad's house, he was happily eating ice cream on the dock while Cara fished.

As she'd chatted with her father, Rune had emerged from the fish house with his medical bag, on his way to see his next patient. A rush of emotion had swept through her—as if he'd lifted a boulder off her shoulders.

There were a few other emotions in there, but she didn't want to dig too deep. Rune was her friend. Nothing more.

And weren't friends supposed to support you when you needed it? Maybe she should open up more to the friends sitting around the table right now. They were all still waiting patiently for her to complete her thought.

She cleared her throat. Even though they all knew Jerome, and knew what had happened, they probably didn't realize how deeply he'd hurt her.

"I think that part of me might be broken," she said finally.

Jess squeezed her arm. "Are you talking about Jerome?"

Trust her most intuitive and empathetic friend to get it.

"Yes. Jerome." Even saying his name aloud brought a stab of remembered pain.

Kate frowned, as if trying to place the name. "I wasn't here then. What happened?" Until she'd moved to Lost Harbor recently, Kate had been strictly a summer girl. She hadn't visited much while she was busy building her legal career.

Toni and Jessica exchanged a glance. Both of them had been around during the Jerome time.

"Jerome was a real piece of work," Toni explained. "He seemed perfect at first, right? He was here overseeing an engineering project, something about the tidal flats."

"They were trying to set up a turbine." Lord knew Maya had heard enough details about it to last a lifetime. "He was the chief engineer. Every time a black man comes to town, my dad invites them over, even if he only had a black grandmother he never even met."

"He went hard for you, that's how I remember it," Jessica said. "Flowers, dinner at the Nightly Catch, that surprise trip to Vegas."

"Yup. He gave me the whirlwind sweep-me-off-my-feet treatment. It worked. I fell in love with him. Like, hard. It was every silly fantasy I'd ever had rolled into one. I was even willing to quit my job for him."

Incredible though it seemed at this point—she nearly had.

Jessica tilted her head, anger flashing in her amber eyes. "I forgot about that. He wanted to steal you away from us, didn't he?"

"You're so dramatic. He was on a fast track, that's all. He wanted someone who was going to support his career, not the other way around. That was the only thing we really fought about, but it was a big one. I was ready, though. I was going to quit. Then he got transferred and found someone else."

"Found someone else?" With her dark eyes flashing, Kate looked like she was ready to throttle him—or at least sue him. "Who? Where? When?"

"He told me right before the station's Christmas Eve party. He'd promised to do the Winter Parade with me, so I wasn't stuck in that cruiser waving to the crowd on my own. Everyone knew we were together, everyone expected him to be there. There was even a rumor that he was going to propose *at the parade*."

"Yes, that's true!" Jessica slapped a hand on the table. "I remember that. Sergeant Hollister even ordered a special cake. He made me put a red heart on it with Maya + Jerome inside the heart."

"He *did*? You never told me that." Maya pulled her lower lip between her teeth. It was a sweet thing for Hollister to do, but she'd never heard a thing about it until now.

"After I heard what happened, I rushed over there and turned the heart into a big red-suited Santa Claus. I didn't want you to be reminded of anything having to do with Jerome."

Typical tenderhearted Jessica. As if icing on a cake could make a difference. "Thanks for that. I wish you could have erased Jerome from that entire winter. At every single party, people were asking where he was. I already had presents for him under my tree. He ruined Christmas that year."

Kate leaned back in her chair, balancing her glass of wine on her stomach. "Not just that year, huh?"

"No," Maya admitted. "The holiday season brings it all back. Every year. It sucks. As soon as they put those decorations up on the streetlights on Main Street, I get into a bad mood. The golden bells, the wreaths, the reindeer sleighs. All it does is make me think of Jerome and how he was cheating on me the whole time."

Toni clenched her hands together as if she were throttling someone. "I wish he'd come back so I could kick his ass. Where does he live now? I have some frequent-flyer miles I need to use up."

Maya lifted her glass in a toast. "It's a good thing I'm off the clock. I don't need to be hearing any threats. Besides, I don't know where he lives now. I know he and Leanne got married. He sent my dad an invite."

"Man, that's just..." Toni shook her head in disgust. "You're better off without him, let's just leave it at that."

Of course she agreed with that. No question. After Jerome had broken her heart, she'd turned her focus to her career. Luckily, that had gone very well. *Take that, Jerome the Jackass.*

Kate sat forward and settled her forearms on the table. "Now that we've established that Jerome was a dick who didn't come close to deserving you, I have to ask, why are you still hung up on him? When was that, five, six years ago?"

"Five years ago. And I'm not still hung up on him."

"But you think you can't fall in love again."

"Because I *haven't* fallen in love again."

"But it's only been five years and you've been busy." Kate's logic made sense. And yet...

"It's just...something that happens inside me. I start liking someone and I think it's going well, and he thinks it's going well, and then I just—shut down." Embarrassed, Maya stared at the swirl of red at the bottom of her wine glass. She didn't usually talk about this sad situation. In fact, she never had before.

"Describe 'shutting down,'" Jessica asked gently.

"I...stop finding him attractive. I don't want to kiss him anymore. I find excuses to stay late at work. I don't answer his texts right away. I make myself see the guy, I might even sleep with him. Just to see, you know? See if that'll make me like him again. It never works."

"Aww." Jessica settled a comforting hand on her arm. "It sounds like you're trying to force things when your heart isn't in it."

"Exactly. And that's because of Jerome. It's been that way since he left." She gestured for Toni to refill her glass. "And you know, it's fine. I don't need a man to have a good life. I *like* my life. I'm glad I didn't leave my job. I worked hard for that position. I like being independent. I would have made a terrible wife for Jerome. I don't think about him anymore. But as soon as I start liking someone, those walls just rise on up."

She swallowed over the lump tightening her throat. There was a reason she never talked about this kind of stuff. Because of this. She liked to project calm and authority, not "hot mess."

"Sweetie, why didn't you ever tell us how much it affected you?" Jessica asked the question, but the other women nodded along with her. A quick glance around the circle showed nothing but sympathy and concern.

"Because no one needs to see me have a meltdown. It might upset y'all."

"Why would it?" Kate frowned.

"People need me to be strong. And I am."

"Yeah, you are strong. But that doesn't mean you can't cry sometimes just like the rest of us non-law enforcement types. Maybe if you let yourself grieve for Jerome, you could move on."

"I'm *over* him. There's nothing to grieve about. I'm glad he left. I'm better off. You know what I've been thinking?" Maya ran her thumb around the rim of her glass. "The only thing you can't do without a man is have a baby. I've been thinking I should look into it."

"You want a *baby*?" Toni snatched the glass away from her. "Not another drop for you. I'll take that wine, thank you."

Maya had to laugh. "It's just something I'm thinking about. I haven't done anything. Relax, everyone."

Her comment had sent shockwaves through the little group. Good—at least they weren't quizzing her about her love life anymore.

Kate clapped her hands together. "If you ask me, you'd be a phenomenal mother, Maya. If you decide to do that, I'll support you one hundred percent. Babysitting, vomit cleanup, whatever you need."

Uh oh, what had she gotten into here? She wasn't really serious about the baby idea. But maybe she was. A few times lately, she'd woken in the middle of the night with a longing she couldn't pin down.

"That's sweet, but don't go planning any baby showers, please. I can't make any decisions while I'm under the influence."

"The wine?"

"The holidays," she corrected with a smile. "They mess me the F up."

Her little joke lightened the mood and her friends all relaxed back in their chairs.

"That's why all I want now is a little company for the holidays. Is that too much to ask?"

Toni got to her feet and opened another bottle of wine—a chocolate merlot that meant things were about to get serious.

"I guess we're back to square one, then. Maya's mystery date." She popped the cork with one smooth move. "Maybe we're overlooking the most obvious choice of all."

"Go solo like I do every other year?" Maya asked.

"Nope. What about the hunk right under your nose?"

It took a moment for Maya to figure out who she meant. "You mean Rune?"

"Is there another hunk living on your dad's property?"

"He's just a friend. Besides—" She broke off, shaking her head.

"Besides what? If there's something wrong with him, better tell me because every single girl in town is asking about him." Toni set the bottle down on the table, while Maya tried to shove aside the image of Rune as Lost Harbor's newest chick magnet.

"That's what's wrong with him. He's too attractive. Girls always loved him, even when he was a kid. I think that's why we became friends, because I got into a fight with him. But no matter how much I glared at him, he just wouldn't stop trying to be friends with shy Maya Badger with her braces and her purple bear barrettes."

"I already liked him, but now I like him even more," Kate declared. "Just imagine showing up to Mrs. Bellini's cookie exchange with Rune Larsen, hunky nurse. If that wouldn't wipe away all those Jerome memories, I don't know what would."

The image that formed in her mind was hard to resist, that was for sure. Everyone in town was curious about Rune. Why wouldn't they be interested in a handsome, friendly, effortlessly sexy man like Rune? "I don't want to mess with our friendship. And he's living at my dad's. It could get awkward."

"Not if you set the terms at the beginning." Trust Kate to take the legal approach.

"You're going to draw me up a contract?" said Maya dryly.

"Absolutely. Holiday Dating Agreement. Item One: Both parties shall be available for any and all holiday events unless otherwise specified."

Jessica laughed with delight, while Maya shook her head at their silliness. "Item Two: There shall be no flirting with parties not included in the agreement," Jess chimed in. "We don't want a repeat of the Jerome fiasco."

With a snort, Toni added, "Item Three. Bonus points for party clothes that show off those muscles."

"Don't forget item four." Maya figured she might as well get in on this too.

"Go for it," Kate urged. "What's item four?"

"No falling in love."

Her friends all booed and gave the thumbs down to that one. But as far as she was concerned, it was the most important item of all. Her relationship with Rune was far too enjoyable to risk ruining it with love, even if she were still capable of it.

No, she'd stick with friendship, respect, and flat-out ignoring her secret attraction to him. Someone on that app would do just fine for a temporary holiday boyfriend.

CHAPTER EIGHT

About two months until Christmas ...

RUNE GOT the feeling that Maya was avoiding him. He tried to time his sessions with Harris Badger to match Maya's daily visits. Sometimes it worked, but often he'd walk into the lingering scent Maya had left behind—the scent of cocoa butter and missed opportunities. Harris was always in a good mood after a visit from Maya, while Rune would be frustrated that he'd missed her.

He kept inviting her to the little fish house, but he noticed that she usually accepted only the invitations that included Cara.

Like picking the last currants in the woods bordering the property. Or helping Cara pull together a Halloween costume for the upcoming Haunted Harbor event. Or when she stopped by to explain "termination dust" on the day the first dusting of snow appeared on the high peaks across the bay. Apparently it meant that summer was officially "terminated."

Friend stuff. Because they were friends. Old friends. Good friends. The kind of friend you wanted to catch a glimpse of whenever you could. The kind who made your pulse pick up. The kind you pretended you didn't want to tumble into your bed.

Luckily, his work kept him quite busy. In a town like Lost Harbor, most people lived far outside the city limits. He spent an absurd amount of time driving to see his patients, and then making his way down long gravel roads to reach off-grid homesteads. Avoiding pet goats and piles of moose poop got to be second nature, as did delivering lectures on proper sanitation after using the outhouse.

Several of his patients were elderly with some great stories to tell about Lost Harbor and the earlier days of the town, before there was even a highway that led to it. He heard tales of how the mail used to come only once a month. Supplies arrived either by boat or small plane. In the old days, Misty Bay would freeze over and dog sleds would travel back and forth to Lost Souls Wilderness. Winter storms still battered the little harbor town, but according to the elders, they used to be even more massive and destructive.

From what he could tell, Lost Harborites were a rugged, independent lot who prided themselves on their ingenuity and ability to persevere. He respected the hell out of them—even if they tended to sport more facial hair than he was used to.

Some of his patients already knew details about him and Cara, such as the fact that they were living in Harris' guesthouse. They asked after Harris' health. They wanted to know how Cara liked the school so far.

The first time someone asked him about his sister, it worried him. It could be dangerous for too many people to know about them. It could make it that much easier for the stalker to locate them.

But in a town this small, there was no avoiding it, so he got used to the curious questions.

As he was currently telling Mrs. Holt, who'd gashed her arm

during the search for her yak and needed help changing out her bandage, "If Cara could literally sleep at the high school, she would. That's how much she loves it."

"I hear they love her too. So many of the boys are already in love with her. Is she allowed to date?"

"She's almost seventeen. If she wants to date someone, she can. But so far she's just getting to know the community."

That was the most tactful way he could put it. Cara had discovered her flirtatious side and had texts and phone calls coming into her burner phone at all hours of the day. He hoped it meant that she felt comfortable here in Lost Harbor, and that she was finally getting a taste of normal teenage life. It might not last long, after all.

"Ouch, that hurts," Mrs. Holt complained as he gently unwrapped the bandage from her arm.

He eyed the wound, which was beginning to pucker around the edges. "It's healing nicely. Good work, Mrs. Holt. I think we can leave off the antiseptic, but I'm going to rewrap this so you don't bonk it while you go through your day. What's the news on your yak?"

He offered the question as a way to distract her from his movements as he re-bandaged her arm.

"He's just so ornery, that creature. I thought he'd be back by now. He's probably on a bender somewhere. I'm used to that. He used to disappear for a few days and I always knew where to look. His boat."

Right. The reincarnated yak. He humored her, since it certainly wasn't his place to question her beliefs. "I suppose you've looked there already."

"Lucas sold the boat. I wasn't sorry to see it go. That boat caused me more trouble than I can say. You tell Harris we want him back at stitch-and-bitch as soon as he can. Otherwise we're going to come to him."

Everyone knew Maya and Harris. Every time he came back to the property, he had a handful of well-wishes to pass along—mixed in with some invitations. Potlucks. Cookie exchanges. Stitch-and-bitch meetings. Progressive dinners.

"What's a progressive dinner?" he asked Maya as he delivered the invitation on a day in late October.

She was unwinding a scarf from her neck; he recognized Harris' distinctive color choices. Yellow and purple always showed up in his knitted projects. Maya hung her coat and scarf on the coatrack and patted her hair back into its proper shape.

"Don't tell me someone roped you into one of those."

"You, not me. Don't worry, I accepted on your behalf."

She turned her best death glare on him, but he just stuck his hands in his pockets and whistled jauntily. "What's the matter? It sounds fun, whatever it is."

"How can you say it sounds fun when you don't even know what it is?"

"Because it has the word 'dinner' in it. You could use a meal out. You work all the time."

She ran a hand across her forehead, as if smoothing out the skin. Not that it needed smoothing; her skin was perfect, in his opinion. "Maybe, but that's not a meal out. That's a meal in which I have to cook something. How's Dad?"

"He's watching Antiques Roadshow, so he might be getting a little riled up. On the bright side, he had a haircut. That always puts him in a good mood."

Maya frowned slightly. "Vicki came today? That's like the third time since he got back. He doesn't get his hair cut that often."

"She says she doesn't mind making house calls, when it's for a handsome veteran like Harris. Honestly, I think I noticed some sparks."

An expression almost like panic flashed across her face. "Don't be ridiculous."

Did Maya have a problem with her father's hair stylist? In Rune's view, Vicki was a kind, vivacious woman who seemed to really care about Harris. She'd brought him a cranberry muffin from Sweet Harbor Bakery and a decaf latte with extra foam. He'd lit up with the biggest smile Rune had seen yet.

He changed the subject. "So what did I sign you up for without realizing it?"

"A progressive dinner is when you go from one house to another and each host serves a different course. Appetizers at one place, cocktails at another, dessert, after-dinner drinks, on and on. It's a nightmare for those of us who like to eat and move on with our lives. I don't have time to draw a meal out over an entire evening." She poked him in the chest. "You have to get me out of it."

"Are you sure? Because you could still use some social in your life. All I ever see you do is work."

"That's completely untrue. I just came from a drink with Toni at the Olde Salt."

A-ha. That was why she seemed more...unfocussed than usual. A little softer around the edges. Looking at him a little bit differently than usual. As if she was seeing grown-up Rune instead of little boy Jay-Jay.

Occasionally he caught spontaneous flashes like that from her. To be honest, he lived for those moments.

"Cool. I mean, it's no *Antiques Roadshow* but—"

From the living room, they both heard Harris shout, "Too low, you idiot! Too damn low." Maya let out a giggle, which was a surprisingly girlish and endearing sound for her to make.

"There's something I want to talk to you about," she said, tugging him by the elbow into Harris' kitchen.

"Still mad about that dinner invite? Because I didn't actually accept it for you. I was just seeing if I could trick you into actually doing something fun for yourself."

She waved a hand at him as she opened the fridge and took out a pitcher of Kool-Aid. Harris loved his Kool-Aid, though Maya was more of a soda drinker. She poured herself a glass and guzzled it down. "Not necessary. I'm in charge of my own fun."

"Then you might want to fire yourself. Maya, remember how much fun we used to have in Hawaii?"

"When we were kids and had no responsibilities, you mean?" She washed out her glass and stuck it on the drying rack.

"We all have responsibilities," he pointed out. "It doesn't mean we have to take everything so seriously."

"But that's you. You always were the best at goofing around. I was the good girl. Still am." She smiled at him smugly and hoisted herself up on Harris' counter. "Except when I'm breaking my father's rules in his own house. It's a good thing he's busy yelling at his TV screen right now."

"You rebel. I should report you to the authorities."

Her lips quirked. He loved watching the way his teasing affected her. It was almost as if no one really joked around with her anymore. They were all too daunted by her position as police chief.

"So what did you want to talk to me about?" He propped his hip against the counter. "I have to pick up Cara soon, but I have a few minutes."

"Where's Cara?"

"She has a new friend. Maggie, the girl from Lost Souls Wilderness. Maggie's showing her the wonders of this thing called a cheeseburger at the Burger Queen. Cara's playing along like she's never seen one before. She's such a good sport, my sis." He waited for her to say more. "Are you stalling?"

She swung her legs against the counter, her stockinged feet hitting the side. Harris didn't allow shoes in his house, so everyone either wore house slippers or socks. He also didn't care for bare feet, which had upset Cara the first time she'd waltzed in after fishing on the dock.

"A little bit," she admitted. She started to say something, then stopped, then shook her head at herself, then tried again. "You're still good with boats, right?"

He lifted his eyebrows. That wasn't what he'd been expecting her to say. "Yes, of course. Boats, paddleboards, fins, anything ocean-related. What do you need?"

"I need someone to pilot a boat around a few of the coves across the bay. I don't want word getting out to anyone." She hesitated before continuing. "It's connected to the Lost Souls investigation."

Oh. So this was a work-related situation. That was disappointing. But if that was what it took for Maya to stop avoiding him, he'd take it. He really missed the old days when he and Maya had been two peas in a pod, playing on the beach and drinking water straight from the coconuts. He remembered so much laughter and telling of secrets and just all-around joy. What would it take to bring back that kind of connection to Maya?

"Whatever you need," he told her. "Working around my schedule, of course. Do you have a boat in mind?"

"We can use Dad's. It would make him ridiculously happy if we did, actually. He never understood why I didn't follow in his boat-crazy footsteps."

"Are you going to fill me in on our mission?"

"It's on a need-to-know basis." She rolled her shoulders to release tension.

"Got it. So that's it? That's all you wanted to ask me?" He got the feeling that wasn't what she'd intended to ask him at first. But he knew from the old days that Maya did things when she was good and ready, and not before.

"Should there be something else?"

"You could ask for a little help with those tight trapezius muscles."

Her dark eyes flew to his, surprised.

He flexed his hands out in front of him. "Come on, let me get some of those kinks out for you. You can try out my nursing skills for yourself."

He thought she might decline, based on the walls she kept putting up. But she must have really needed a shoulder rub, because she stepped in front of him and turned her back. Gently he moved her hair over one shoulder.

"Remember the time I put those puffs in your hair?" he asked as he placed his hands on her shoulders. So finely formed, those shoulders. Almost a work of art. With his thumbs, he tested the tautness of her tendons. Ouch. She could definitely use his help.

"I don't think I've ever laughed so hard," she murmured. "I came out of there looking like a mutant hedgehog that got caught in a storm."

He started gently, stroking the slope of her neck down to the shoulder joint. She relaxed under the touch and let out a sigh. "That feels great, Rune. But don't you have something else you should be doing now? I'm not your patient."

"Right now you are," he said firmly. "Haven't you heard about caretaker fatigue? You can't tend to your father if you don't take care of yourself. Just relax."

"What about Cara? Don't you have to pick her up?"

"I'll let you know when I have to go. She and Maggie are probably making friends with the crows begging for French fries. She's going to text me when she's ready."

Maya dipped her head so her chin met her chest, exposing more of the smooth brown lines of her neck. He switched his attention to the two tendons that ran up to her occipital muscle. Stroke, knead, release.

He propped his rear against the kitchen counter and drew her along with him. She allowed herself to be pulled closer, so they were separated by a bare inch or so. Her skin felt so satiny under his stroking, and he found huge satisfaction in the way her tight muscles relaxed.

She deserved a back rub every damn night. Someone in her life should be on full-time back rub duty.

With a pang, he knew that person couldn't be him. Time was already ticking away. Any day now they might see some sign that the stalker had located them.

He shoved the thought away and focused on the delightful task in front of him. When that man showed up, he'd deal with it. Until then, he was going to enjoy every second he got to spend with his childhood buddy.

Funny thing, though. If Maya was just a childhood buddy, would he be feeling desire spread through his system like a slow infusion of top-shelf brandy? Would his cock be stirring to life?

Get a grip. You're a nurse right now. Not a teenage boy hot for a girl. Distract yourself.

"Why'd you decide to become a police officer?" he asked her. "It's like you picked the most stressful job you could find in a place that's mostly peace and quiet."

"Ha. It wasn't about the stress. It was about the challenge." Her voice was low and husky, almost dreamy, and it sent another shot of desire into his veins. "It's actually kind of dumb, but there was this kid in high school who tried to bully me. He was pretty racist, to be honest. We despised each other."

He tensed at the thought of someone bullying Maya. "Is he still in town? Can I beat his ass?"

She shook her head slightly. "He's different now. He wrecked his car and it really messed him up. Recovery was a bitch, but he came out with a new attitude. Very lovey and tearful. He actually apologized to me for the shit he did in high school."

"I've seen that kind of thing happen." He moved his hands to the front of her shoulders. "A medical crisis can really change a person. Not always, but sometimes."

"Yeah." She moaned as he worked on the pressure point at the tip of her shoulder joint. "That's fricking amazing, Rune. I could fall asleep standing right here."

He smiled, picturing himself carrying her to the couch. Or maybe even to his car so he could drive her home. Where they'd be alone.

Until Cara texted and he had to leave.

"Don't sleep yet. Go on with your story."

"Right. So they held a job fair at our high school, and the Lost Harbor police gave a pretty decent presentation. My nemesis was super-interested in applying, and I thought about what it would be like if he was the face of law and order in Lost Harbor. It would have been terrible. So after he'd moved on to the fish-processing table, I talked to the LHPD. They had these aptitude tests we could fill out. They told me I scored better than anyone. They wanted to recruit me. And they told the bully dude that he'd be better off fishing. So they showed me where to sign up for a training program in Anchorage and offered me a job."

"And you liked it? I always thought you'd be a writer because of all the books you read."

She laughed—probably at the doubt in his voice. "I liked it a lot. I was good at it. Really good. It pushed my buttons for two reasons. I like being the voice of reason and authority. Always have."

"Won't argue with that. If I'd listened to you, I wouldn't have a jellyfish scar on my belly."

"You *still* have that?"

He bit back the urge to offer to prove it. With Maya and her barriers, he had to be careful.

"What's the other reason?"

"Whatever I did, I wanted to be excellent at it. I wanted respect, you know?"

"You definitely have that."

"Yeah. It took some work, but I got there." He loved hearing the pride in her voice. "It helped that everyone knew my father. The Coast Guard gets a lot of love around here..." She trailed off as he angled her head down to massage the last traces of tension at the base of her skull. Instead of words, she let out a moan of appreciation.

Since she couldn't see him, he allowed himself a smug grin. Police Chief Maya Badger might be an independent woman who prided herself on keeping her cool—but she liked a good back massage as much as anyone.

"What about you?" she murmured. "You like being a nurse?"

His phone beeped, breaking the moment. "We can talk about that later." Reluctantly, he withdrew his hands from her warm skin. "I have to pick up Cara."

Maya lifted her head and turned it from side to side. "So much better. Thank you, Rune. You know she's old enough to drive herself in Alaska, right?"

"We're looking into it. I don't like the idea of her driving alone."

Her eyes, the deep dark color of honey melting under the sun, captured his, their expression unreadable. He thought he detected sensuality in her gaze, but that could have been wishful thinking. "Tough to be your sister's twenty-four-hour guardian."

He shrugged uncomfortably. He didn't think of it as "tough." It was just the way things were. The way they had to be.

"See you soon, Maya. Call me when it's time for your secret boat mission."

He headed for the Arctic entry and collected his jacket from the peg. She followed after him, padding across the floor in her striped socks. "Don't say anything about that, okay? Not even to

Cara. I want to keep this entirely off the town radar. That's why I need you."

"Got it."

So that was why she needed him. Not because she trusted him or wanted to get him alone in an ocean-going vessel. But because he wasn't part of the town grapevine.

But hey—on the bright side, they would, in fact, be alone in an ocean-going vessel. So there was that.

CHAPTER NINE

How was it possible that she could command respect as a police chief and yet not have the nerve to ask Rune to be her holiday date?

Maya bustled around in the *Egret*, her father's twenty-six foot, twin 200 horsepower engine Sea Sport Kodiak, getting it ready for the trip into the bay in frigid twenty-degree temps.

She'd been on the verge of doing it last night in Harris' kitchen. After another fifty-two dating app busts, she'd deleted the app. She'd talked herself into just...throwing the idea out there to Rune.

But at the last minute she'd chickened out and gone for the boat request instead.

Coward.

But her need for a pilot was real. Finally...*finally*...she'd heard from the FBI. Agent Dick Clement.

"We intercepted a communication about a drop-off in Lost Souls Wilderness. Can you check it out for us?"

"You have a location?"

"Coordinates and a rough time window, that's it."

"Send them over." Since she was on the phone, she'd done an invisible happy dance. "Does this mean you're actually opening a case?"

"Don't get ahead of yourself, Badger. Monitor this drop-off and we'll talk. It could be nothing. Believe me, you don't want your name on something that turns out to be a big waste of our time."

She'd had to clench her teeth to keep back everything she'd wanted to say to that.

But now that Rune had agreed to be her boat pilot for this mission, maybe she could try again. It shouldn't be so hard! But it felt like the first step in a risky direction.

The *Egret* rose and fell as a departing boat's wake rippled under her hull. Maya grabbed onto a hand hold, even though she knew there was no danger. Harris used the *Egret* for fishing and getting out on the water on a sunny day, and of course had trained her in the basics.

But boating—not for her. She always got seasick on the water. Her father had offered her all kinds of prevention techniques—an acupressure bracelet, Dramamine, deep breathing, fixing her gaze on the horizon until her eyes dried out. None of it had worked completely, so she preferred to stay land-based.

Even the smell of the harbor—a little fishy, a little salty, a little diesel-y—made her slightly nauseous.

Lucas Holt, the harbormaster, ambled down the float toward the Egret. He wore a Helly Hansen jacket and a thick knitted watch cap that set off the strong lines of his face. She and Lucas had dated in high school; in fact, he'd been her first heartbreak, before she knew what heartbreak really was.

Now he was engaged, with a new family.

"I must have eaten some bad crab cakes at Captain Crabbie's. Is that really our very own ocean-hating police chief heading out to sea? Official business?"

She unscrewed the cap of the gas tank and checked the level. This wasn't great, that she'd been noticed before she even left the harbor. But maybe it was better this way. Whatever she told Lucas, he could tell other people who asked.

"This is strictly personal," she told him. "Rune hasn't seen Misty Bay yet, and we're running out of time before winter sets in."

She shivered at the very sound of the word "winter."

Lucas eyed her four-inch-thick parka and thick winter gloves. "You might have already missed that window."

Shrugging, she screwed the cap back on the tank. "Better late than never. Rune really wants to see the bay. You've met Rune, right? The travel nurse?"

"My mother has. She raves about him."

On cue, Rune hurried down the boat slip. In his rubber fishing boots and Carhartts, he almost looked like an Alaskan. "Sorry I'm late. Last-minute infusion emergency."

"Rune, this is Lucas Holt, the harbormaster. I was just telling him how much you've been wanting to see the bay."

He didn't miss a beat. "You bet. Nothing like the Pacific Ocean on a twenty-degree day. Something to tell my grandkids about. It's a Bucket List item, for sure."

Lucas narrowed his eyes suspiciously. "Do you know much about boats? I know they're not Maya's thing. Let me see if Megan can take you guys out on the *Forget Me Not*. I'll call her right now."

"No." Maya groaned inwardly. This was exactly what she'd been worried about. Lost Harbor was a small town to start with, and the harbor community itself even more so. "Rune is a very experienced boat pilot. He grew up on Oahu. He knows everything about boats."

Lucas looked Rune up and down, but with more respect than before. "Alaska waters are a lot different from Hawaii's."

"Hey, the humpback whales go back and forth. I think I can handle it." Rune stepped onto the gunwale, then onto the deck. From the way he instantly got his balance, it was obvious he was a natural on the water.

Lucas hung around a few more minutes as Rune familiarized himself with the controls and the gauges. "All right then. Stay safe out there."

"Stop worrying." Maya shooed him away. "You're the harbor-master, not the harbor mother hen."

"Ha ha." But he relented and headed back to the ramp that led up to the boardwalk. Over his shoulder, he called, "Don't forget the Haunted Harbor party. Command appearance. No excuses."

She cringed at the reminder. She considered the Haunted Harbor party to be the kickoff of the holiday "relive the Jerome disaster" season. They'd gone together, and in fact had kissed for the first time behind a fake gravestone.

"That's not how people usually look after they get an invitation to a party," Rune observed as he tested the wipers that kept ocean spray from completely coating the windshield.

"I don't want to talk about it," she grumbled. "Come on, let's go before someone else shows up."

She handed him the key and he started the engine. He looked out at the sullen gray water of the harbor and the low overcast clouds trailing across the sky overhead. "I like our cover story, by the way," he said dryly. "Makes total sense that I wouldn't be able to wait for a warm, sunny day to see the bay."

Laughing, she patted him on the back. Even through his thick fleece-lined jacket, she could feel the hardness of his muscles. It made her think of the strength in his hands while he'd worked the tension out of her neck. She hadn't slept so well in weeks. Not since her father had gone into the hospital.

"Just go with it. Everyone knows I never willingly go out on the water. It's the only thing that makes sense."

"You're the boss. Really curious what this is all about."

"All in good time." She went back onto the deck to cast off the lines. "Ready," she called to him.

She stayed out on the open deck while Rune slowly steered the boat out of the slip. The fumes from inside the cabin tended to trigger her seasickness. As they glided through the harbor, she fixed her gaze on the horizon—the snow-dusted bulk of the mountains on the other side of the bay.

As they exited the harbor and gained speed, the icy wind bit at her cheeks and nose.

Okay, she could admit it. This was crazy.

She abandoned the open deck and ducked into the cabin, where Rune was whistling at the steering wheel, legs braced apart.

"Doing okay?" he asked her.

Not wanting to lie, she didn't answer that question. "Head for these GPS coordinates." She rattled off the numbers Agent Clement had given her. He punched them into the GPS and swung the wheel to the east, toward Far Point.

"Are we meeting someone out there?" he asked.

"Not exactly." She hesitated, not sure how much to tell him. She knew he was discreet; he had to keep all his patients' information confidential, after all. With all of his experience dodging the stalker, he knew how to handle himself. And then there was the time in Hawaii when they'd walked through a forbidden lava tube and he hadn't told her father.

She could trust him.

"What I'm about to tell you is completely confidential," she said seriously. "You cannot say anything to anyone."

"You have my word."

"I've been trying to get the Feds to come down and investigate some suspected criminal activity in Lost Souls. But I've gotten nowhere with that. I've started taking in personally, to be honest. It's like they don't trust a young black female police chief. Go figure."

"Idiots."

Major points for his instant backup. "Anyway, they finally got hold of their own red flag and they want me to check it out. The coordinates are from a little cove just past Far Point. We're supposed to get close enough so we can see if anything's going on, but not engage. I brought my zoom lens in case I can get some pictures. We have to make it look like we're just sight-seeing or something so we don't burn the source. We can always pull out my dad's fishing rods if we need to make it look more real."

Rune listened closely, frowning all the while. "If they get a glimpse of you, won't they recognize the police chief?"

She gestured at her own bundled-up body. "No uniform, a bulky hat, a scarf. They'll barely be able to tell that I'm human."

Her joke didn't chase away his expression of concern. "Even so, I think you should stay out of sight. You can take pictures from inside the wheelhouse, right?"

"I'm not going to hide away." Irritated, she dug around in her dry bag for her camera. "You have no idea how frustrating this whole case has been. They won't even admit there *is* a case. If this is the only thing they want me to do, I'm damn well going to do it."

He snorted, spearing her with an amused sidelong glance. "Hit a nerve, did I? Fine. I just want to volunteer my services as a complete stranger that no one's going to recognize."

A wave crashed over the bow. The impact shivered through the *Egret*. Maya gagged as the first surge of seasickness hit. She staggered to the bench and sat down, gripping a handhold as if her life depended on it. "Let me know when we get close," she said tightly. "I'll be staring at the horizon until then. That faraway one, that doesn't keep rocking up and down."

"Want me to slow down?" The swells didn't seem to bother him. He shook his hair back from his face, a picture of exhilaration with his braced legs and flashing eyes. Like when he used to bodyboard right up onto the sand at her feet.

"No," she managed through gritted teeth. "I don't want to miss the window when they're supposed to be there. Lucas already delayed us."

She went quiet after that, focusing on keeping the gorge from rising in her throat. How could the daughter of a lifelong Coastie be so prone to seasickness? Maybe her mother had suffered from it too. She didn't know.

"Does it help if I talk or is it better if you suffer in silence?" Rune asked over his shoulder, not taking his eyes from the churning waves ahead.

"I honestly hate you a little bit right now," she groaned. "You're having fun, aren't you?"

"Hell yes. I haven't been on a boat in a while. Sorry, do you want me to look more miserable? I can fake it."

"No. It's fine." Would it help for him to distract her with conversation? It was worth a try. "Talk to me. Was it hard switching from EMT to nurse?"

A white froth of ocean spray splashed across the outside of the cabin enclosure. She tightened her grip on the handhold.

"A little." Expertly, he kept the *Egret* headed into the waves instead of letting them hit the side of the boat. Harris would be proud. "I liked the adrenaline of being a paramedic. You know me, I like action. Home-visit nursing has a slower pace. But it has its good parts too. When you're a paramedic, you never get to know anything about your patients. You never see them again after you get them to the ER. Now I get to know all about them. A little too much, sometimes. But that's okay. People are so grateful for the help. They bake me cookies, they crochet me little handmade gnomes, they set me up with their granddaughters."

Okay, now that was interesting. "I've never heard of scamming dates through home nurse visits."

"I haven't *gone* on any dates like that," he corrected with a laugh. "But it's kind of them to try."

"Why don't you have a girlfriend? You were always such a girl-magnet." This was something she'd been wondering about for a while, but apparently it took being about to vomit on her dad's boat to actually ask about it.

"I have *girls*," he said lightly. "Girlfriend implies longevity. It's hard to do that when I have to move every few months."

Of course. She kept forgetting that he was not long for this part of the world. "Do you think things will change at some point for Cara? Will she go to college?"

"You mean, how long do I have to be her bodyguard? I don't have an answer to that." A seagull hovered over the deck, then flapped away when he realized they weren't carrying any fish. "We'll see what things are like when that time comes. We're hoping he moves on to another obsession, like toy trains or Fortnite. Or, if we get lucky, he'll slip up and do something he can be arrested for. I'd love to stop him from ruining some other girl's life."

Hearing the frustration in his voice, Maya vowed to herself that she'd do everything *she* could to make that happen—if she had the opportunity.

"If it's any comfort, Cara seems like a pretty happy girl. Especially considering the circumstances. You're a good guardian."

He glanced over at her, looking touched. "Thank you. We manage. But that's mostly due to her. She's so good-natured. I don't know where she gets it."

"What are you talking about? You're good-natured too. You always had the best smile, like a toothpaste commercial. That's why all the girls loved you. You were the hot ticket of fourth grade."

He snorted. "Guess I peaked early."

"Uh...I don't think so." She ran her eyes up and down his strong form, so sexy the way he manhandled the wheel. Long lean legs, muscular thighs braced apart—he made her mouth water.

And not in the seasick way.

Her scan of his body brought her back up to his face—where she got busted by his amused smoky green eyes.

Quick. Change the subject. "Why'd you decide to be friends with me back then?"

"You mean after I saved your life?" He turned back to watching the ocean rocking them up and down, side to side.

"Here we go again. Okay, yes, after you saved my life. Which you might be doing again, right now." The boat slammed into the valley between two waves.

Again, he seemed unbothered. "Why did you want to be *my* friend? I was a scrawny little hyperactive rule-breaker."

"But you were always so much fun. I was more serious."

"Maybe that's part of it. We were so different back then. You were calm and sensible—until I started getting you into trouble." He gave a Dr. Evil laugh. "Besides, you were fun too. You made me laugh."

A blast of wind found its way into the cabin, and she shrank into her parka. "Are you laughing at me right now?" she asked dryly. "Seasick and miserable?"

"A little." He grinned at her, then shook his head. "No, of course not. You know what's funny? We're not as different now. Becoming a full-time guardian made me a lot less of a goofball."

"I hope you still have some Jay-Jay in you. I miss that little kid."

"Want me to bring him back? Say the word and I'll do those

hula dances that always made you laugh. I used to do anything just to make you laugh. It was always a good day when you flashed those braces at me."

She ran her tongue across her teeth, remembering the feel of those braces. "I hated those things."

"Do you remember when we kissed behind the lifeguard stand? When we were making fun of all the teenagers?"

Stunned, her mouth fell open. She'd forgotten all about that! She and Rune had *kissed.* Just a kid kiss, obviously. A quick planting of lips against lips. But *still.* She'd forgotten all about it until just now.

Rune looked over at her and gave a double-take. "Wait...you forgot about it? Don't break my heart like that."

"No, I just...okay, yes, I forgot. We were nine! And my Dad would have flipped. I probably blocked it out."

Turning back to his navigating, he shook his head ruefully. "Damn, that hurts, Maya. That was my first kiss."

"Well, mine too. Until my next kiss, which I guess I *thought* was my first..." She trailed off at Rune's look of outrage.

"I didn't even get credit for being your first kiss? I demand a recount."

She burst out laughing. "You want me to track down Jimmy Melkov and inform him that he was, in fact, my second kiss, not my first?"

"If it's not too much trouble."

Torn between laughing and rolling her eyes, she realized with a start that she'd forgotten all about her seasickness. Apparently talking about kissing was the magic pill she'd been looking for all this time. "I'll consider it."

"You'll consider it. That's what you tell people when they come to you with wacky ideas about how to keep the peace in Lost Harbor, isn't it?"

He knew her so well. How *did* he know her so well? It was

strange, really, that she felt a kind of bedrock familiarity with Rune when they were different in so many ways. Starting with skin color, of course. Gender. State of origin. Family background. And yet—they both knew the pain of a missing parent. They both felt like outsiders at times. Maybe all that time they spent together as kids had made her comfortable with him on a cellular level.

"It might be," she admitted. "But don't tell anyone my secrets."

"I take patient confidentiality seriously."

She tilted her head at him with a patented Badger family skeptical frown. "Patient?"

"That neck massage last night. Once a patient, always a patient."

Right...that massage. All the sensations from last night came surging back. The gentle skill in those strong, practiced hands of his. The way his warmth sank through her skin into her muscles. The way her entire body succumbed to the floating bliss he generated with each stroke.

She cleared her throat. "Good to know."

Time to change the subject again. This was getting entirely too awkward. Her cheeks were flushing and she felt overheated in her parka. That was definitely a first—since when did she ever feel too hot on a boat on the ocean in late October in Alaska?

She pointed up ahead. "That spur there, with the crag that looks like Abraham Lincoln, that's Far Point. The cove should be just around the other side. It's open ocean out there, so it'll be a lot rougher. And most casual boaters don't go past Far Point. So we have to look like we didn't intend to go that far."

"How should we do that?"

"Keep the boat pointed toward Mount Sage." She gestured at the outline of the volcano on the horizon. Its flanks gleamed white with fresh snow. On foggy days the mountain couldn't be seen, but today it stood out against the overcast sky. "Let's make it look as if we're trying to get a good shot of the volcano."

"Got it."

She dug out her binoculars and kneeled on the bench that offered the closest view of Far Point. If she stayed close to the handhold, she might be hard to spot if someone onshore was also checking them out with binoculars.

As soon as they rounded the point, everything changed. The wind whined at a higher volume, and the waves slammed even harder into the *Egret*, making the entire boat shudder from stem to stern. Maya's pulse raced at triple speed.

This is Dad's boat, she kept telling herself. *He keeps it in perfect shape. No one maintains a boat like Dad. He wouldn't let us use it otherwise.*

Neither of them spoke as they drew closer to the coordinates Agent Clement had sent her. It was too difficult to talk above the drone of the engine, the slap of the hull against the water, the hiss of spray splashing over the sides and the occasional lonely cry of a curious seagull.

Now that their fun kissing conversation was over, the seasickness clawed at her throat. But she refused to give in to it. She trained her binoculars on the shoreline. The rise and fall movement of the boat made it hard to focus. Everything was a blur of forests and rocks.

"We're about as close as we're going to get to those coordinates," Rune said quietly.

"Okay, slow us down. Here." She dropped the binoculars for a moment to hand him her bag, which held her camera. "Pretend you're taking a picture of the mountain."

He throttled down the engine into an idle and took the bag from her. "I'm going to actually take a photo, just in case anyone questions us."

"Fine," she said absently as she refocused on the shoreline.

Now that the boat was idling, she could sync to its motion a little better. Up and down, up and down. Up was when she got the best line of sight to the hidden cove.

Movement. On the shore. A bear? No, the bears were hibernating by now. Had to be a person. Yes. A person. Two people. And there—a boat anchored behind a little island of rock. She couldn't get a fix on any faces or other identifying features of either the people or the boat.

But that wasn't her mission. She was merely supposed to confirm that the coordinates were legit. That the information the agent had intercepted was real.

Mission accomplished.

But she wanted more. "Hand me my camera." Without looking behind her, she held out her hand. Rune set the body of the camera into her palm. With the zoom lens on, it was quite heavy. She lifted it to her face and quickly switched out the binoculars for the camera.

It took a moment to adjust to the different focal length of the zoom lens. When she did, she saw that something had changed— the two men were looking right at her.

"Shit." She dropped the camera onto the cushioned bench at her side. "Shit. They're looking at us."

Rune was still next to her, one hand on the steering wheel to keep the boat steady.

Without thinking too hard about it, she rose to her feet and grabbed Rune by the collar of his jacket, pulling him close. "How about a fake kiss?" she asked quickly. "Just make it look good from a distance."

He flashed her a pirate grin and cupped her face with his free hand. "My pleasure. I'm an excellent fake kisser."

"Come on, hurry."

He bent his head over hers, but he still didn't go for the kiss. "You can't hurry a fake kiss, or it will *look* fake. We're flirting, we're completely caught up in each other, we don't even care that we're drifting on the open ocean. Keep looking at me, just like that except without the 'what the hell are you talking about' expression."

She smothered a laugh and relaxed her face into a dazzled smile. As if Rune was the most wonderful thing in the world, better than chocolate and bubble baths combined.

He blinked, as if she'd momentarily thrown him off his game with her smile. A personal triumph, she figured.

"That's...good," he said, a little more strained than before.

For a fake kiss, he sure was overthinking it. They needed to get this thing done.

She took command and wrapped her hand around the back of his neck. Tugging him down, she offered him her mouth. "Let's do this," she hissed. "Tick-tock."

Honestly, why did she always have to be the one with any common sense? If those men onshore had binoculars, they were already watching. To throw them off, she only had a few moments. If the men thought they'd been busted, they might rework their entire comms system. The lead would be worthless. The source would be burned. The case back to square one.

And then all thoughts of logic flew from her mind as Rune claimed her lips with a kiss that sent shock waves through her system. Warmth...sizzle...sunshine...all of it swirled together in a rush of brilliant pleasure. His lips were firm and generous at the same time, as if they were inviting her into his world. A world where she would be queen and he would be whatever she needed.

A kind of exhilaration swept through her and she parted her lips for more. He gave it to her, sweeping his tongue inside the cave of her mouth, where every surface tingled and warmed at his touch.

Fake kiss, my ass.

This was the real thing and she couldn't get enough of it. She drank him in as if she'd been starving for this, pining for it. Her mind—always working, always on guard—let go like an anchor releasing her to drift on the current. She lost herself in the flood of pure physical joy.

She staggered as the boat got slammed with a supersized wave. Rune held her tight so she didn't lose her balance. "I need to steer this thing," he murmured against her lips before turning back to the helm.

"Yes. Yeah. Of course." She ran her tongue across her lips, tasting salt from the spray and sweet from Rune. She plopped down onto the bench as he wrestled with the wheel. Picking up her binoculars, she focused on the spot where the two men had been.

They were gone—or maybe her angle had changed and she couldn't see them anymore.

She dropped her glasses and sighed. Hopefully she hadn't messed anything up by making them suspicious. "Go ahead and pick up speed. Let's keep going toward Mount Sage for a bit."

"Roger that."

Was his voice a little gruffer than usual? Was it the effect of the salt in the air?

He put the boat in gear and they cruised farther into the bay. She watched the little cove as it receded into the distance, swallowed up by the greater landscape of forests and rugged outcroppings.

What now? How to handle this? She and Rune had kissed, and there was no way she could forget about it the way she had when she was a kid.

Maybe never mention it again?

Or maybe *do* it again?

The tempting thought hovered out there like the promise of an ice cream sundae after a long week. *Treat yo-self,* she could imagine her cousin Reecie in Anchorage saying. *Go for it*, Kate would urge. *I knew it*, Jessica would say.

"Tell me when you're ready to head back," Rune said. "It's your call." His voice had returned to normal. She wondered what he was thinking about this situation. Then again, he didn't over-think things like she did. He probably wasn't worried about it at all. He probably kissed people all the time—all those non-girl-friend "girls" he'd talked about.

"I will," she told him. "Give it a few more minutes."

"The other thing is your call too," Rune said softly, his attention still on the choppy water ahead.

"What are you talking about?"

"I know you're trying to decide what to do about that kiss. I can see your wheels spinning from here."

"I'm not—okay, I am. I didn't intend for it to be like that."

"It's my fault." His voice shifted to a jaunty cheerfulness. "My pride was hurt that you forgot the first kiss. I was aiming for 'best kiss.' One that you wouldn't forget. That's all."

It wasn't all. She could hear it in his voice. It was so much more complicated than that. Friendship, attraction, sizzle...all that, lined up against her better judgment. But even so, it touched her that he was trying to make the whole thing easier for her.

"*Best* kiss? Isn't that a little arrogant?" She adopted a teasing tone to match his.

"Second best? Third? Just tell me it wasn't the worst. Gotta start somewhere."

"It wasn't the worst."

That was as far as she could go right now.

And maybe it was the best. Because right at this moment, she couldn't think of any other *specific* kiss that might compete with it.

CHAPTER TEN

They didn't discuss the kiss again. But that didn't mean Rune didn't think about it as they made their way back to the harbor. Hell, the lush softness and heady flavor of her lips might never leave him. He'd never forgotten the first kiss, after all. Why would he forget this one, when he was a full-grown adult and she was a beautiful, fascinating all-grown-up woman?

But she obviously didn't want to talk about it, so he let it be. Maya had her reasons. He had to respect them.

After they got the *Egret* squared away in its slip, they unloaded their bags onto the float.

A scraggly looking dude riding a bicycle stopped on the boardwalk above them. Rune squinted at the bike—was that a chicken perched on the handlebars?

"Chief Badger!" The man waved at them. "Get any fish?"

"Hey there, Boris. No sir, no fish for us. We got some photos of the volcano though."

"She about to blow?" His eyes went wide with alarm. He wasn't "all there," Rune realized.

"No no. Calm as can be." Maya shouldered the last bag and

stepped onto the float. "How are things here in the harbor? Anything to report?"

"Nothing much. Calm as can be." He repeated her phrase back at her.

"All right then. Keep up the good work."

The man's face lit up with an eager grin. "I will, Chief." He kicked his bike into motion and pedaled down the empty boardwalk.

"Boris Clancy," she explained. "He's a fixture around here."

"That was kind of you," he said softly.

"Everyone needs to feel useful. He's been through a lot in his life."

She led the way up the ramp, which was tilted at a steep angle because the tide was so low.

"You're not a typical police chief, are you?"

"I don't really care what other chiefs are like. I live here and I know this community. That's what I care about. Someone like Boris, he's had trauma in his life. Just because he's disabled doesn't mean he shouldn't get respect like anyone else. If I see someone hassling him—sometimes a kid or a tourist will make fun of his chickens—I step in. But if he goes on a bender and crosses a line, he'll find himself in that holding cell. He's been there plenty of times. That's how you serve and protect. You have to know your people and consider them your charges. *All* of your people. Everyone wants to be safe and respected. That's what I aim for." She caught herself with a shake of her head as they reached the boardwalk. Most of the shops and restaurants were boarded up for the winter, giving it the look of a ghost town. "Don't get me started on all that. It's a pet topic. Did you get some good photos of the volcano? I'm kicking myself for not getting a shot of that cove."

"I got one."

"Got one what?" She dug into her bag for the camera, which she'd already packed into its case.

"I got the shot of the meeting in the cove. Not sure how much I got, but I'm pretty sure two people and a boat should show up. Maybe your FBI dude can enhance the photo. I've seen that in movies, no idea if it's actually a thing."

She looked at him as if he'd just descended from Heaven on a cloud. "You *got* the shot? Seriously?"

"I think so. I tried, anyway. You'll have to see for yourself how it turned out." He dug his phone out of his pocket to check the time. "I have to pick up Cara."

"I might see you up at the property. My dad wanted me to come over tonight."

"Ahhh." He knew what that was all about. Harris had been talking about it for a few days—but had sworn him to secrecy until the right moment.

"What does that mean?"

"Nothing. It's just a sound." They reached the gravel lot where both their cars were parked. A crow pecked at a piece of roll someone had dropped. It flapped its wings and hopped a few inches away. As soon as they'd passed by, it reclaimed its prize. "I'll see you later."

"And I will be finding out what that 'ahhhh' was all about. If it's something about my dad's health, you better tell me now."

"It's not," he said quickly. "Harris doesn't even need me anymore. I just stop in to say hi now and then. It's a routine we have. I check his vitals, he asks what I had for breakfast and offers me leftover buttermilk pancakes with the butter and syrup he shouldn't be eating."

She sighed. "I know. His diet is the worst. But he just won't listen to me."

He reached his car and opened the trunk to toss his bag inside. "Welcome to the frustrating life of a home health nurse."

"I wish I could just arrest him and make him eat right," Maya grumbled. She was so cute in her homemade purple hat and the bulky scarf wrapped around her neck that he wanted to sweep her into his arms right there in the parking lot.

No, he wouldn't be forgetting about that kiss anytime soon.

"It's always an option." He hovered next to his car door, reluctant to say goodbye. They'd taken a big step closer with that boat ride, and that kiss. But had it actually been two steps backwards? Would she start avoiding him even more now? He didn't know how to make it clear that he just wanted to be around her. Friend, pilot, kisser, whatever.

Kissing was best, but not required.

"Thanks for helping out, Rune." She buried her hands in her parka pockets as a gust of wind caught her. "Piloting the boat, giving me a cover story, getting that photo. I really appreciate it."

"Happy to help," he said neutrally. "Serve and protect, right?"

She smiled at that. "That could be your motto too. You serve your patients and you protect Cara."

"Two peas in a pod, just like before." He winked at her and got into his car, then backed out of the lot.

He whooshed out a long breath as he headed away from the harbor. How long could he pretend that she didn't affect him? That they were just old buddies?

Yeah, after that kiss, that ship might have sailed. So to speak.

CHAPTER ELEVEN

The moment Rune picked her up at the high school, Cara launched into one of her nonstop chatter-rants. The audition for the Christmas play that she'd messed up. The girls who had called her Toothpaste Barbie because of the way she smiled. The teacher who had it in for her because she'd dared to question her definition of "colonialism." The coach who wanted her to try out for the ski team even though she'd never so much as put on a pair of skis.

It was all so *normal* that he could have cried. Not a single thing about a letter slipped into her backpack or a weird message passed to her by another student. Nothing about dried flowers appearing in one of her textbooks or a drawing of herself tacked onto a bulletin board at the Laundromat.

All of those things had happened at some point over the past two years. He had no idea how this twisted man was able to get so close to Cara without being tagged as someone suspicious. Or why Cara didn't spot him herself. She knew what he looked like. He must be really good at masking his appearance.

They had a few errands to do in town, which gave Cara that

much more time to spill everything that had happened to her that day. Unlike most teenagers, she didn't hold back much. Maybe it was because they were siblings, or maybe their unusual situation explained it. But she didn't seem to hesitate to share her troubles with Rune.

They picked up some groceries at the market, including a list from Harris, then stopped by Eller's for a new printer cartridge. They picked up a new cable needle for Harris at the yarn store. Everywhere they went, they ran into someone who either knew Rune from his rounds or Cara from school.

Wild how they'd become part of this community so quickly.

Everyone wanted to know how Harris was doing. Everyone wanted to know how Cara liked school. And everyone had a party to mention. "Are we going to see you at Haunted Harbor?... The Winter Parade's looking for float designers...Are you spending Christmas in town?...Where are you having Thanksgiving?"

"They really like the holidays here," Cara said gravely when they were finally on the road to home.

"It's a long winter, that's what they say. A long, dark, cold winter. Anything to brighten things up. Speaking of which, how are you feeling about this long, dark, cold winter closing in? Are you ready to make a break for the sunshine?"

She looked at him in horror. "You want to leave already?"

"No, but I want to check in with you. You're good here?"

"Really good. I don't want to leave."

"You mean, not yet," he corrected.

She didn't answer, which set off some alarm bells. Was she getting so attached to this little town that it would be tough to leave? He could understand if she were. Lost Harbor had a quirky charm about it. It was both humble and endearing, with its eccentric residents and magnificent setting. Perched on the edge of the bay, the only dot of civilization with miles of wilderness on all sides, it would be a hard place to forget.

He'd heard the legend of how it had been named. An expedition of explorers had run across the long arm of land that formed a natural harbor. But when they tried to find it again, they couldn't. The bay had filled up with mist.

Hence, Lost Harbor. And Misty Bay.

He could only hope that the "lost in the mists" quality would help shield them from Stalker Chad.

When they reached the property, he saw that Maya's car was already parked in the driveway, along with a red Jeep that belonged to Vicki.

Even though he'd just seen Maya, his heart gave an eager jump at the prospect of seeing her again so soon.

After all...they'd kissed. There was no taking that back. It was no kid kiss. Not a fake kiss. It was the real deal, and Maya might have awesome powers of self-command, but she wasn't someone who lied to herself.

"Harris wanted me to stop in," he told Cara as they got out of the car. "Want to come with?"

"Sure. Be right in."

She was texting someone on her phone, so he let her be and headed for the front door. Harris had already mounted a wreath there—an autumnal version with elderberries and willow branches. Man, they really did celebrate the seasons around here.

He knocked on the door, then pushed it open and went inside. As he stepped into the living room, a fierce glare from Maya almost stopped him in his tracks. Over her shoulder, he spotted Harris in his recliner, with Vicki perched on its broad arm. Vicki was at least part Alaska Native and a good ten years younger than Harris. Her dark hair was swept to one side, revealing hoop earrings. Her hand rested lightly on Harris' shoulder.

"Rune, can I speak with you in private?" Maya said to him through clenched teeth.

Oh shit. Obviously she'd just gotten the news about Harris and Vicki's new relationship.

"Hi Harris! Hi Vicki," he called to them as she marched him into the guest bedroom.

As soon as the door was closed, she whirled on him. "Why didn't you tell me this was going on?"

"I warned you. I told you I'd noticed sparks."

"This is a lot more than sparks. They're...they're...like a *couple*." She could barely say the word, it seemed. The outrage on her face would have made him laugh if that wouldn't have infuriated her even more. "Did you know that?"

"Harris wanted to tell you himself. That's his prerogative."

"They're going to the Haunted Harbor together!"

"Okaaaay..." He wasn't sure why that part was especially bad, but apparently it was.

"He was supposed to go with *me*. It was going to be his first big outing since the surgery."

"Well, you know how some kids are about going places with their parents." He tried a tentative joke, but she didn't seem to think it was funny.

"She'll probably be going to the Cookie Exchange with him too."

"I...couldn't say." Especially since he had no idea what a cookie exchange was. He tried putting a hand on her arm. "What's the problem, Maya? Is it something about Vicki? She seems to really care for him."

"Vicki is..." She wrenched her arm away from him and paced toward the window. "She's a lot younger than him. What's in it for her? She might be after his retirement. Dad's got a pension from the Coast Guard and he owns property. All his mortgages are paid off. He's a catch."

Somehow he didn't think this had anything to do with Harris Badger's finances. "Vicki owns her own business. She told me that she opened her salon when she was in her twenties. I don't think she's hurting for money. That red Jeep of hers is all tricked out, did you see it?"

"Exactly. *Red. Jeep.* Seriously, can you see my dad with someone who drives a *red Jeep?*" She threw up her hands. "Also, she's really into essential oils. Did you notice that it smells funny in there? She set him up with this damn infuser that's supposed to relax him."

"That smell is lavender. It's aromatherapy. A lot of patients respond well to it."

"I don't trust it. What if it's brainwashing him into liking her? Smells can be very powerful. I should send those oils to a lab and get them analyzed."

He couldn't help it anymore; he burst out laughing. "Maya, are you hearing yourself? You want to launch an investigation into *lavender oil?*"

She narrowed blazing eyes at him, as if ready to launch a grenade his way. Then slowly her expression relaxed and she rubbed the heel of her hand into her forehead. "You think I've lost it."

"I think you're upset, I'm just not sure what about. Don't you trust Harris to choose his own date for the cookie exchange, whatever that is?"

"You don't understand. Dad doesn't 'date.' Ever since my mother died, it's just been him and me. He always said he only had time for the important things, and that was work and me. That's why I'm such a Daddy's girl."

"But you're all grown up now. Far as I can tell, he has a pretty busy social life. He always has people coming through here with casseroles and brownies."

"My dad is a popular guy, but that's—"

"Once I came for an appointment and he was in the middle of a jam session."

"He plays the fiddle with Darius Boone and a few other people. They're pretty good." The pride in her voice made him smile inwardly. She spoke about Harris almost as if he was her child instead of the other way around.

"Are you having trouble letting go, Chief Badger?"

"I'm worried about him!" she cried. "He nearly died." Her breath caught and she pressed her lips together, as if determined not to let any other sign of weakness appear.

He ached to hold her in his arms and comfort her. But coming so soon after their kiss, he didn't want to push his luck. "That must have been terrifying," he said gently.

She allowed herself a nod. Just one. "It was." A world of terror shone through those two words.

What could he offer her to show his support?

"How about this. I'll go to the Haunted Harbor with you. We can keep an eye on Harris and Vicki. We'll be like the parents spying on their teenagers."

Her eyes flew to meet his. There was something in their rich brown depths that he couldn't quite identify. Surprise? Amusement? Yes, it must be amusement because she let out a sudden laugh. "You're inviting me to the Haunted Harbor?"

"Yes," he said cautiously. "Something wrong with that?"

"How about the cookie exchange? Would you go to that too?"

"Well, sure. Why not? I like cookies. Unless 'cookies' is code for 'fish guts' or some other weird Lost Harbor thing."

"No, it's pretty much just cookies. Maybe some brownies, lemon bars, that sort of thing. We'd have to bring something that we baked. Usually my dad does that."

"I can bake. I've made birthday cakes for Cara."

"No mixes allowed. They're very strict about it."

"You'll have to get me the rule book. So is that a yes?" he

asked cautiously. Something was still off. "Why do you still have that weird look on your face, like I just dropped in from Mars?"

"It's just..." She shook her head and tucked her hands into the back pockets of her jeans. The motion brought his attention to the curves under her red sweater, which made him remember the feel of her body pressed against him during their kiss. Intoxicated, that was how he'd felt. Almost drunk. "Okay, I was going to ask you this before."

"Ask what?" He dragged his focus back to her face.

"I have a situation."

Disappointment twisted in his gut. This was probably about something else involving her police work. Maya was nothing if not dedicated to her job. Lost Harbor was lucky to have her.

"Whatever you need, Chief," he said lightly.

"No no, this isn't anything like that. I—"

He watched, wild with curiosity, as she hauled in a long breath.

"I need a boyfriend."

CHAPTER TWELVE

To put the cherry on top of that embarrassing moment, a knock came at the door.

"What's going on in there?" Harris called. "Vicki has to go home. You going to come out and say goodbye?"

Maya heard the hurt in his voice, and it broke her heart. Why was she acting this way? If her dad wanted some company and possibly a little romance, she should be happy for him.

Strangely, now that Rune had offered to take her to the Haunted Harbor, her resistance had eased. At least a little bit.

"Sorry, Dad. Be right out." She lowered her voice so her father couldn't hear. "Want to finish this somewhere else?"

Rune nodded, still looking bemused. "Want to go for a drive? I just have to tell Cara first."

"Sure." She schooled her face into a polite and friendly expression. "How does this look? For Vicki, I mean."

"Much better. Less 'I'll arrest you at the first wrong step' and more 'make sure my dad's home by eleven.'"

That made her smile enough to look more natural as she said a friendly goodbye to Vicki. Rune left—the lucky guy—but Vicki apparently interpreted her politeness as an invitation to become new best friends.

"Come by the salon whenever you want and I'll take good care of you," she gushed. "No charge. You're family now."

"That's nice of you, but I get my hair done in Anchorage." None of the salons in Lost Harbor knew anything about African-American hair, so every two months she went to Anchorage to a friend of her cousin.

"But I've been studying," Vicki said eagerly. "I took a course on all types of black hair—4A, B, and C. You look like a 4C to me. I've been watching YouTube videos and I'd love the practice. I stocked up on some great conditioning products too. Harris can tell you."

Her dad patted his own hair, which looked pretty good, she had to say. His hair didn't take much—a close razor-cut was all he needed. But Vicki had done a decent job getting the edges even and crisp.

"It's nice of you," she repeated, still not ready to accept that offer. Sure, it would be convenient not to travel to Anchorage every two months. But she wasn't about to trust her hair to some ditzy woman with a crush on her father and hardly any experience with black hair.

By the time she escaped out to her car, her jaw was tight from maintaining her polite expression. Why was this so hard?

Outside, she tilted her head up and whooshed out a breath. Night had fallen and the sky had changed into its dazzling star-studded party look. Even though she hated this time of year because of Jerome, she also loved this time of year because it brought back the stars. After a summer of skies in which light lingered until dawn, finally the nights were dark enough for the moon and the stars to shine.

That was the thing about Alaska. No matter what drama or emotional turmoil she was going through, there was always something beautiful to distract her. The sky, the mountains, even the cold wind cutting across the bay—it all reminded her that this too would pass. Harris had taught her that, actually. One more gift from her father, her best friend.

"You survived." Rune was leaning against his car, waiting for her, his arms folded across his broad chest. "She's a chatty one."

"Sure is. I don't know how Dad stands it. We're both on the introverted side."

"Sometimes introverts like people who are more social. It means they don't have to worry about carrying the conversation."

Maybe that was part of why she and Rune got along so well. He'd always been more gregarious than her. That was why he made friends wherever he went, whereas she chose her friends more carefully. It took time for her to trust people.

Was twenty years enough time? With a twenty-year break in the middle?

When it came to Rune, maybe.

He beckoned her toward his car. "I'll drive. It's already warmed up. I just need a destination and a beautiful woman in the passenger seat."

Such a sweet-talker. And yet, it worked, lifting her spirits as she moved toward his car. "Haven't we known each other too long for flattery?"

"Define flattery."

She got into the passenger seat and settled back with a sigh. What a long-ass day this had been. "There's a pretty spot down the road a bit," she told him once he was in the car, door closed. "Just turn left and go until I tell you."

"You got it."

They drove in silence until they reached the turnoff to a lot someone had abandoned years ago. They'd put in a driveway but never gotten around to building anything else. It had a sweet view of the mudflats that stretched from the bluffs toward the ocean. They gleamed ghostly silver in the starlight, save for the moments when the beam of the lighthouse swept across them.

Rune turned off the engine and took in the sight. "Wow. I bet you never get tired of the views around here."

"I don't," she said honestly. "Sometimes I take it for granted or don't pay attention because I'm so busy. But as soon as I get a moment to breathe, I get blown away all over again. I don't think I could ever leave here for too long. I know Dad never will. My aunt in Jamaica wants him to, but he says he's an Alaskan now and she can save her breath."

Why was she talking about this? Now that the moment had come, she was actually nervous. How ridiculous. This was *Rune.* Back in the day, he'd let her bury him in the sand and make him look like a mermaid with boobs. He would never judge her.

"Come on, let's walk a little." She jumped out the car and found the little footpath that meandered along the edge of the mudflats. The door slammed behind her and Rune arrived at her side. The earthy scent of ocean mud drifted from the flats.

"Just to be clear," she told him, "when I said 'boyfriend,' I didn't mean a real one. I wouldn't ask that. Your friendship is very important to me."

"Got it," he said neutrally. "So what did you have in mind? Imaginary boyfriend?"

"No, just a fake one. For the holidays."

"A fake holiday boyfriend. They don't carry those at Eller's?" His dry tone made her laugh.

"They ought to. I'll put it in the suggestion box."

"Okay, well, I'm not saying no, but why do you think you need a fake boyfriend? Chief Badger doesn't need a sidekick. You stand on your own."

She sighed. "You don't understand. I've have a bad relationship with the holidays ever since my ex dumped me on Christmas Eve."

She risked a glance toward Rune to see how he was taking all this so far. Not much showed on his face other than anger at the info she'd just dropped.

"That's a dick move."

"Well, he's a dick. Which I suppose makes me a sucker because I fell for him and overlooked a whole bunch of red flags. I learned my lesson. But that's not the point now. The point is that the holidays are not fun for me because of him, but everyone else in Lost Harbor goes nuts for them. It's one party after another."

"I've noticed," he said. "Three people have asked me what we're doing for Thanksgiving, and it's not even Halloween yet."

"Yup, that's the way they roll here. Believe me, it's nonstop from Solstice to New Year's. People calm down after that. By then it's all about skiing and sledding and snow shoveling. Everyone starts planning their spring breaks and putting bets on when break-up will start. Until then, I don't want to have to grit my teeth through another holiday season being single in Lost Harbor."

She was rambling again. Revealing her history with Jerome and her vulnerability during the holidays wasn't easy.

Rune's arm bumped against hers as the path narrowed. She stopped and gestured for them to turn around and head back. But he brought her to a halt with a warm hand on her arm.

"Maya, you don't have to explain it all. If you need me to go to a bunch of parties with you, I'm cool with that."

She looked up into his eyes, which gleamed in the starlight, and let out a breath as the tension left her body.

"You are? Even though it's not exactly real?"

The lighthouse beam swept across his face, turning shadows to light, then back again. "I can't be a real anything, not while we have this stalker breathing down our necks."

"That's true." She didn't like the reminder that he wasn't

going to be here for long. "He'd better not show up before the holidays are through, or I'll have to kick his ass."

"You have the green light from me, if that counts."

She didn't need anyone's green light to protect her town, but it was cute that he mentioned it. "We can decide on some ground rules if you want. Mission parameters."

"Mission parameters," he repeated with amusement. "I'd like to hear those, sure."

"As the police chief, I need to make sure I hold onto people's respect. So here's the main one. You can't go flirting with anyone else."

His eyes darkened, as if she'd offended him. "You think I'm some kind of player?"

"Rune, girls always chase after you. Even when you were a kid. Everyone in Lost Harbor is curious about the hot new male nurse. Don't act like you don't know."

A muscle in his jaw ticked. "First of all, 'male nurse'? Seriously? This isn't the 1980s. Second, have you seen me flirt with anyone since I've been here? Or date anyone?"

"No, but—"

"Maya, in case you haven't gotten it yet, I'm not that carefree, barefoot kid anymore. When that pervert started going after my sister, my life changed. Overnight. I had to put Cara first and everything else last. I grew up fast. Late, but fast." A smile tugged briefly at the corner of his mouth. "If you'd caught me three years ago, yeah, I would have said I was kind of a player. But I'm nothing like that anymore."

This was a side of Rune she hadn't fully witnessed before. Dead serious, almost hard-edged, his usual easy manner gone.

To be honest, he was extremely attractive to her like this. She liked his more lighthearted side too. But this—this was catnip to a sober-minded police chief like her. A thrill of attraction traveled from the roof of her mouth deep into her belly. Suddenly dry-mouthed, she cleared her throat.

Back to business.

"I don't want to cramp your style, that's all. Jerome, he..." She looked away briefly, then back at him. "He humiliated me. I can't do that again."

He reached his hand out to cup her chin, his touch gentle but so strong. "You gotta trust me, Maya. I know you do, or you wouldn't be asking me to do this. Right? So trust yourself. Trust the part of yourself that trusts me."

Either he was really good, or that totally made sense. She nodded and he dropped his hand. She missed its warmth immediately. Her chin tingled. "So do we have an understanding?"

"Almost." He flexed his hand, as if he could still feel the same sensation she did. "What about the kiss?"

"The kiss on the boat?"

"Or any other kiss. Am I the kind of fake holiday boyfriend who kisses you or the perfect gentleman kind?"

"You don't have to worry about it. No one kisses anyone at the cookie exchange. They're too busy eating."

"What about the Haunted Harbor? We're going to have to kiss."

"We will? Where's your logic?"

A smile tugged at his firm lips, the lighthearted Rune coming back to play.

"Maya, Maya, Maya...I can tell you haven't thought this through. That's okay, it's outside your police chief area of expertise. Here's the problem. Everyone here knows we're old friends."

"So?" What was she missing? How complicated could a fake holiday boyfriend situation be?

"So they're going to think we're just buddies. Is that what you want? You said you wanted a fake boyfriend, not just an old friend playing plus-one."

"Yes. Exactly. I know it's silly, but when people get that pitying look on their faces, I think about Jerome and—"

"I get it. We have to make more of a statement."

"Like a press statement? Sergeant Hollister usually—"

"Stop being a police chief for a moment. We have to make it clear from the start that we're not just old friends going to a party together. A long, passionate kiss should do it. In front of Mrs. Holt or Toni or someone else in the gossip supply chain."

He sure was throwing himself into this project. His enthusiasm touched her to the core.

"I guess I'll just trust you on that."

"I'll start dropping hints to some of my patients. People get chatty with their hot male nurses." He sent her a sidelong smile with that comment.

"I'm sorry I called you—"

"Hey, no worries. We have more important things to figure out. Here's another one. What do we tell Cara and Harris? I don't want to lie."

Crap, he was right, she really hadn't thought this all the way through. She couldn't lie to her father about Rune. But maybe there was a way they could fudge things.

"We did already kiss," she said slowly. "That wasn't a lie."

"It felt real to me. And you remembered it this time, so there's that."

She made a face at him. As if she could forget that kiss. Come on. "So we can just tell people that we're...seeing where it goes. That's all we have to say. If Harris or Cara wants to know more, we can say that we kissed, and we're taking things one day at a time."

"One party at a time," he corrected with a grin.

"Right. Haunted Harbor's up first. The cookie exchange is the next weekend. Then there's the Harvest Festival and—"

He threw up his hand. "One party at a time. Please, for the love of God."

"Sorry. I really appreciate this, Rune."

"Babe, it's no hardship. I like parties and I like Maya Badger." He gave her such a tender smile that her knees went a little weak.

"Babe?"

"Just practicing. We have to look...intimate."

Intimate. Now that was a word that made her a little nervous, especially when he dropped down to that deep growly voice. But Rune just meant that there would be some kissing involved. She could live with that.

No—she looked forward to that.

"Okay, then. We have a plan." She stuck out her hand to seal the deal. He shook it solemnly. The way he took her seriously and accepted things on her terms—she really appreciated that.

"One last question," he said. "This Haunted Harbor party. Do we have to wear a costume?"

"Are you trying to give me a nervous breakdown? I don't do costumes. I'm the police chief. I have my dignity to uphold."

He cocked his head at her. "I can't tell if you're joking. I can see why you wouldn't go as a slutty stripper or something, but what's the fun in no costume?"

"I do the same thing every year. I have a set of vampire fangs and a black cape. I go as Chief Dracula."

"The same costume every year?" He shook his head sadly. "You need more than a fake holiday boyfriend, Maya. You need a new attitude. A fun infusion."

"A *fun* infusion?" She laughed at that. "Is that one of your hot male nurse lines? Does it work?"

He shrugged off her teasing. "Leave the costumes to me. I got this."

"Fine, but I need to stay warm. That's my one condition."

She remembered all the times when Jay-Jay had thrown himself headlong into some crazy scheme—selling coconuts to tourists or chasing a wild pig into a lava tube. Rune had that same look in his eyes now, that thirst for adventure that crashed through every obstacle.

Which meant—there was a good chance she'd gotten in *way* over her head with this plan.

CHAPTER THIRTEEN

Party number one. Haunted Harbor.

RUNE KEPT his promise about the costumes. He used his own medical equipment to dress as a hot nurse—the female kind. Big fake boobs and all.

Maya laughed so hard when she saw him that she nearly peed her pants, just like in the old days. Just like then, it made his day to get her laughing.

For her, he found a fake fur Dalmatian stole at the thrift store, a form-fitting black floor-length dress and a cigarette holder—she made a fantastic Cruella de Vil.

"This dress is tight," she complained, plucking it away from her curves.

"But toasty warm, right? It's superfine wool, lined...and you look superfine in it." He grinned and adjusted his boobs. "I met your one condition, so no complaints, lady."

"Oh, fine. Maybe no one will recognize me."

The Haunted Harbor event took place on the Coast Guard

cutter *Midway*. The sailors cordoned off a section of the lower deck and went all out with Halloween displays for the kids. Things like fake graveyards with ghosts rising from freshly dug graves on cables attached to pulleys. Ensigns in full zombie makeup jumping from behind hatch doors. Skeletons dropping from the ceiling.

The adults were invited to a private party in the captain's lounge. Which was where he and Maya staged their fake hot-passionate kiss. His "hot nurse" costume made it funny too, but everyone bought their act nonetheless.

As he held her in his arms, her dark honey eyes laughing into his, he wasn't sure if the harder acting job was for the audience—make it look passionate—or for her—make it look fake.

Quite a tricky balancing act.

But the kiss did its job. He could practically hear the news spread like wildfire around the cutter. *Rune and Maya...saw that one coming...she says they're just seeing where it goes...*

The next week, his patients had all kinds of questions for him. Warnings too.

"You'd better treat her right."

"Maya deserves a good man."

"Not like that Jerome. Did you hear what he did on Christmas Eve?"

"He got married just a few months later, to the McGee girl. Leanne."

What kind of person would dump Maya during the holidays...for someone just out of high school? And someone right in Maya's backyard? Without even meeting him, Rune already despised Jerome. Anyone who would hurt Maya deserved nothing but scorn.

But he had to wonder—did Maya still have feelings for him? Was that why she hadn't had a "real" boyfriend since then?

PARTY NUMBER FOUR. Mrs. Bellini's cookie exchange.

NEITHER RUNE NOR Maya had time to bake anything, so Rune paid Cara to make brownies for them to bring. Hand in hand, he and Maya squeezed the platter between some Mexican wedding cookies and a pan of creme brûlée.

"Do we have to sample everything?" he whispered, looking at the array of homemade sweets—dozens of them.

"God no. I want you to survive the night. We have the Harvest Festival coming up next."

"You really need to send me a spreadsheet." He chose a plain old chocolate chip cookie and took a nibble. "How was your week? It's a good thing we're fake boyfriend and girlfriend, or I might never see you."

"Fall is always a busy time." Maya was eyeing a gingerbread cookie shaped like a boot. Or maybe it was a stocking.

"I had to check the police blotter to see what you're up to."

"You did not." She glanced up, cookie in hand.

"Yup." He recited the most recent blotter item. "*Police called to the scene of a break-in. The culprit was revealed to be a young black bear. He was tranquilized and the forest service was called.*"

"It was quite the drama."

"Oh, and I saw that the reward for Mrs. Holt's yak has gone up."

"Three hundred dollars. Boom." She licked rock sugar from the gingerbread stocking. His groin tightened in response.

To distract himself, he recited more blotter items. "*Two vehicles collided on East Mountain Road. Both drivers were found to be inebriated and were arrested. They were also both discovered to* be *unclothed and also married to each other. Citations were issued."*

"Relationships." Maya shook her head sadly. "Whatcha gonna do?"

He chuckled. "And then there was the bonfire on Seafarers Beach. Kids threw jellyfish at each other? I think I would have had fun growing up here."

"We would have had fun if you had."

The promise in her eyes drew him in, like a magnet he couldn't resist. He brushed a kiss onto her mouth, tasting sugar and ginger and the thrill of a sigh from her parted lips.

This kiss didn't feel like something between old friends. It sent a charge of lust right into his bloodstream. It made him want to drag her off to a corner and take that kiss deeper. Make her burn with the same desire firing his blood.

Take it easy, fake holiday boyfriend.

He ended the kiss with a wink, as if to say, *All part of the act.*

Her tongue slid across her lips. Surprise? Enjoyment? He couldn't tell. "So you think we need to kiss at every party?" she murmured.

"To be safe," he said solemnly.

PARTY NUMBER DOZEN-OR-SO. *The Harvest Festival.*

SHE SEEMED TO AGREE, because at the Harvest Festival, surrounded by hay bales and winter squash displays, she kissed *him*. He slid a hand onto the slope of her lower back and rested it there until her body swayed toward his.

"What are you doing?" she murmured against his lips.

"Making it look real."

"Hmmm. Good thinking." Her husky whisper seemed to travel into his brain and set up shop there. He wanted to hear that whisper in bed. When they were both naked. Maybe after he'd made her come apart.

But for now...it was progress.

"So how was your week, fake boyfriend?" she asked after they drew apart.

"Busy. Lots of sprained wrists, broken bones, torn ankle ligaments. It's getting icy out there. I've been taking on some more shifts with the volunteer fire department. Feels good to get the old muscles moving again."

Maya smiled up at him. "Darius mentioned that. He said you're a huge asset."

"Are you sure he didn't say 'huge ass'?" he joked. "Just checking."

"No, he really appreciates the time you're spending."

"It helps me, too. I've been talking to the crew about Cara's stalker." He'd decided to clue the entire department into what was going on. The more eyes, the better. So far, there'd been no sign of Stalker Chad—but he knew better than to relax.

"What have you told them?"

"To keep an eye out for a stranger in his mid-thirties who's former military. That's about all I know. I passed around the photo. Didn't ring a bell for anyone."

"How's Cara doing?"

"She got that role in the Christmas play that we helped her rehearse for. You know, back when you had time."

Maya made a face. "I know, it's crazy. I guess you can see why I don't have a real boyfriend."

"No, not really," he said, honestly. "Why don't you?"

She shot him a funny look. "Lots of reasons, I guess. Jerome thought I gave my job too much attention."

"Forget about him." He pulled her against him again, so

passionately he knocked a scarecrow off its perch on a hay bale. "Jerome's about as smart as that scarecrow. Feel like checking out the hay bale maze and pretending to make out?"

"How do you *pretend* to make out?"

"I'll show you."

***

PARTY NUMBER TWENTY-SOMETHING. Veterans Day visit to Lost Harbor Assisted Living.

RUNE HAD to put their simmering attraction on pause for the Veterans Day event. He helped Maya deliver flowers to those veterans who lived at the assisted living home, and joined her to chat with them. He and Maya didn't flirt, didn't kiss, didn't even hold hands, and yet he felt their connection deepen.

Something about watching her interact with the vets—with so much attentiveness and respect—really did it for him. They all knew her; clearly this was something she did every year, and maybe even more often than that.

"I'm not sure that counted as a party," he murmured to her on the way out. "But I'm glad I came."

"I'm glad you did too." With a radiant smile, she took his hand. "They loved having someone new to tell their stories to."

"Good stories, too." Except the feel of her hand in his chased them right out of his head.

***

PARTY NUMBER "HE'D LOST COUNT." Shabbat Eve dinner at the mayor's house.

. . .

AAAAND...IT turned out that Shabbat meals were even less make-out friendly than visits to veterans. But he did learn that Maya looked beautiful in candlelight. Not that he was surprised, of course. She took his breath away in everything he'd seen her wear, from the maroon scarf she'd worn to a skating party, to the little black dress she'd rocked at cocktails with the town council members.

Damn, these parties were just about killing him.

PARTY NUMBER ELEVENTY-BILLION. Sadie Hawkins Day Dance

AT THE SADIE HAWKINS dance at the high school—Maya was chaperoning—Rune decided it was time to make a move. No more pretend make-out. He was ready for the real thing.

He pulled her onto the dance floor for a slow dance. Gliding his hands up her sides, he found the swell of her breasts with his thumbs. Her breath sped up but she didn't stop him. He stroked his hands back down to her hips, snug in a tight black dress, and tugged her against him.

Against the erection pushing against the fly of his nicest linen trousers, the thin ones that didn't do a thing to hide his arousal.

"What are you doing? People are watching." And yet she didn't pull away, he noticed. She stayed right where she was, and maybe even pushed a little closer.

"No one's watching us. We're the chaperones. We're like wallpaper. Right now, anyone over the age of eighteen is invisible to them."

He felt her head turn as she scanned the dance floor. The theme of the dance was "Paris at Night," which meant a cardboard Eiffel Tower and strings of twinkle lights hung from the ceiling of the high school auditorium. Most of the girls were wearing black party dresses, but the boys mostly wore their regular clothes, although a few were wearing vintage tuxedoes.

One boy had gotten very creative and dressed half of his body as a woman and half as a man. When Rune complimented him, he explained that he'd invited himself to the dance, and since the girls were supposed to invite the boys, he'd dressed as both.

Many of the teenage girls had just invited their friends, and were now dancing in little groups with each other.

The twinkle lights didn't cast much illumination, which meant that he probably wasn't the only one taking advantage of the dimness.

"I guess you're right," she concluded. "They have better things to think about than a couple of ancients like us."

One of those teenage couples nearly collided with them, and he swung Maya out of the way. She clung to his shoulders. "My hero," she said breathlessly when they were clear of the potential collision.

"That's what I want to hear. Nurse Rune to the rescue."

"Seriously. Collisions aside, do you know how tedious this dance would be without you here?"

"How could *Paris at Night* ever be called tedious?"

"When it's filled with teenagers trying to sneak alcohol into their fake champagne. Excuse me, I'll be right back."

She ducked under his arm to bust a boy with a flask tucked in the back pocket of his pants. Rune watched, wrestling his arousal back under control, as she sternly lectured the kid. Always on the job, Maya Badger. Even when she'd been trembling in his arms a few minutes ago.

"Didn't you ever sneak a drink during a school dance?" he asked when she slipped back into his embrace.

"Of course I did. Jessica and Toni and I tucked little airplane-size bottles of vodka in our bras for prom. Chrissie too—you don't know her, she moved away. But we got busted when one of Jessica's bottles broke and the school nurse had to pick glass out of her cleavage."

He cracked up just picturing it. "That sounds like Jessica."

"Yeah." The affection in her voice fit with everything he knew about their friendship. "She's a goofball, but you gotta love her. I don't see her as much now that she's with Ethan. It's the end of an era."

"End of an era?"

"Our little friend group is pairing up. Kate and Darius, now Jessica and Ethan."

If you asked him, Maya and Rune had a certain ring to it. But he kept that to himself. He was just the fake holiday boyfriend who was going to be leaving in the near future.

"I've been thinking about you not having a boyfriend."

She snorted softly. "Can't wait to hear this."

"After Jerome, maybe you're done with all that."

"All that? You mean, men?" Her wry tone made him smile. They danced past the cardboard Eiffel Tower, which was leaning precariously to one side. He paused to straighten it, then waltzed onward.

"Men. Romance. Sex. That sort of thing. It's the 'I don't need a man I have a vibrator' vibe."

She smacked him on the shoulder as she laughed, the sound buried against his chest. "You did not just say something about my vibrator."

"There you go. I knew you had one."

"Of course I have one. But it's none of your business. We're not talking about my vibrator at a freaking high school dance."

"Good point. So when can we talk about it? Because I feel it's something we should discuss."

She was still laughing, probably from sheer embarrassment, but he'd take it. "Why do we need to talk about that?"

"Because it's interesting. *You're* interesting. Your love life is really interesting, especially now that I'm sort of part of it, in a fake-holiday-boyfriend kind of way. I mean, if a vibrator could do everything a man can, you wouldn't need me. You could dress it up in a tux and have it play chaperone with you."

She let out such a burst of laughter that two nearby couples actually noticed them. They looked away immediately, as if they were afraid to catch the eye of the mighty police chief.

"Obviously, a vibrator can't do it all. Just the most important stuff."

Oh sweet lord, hearing her talk about her vibrator was giving him a serious stiffie.

"And it can't break your heart," she added softly. "So there is that."

"That's a good point. But not every man is going to break your heart."

"You know that's right. *No* man is going to break my heart. They won't get the chance."

Right. Of course. She'd built up that wall so thick it would take a battering ram to get through.

Or someone sneaking through a back door disguised as an old friend.

Except that he couldn't do that. It wouldn't be fair because he couldn't stick around to follow up. If there was one woman in this world he refused to hurt in any way, it was Maya.

So he went along with her declaration of independence. "Looks like you have the perfect setup. Fake holiday boyfriend plus," they were veering close to a group of girls, so he quickly censored himself, "your other best buddy. You have all the bases covered."

"That's right, baby. Bases one hundred percent covered."

But even as she said that, she pressed her hips against him. His erection surged in response. He gritted his teeth, trying to make it go back down. It didn't work.

God, she was making this hard. If they kept going like this, he wouldn't be able to keep things on an old-friend level.

He'd devote himself full time to becoming the "best buddy" who got to go to bed with her.

CHAPTER FOURTEEN

About a month before Christmas...

EVERY HOLIDAY PARTY they spent together, Maya had a harder time resisting the fierce pull of her attraction to Rune. Unbelievably, she actually looked forward to all the holiday parties. At each one, they went a little further and got a little bit closer.

She loved every minute of it. Fake or not.

The first real snowfall—in which the snow accumulated more than two inches—came a week before Thanksgiving. As always, the combination of freeze-up and the first layer of snow led to an unfortunate number of car accidents. Maya was kept busy with those, along with the two-day search for a missing toddler who'd wandered into the snow and the rescue of a skier who got stuck in a Port-a-Potty.

She couldn't wait to hear Rune's recitation of the blotter write-up on *that* one.

At Seafarers Beach a few days before Thanksgiving, as she

was overseeing the removal of a sea otter that had washed ashore, her phone rang. She stepped aside, dodging a pile of frozen kelp, her boots gripping the icy pebbles

Special Agent Clement was calling from Anchorage. *Finally.* She'd sent him the photos she and Rune had taken at Far Point, but hadn't heard anything back.

"Got news for you, Badger," he said. "We're closing the books on this one."

"*What?* But what about the drop-off? The photos I took?"

"Dead end."

"*Dead end?* Two men and a boat in a remote cove in twenty-degree temps can't possibly be a dead end."

"We identified them as Russian nationals, but they disappeared before we could question them."

Disappeared? Sounded like a screwup to her.

"Listen, as the police chief of the closest harbor town, I strongly urge you to keep investigating."

"Badger, you're way out over your skis on this one. We're done." The frustration in the man's voice echoed her own. "Working out there is impossible. It's too big an area, too fucking rugged. No leads. No evidence of any crime. Frankly, it's making you look bad."

"*Me?*" Her stomach dropped.

"You're the one pushing this. No one else. Some small-town police chief has a hair up her ass. That's what it looks like from here."

She swallowed hard. The idea that she was ruining her reputation stung worse than a...jellyfish. "What about the Aurora Lodge? Have you talked to the manager there? She knows something."

"Kelsey Lewis? Not saying a damn word. We have nothing on her. No leverage. Believe me, I wish we had something concrete. Until we do, my advice to you is to drop this before you make a fool of yourself. If it's not too late."

She chewed at her lower lip and looked across the water at the bulky silhouette of Lost Souls Wilderness. Something was going on out there. She knew it. But was it worth turning into the girl who cried wolf?

"I understand. Thanks, for the update."

"You take care. Keep your head down and this too shall pass."

She ended the call with a savage punch of her finger. Of course the Feds wanted to drop this. She couldn't really blame it on their dismissive attitude toward a "small-town police chief." She needed some damn *evidence*.

Across the frozen beach, Nate Prudhoe approached, brushing ice crystals off the sleeves of his parka. She took a step back. He'd been right up in that sea otter operation.

Nate was one of Maya's closest friends, and had been for years. In fact, in many ways, he'd always reminded her of Jay-Jay. They had a similar openhearted, playful manner.

At one point Nate, who was a firefighter, had hinted that he wouldn't mind a romantic relationship, but she'd still been recovering from Jerome at that point. And besides, she'd never want to jeopardize their friendship. Who else would she play golf with?

Besides that...she'd just never had those kinds of feelings for him. She'd never felt her pulse race the way it did around Rune, or that weird sudden feeling of happiness that sometimes came over her when she thought about him.

Now Nate was married to Dr. Bethany Morrison and had never been happier.

But currently his face wore a grave expression. "I have to get back to the station, but I wanted to warn you about something."

"If it's about ruining my reputation with the Federal Bureau of Investigation, forget it. Too late."

"What? No. Way off."

"Okay, shoot. It's not getting any warmer out here." She stomped her feet to keep blood flowing to her toes.

"It's Jerome. He's coming back to town for Thanksgiving with the McGees."

"Shit." The sound of his name gave her a kick in the stomach. She drew in a breath of frosty air. "When?"

"He might even be here by now. I didn't want you to run into him unprepared." His gray eyes—usually so playful— watched her with concern.

She straightened her spine. "I'm fine. That was five years ago. I'm over Jerome, which is why I never talk about him, and in fact I don't want to talk about him now. But thanks," she added. "It was nice of you to warn me."

He narrowed his eyes at her. "Really? Completely over him? When did this happen? Recently, like in the past, oh, two months or so? Since Rune Larsen showed up?"

Even though she felt her face warm, she shrugged. "Worry about your own life. I got this."

"But my life's perfect now," he complained. "I have to find something to worry about."

"Way to rub it in."

Still teasing each other, they made their way to the parking lot. As soon as she'd escaped into her car, she let her bravado collapse.

She wasn't ready for a Jerome sighting yet. How would it happen? In a small town like Lost Harbor, there would be no chance of avoiding him. She'd run into him at Eller's Drug Store or at Sweet Harbor Bakery buying pies. Or maybe someone would inadvertently invite both of them to the same party.

Which meant—Rune would be there too.

A rush of relief came over her. Relief and a sense of security. Rune would be with her, by her side, and everything would be okay.

FOR WEEKS, everyone in Lost Harbor had been placing bets on when the first snowfall would come. Rune chose Thanksgiving, and missed by a week. It cost him fifty dollars. But the joy of waking up and seeing soft flakes drifting past the little window of his loft made up for it.

He called down to Cara, who ran shrieking into the yard in her bare feet. When he went outside, taking the time to put on boots like a proper elder brother, he spotted her at the end of the dock with her face lifted to the sky. Snowflakes swirled around her, landing on her shoulder and hair like curious tiny butterflies.

"This is amazing!" she called to him. "So much better than Mauna Kea. Can we have a snowball fight?"

"Way ahead of you," Rune called just as his first snowball landed on her back.

Hey, he wasn't *always* the proper elder brother. He still had a lot of Jay-Jay in him.

The snow had another benefit: it would be hard to hide footprints in a fresh snowfall. It would form one more layer of protection from the stalker. However, with each day that passed, he relaxed just a little bit more. Three months after their arrival in Lost Harbor and there was no sign that the stalker knew where they were. Maybe he couldn't travel that far. Maybe they'd managed to cover their trail enough this time. Maybe he'd found another fixation.

Maybe Rune could get his life back.

What would he do if Cara was no longer his responsibility? Sometimes he allowed himself to dream about that. He'd probably go back to being an EMT. Not that he didn't enjoy the home nursing, but he did best in emergency situations. The volunteer shifts he took on at the fire station were the highlights of his week.

But most importantly, he'd allow himself to form a real relationship. He was ready. He wanted to settle down. Taking care of Cara had shown him that he'd be a good parent. And reuniting with Maya had reminded him what a solid connection felt like. That was what he wanted, even if Maya wasn't interested in anything like that with him.

Or was she? He honestly couldn't tell. When they were alone together, she treated him like her old friend. In public, she acted like they were dating. She welcomed his kisses and responded with eager sensuality to his touch. It was confusing as hell.

Then again, a lot of things were confusing in Lost Harbor. He'd heard the saying, *Strange things happen around Lost Souls Wilderness.* He didn't doubt it, especially the more he got to know Maggie, Cara's new best friend.

Maggie was definitely a strange one. She was still learning about living in society as opposed to a cabin in the wilderness. With her welcoming personality, Cara was the perfect person to help her navigate high school. For her part, Maggie showed Cara all kinds of Alaska survival skills.

One day Rune came home from a volunteer shift to find Maggie showing Cara how to shoot a bow and arrow. He'd never forget the horrified expression on Cara's face as she accidentally nicked a squirrel's tail.

"He's okay," Maggie assured her after the squirrel raced up the corner post of the fish house, chattering madly.

"But how do you *know*?" cried Cara. "I didn't meant to hit anything."

"The squirrel said so. He's very unhappy with you, but he's uninjured. Don't be surprised if he drops a spruce cone on your head."

Rune rubbed at the back of his neck, hiding his amusement. Maggie claimed that she could understand the language of various animals. Not every animal—just the ones she'd grown up with in the wilderness.

Lost Souls Wilderness. Where strange things happened.

Cara tossed the bow to the ground beside her. "Forget teaching me how to shoot. I want to learn how to talk to animals. Can you teach me that?"

Rune covered his laugh with a cough. Trust his soft-hearted sister to reject survival skills for an opportunity to chat.

He left them to their fun, two teenagers in cozy hoodies, their cheeks reddened by the wind. He'd never expected Cara to adapt so well to the colder climate here in Alaska. But she'd embraced it completely so far.

Maybe a miracle would happen and they wouldn't have to leave.

In the meantime, Thanksgiving was coming. Jessica was hosting a potluck Thanksgiving dinner at the Sweet Harbor Bakery. That meant the food would be out of this world. More importantly, another party meant another chance to make progress with Maya.

CHAPTER FIFTEEN

Every Wednesday, Maya took a Hump Day yoga class. She looked forward to it all week. Not even the fact that Thanksgiving was the *next day* and she still didn't know what she was bringing would make her skip the class.

She was just about to change into her yoga clothes when Maggie and Cara appeared at her office door.

She groaned. "Is this about Thanksgiving? I haven't decided what to make yet."

Jessica had enlisted the two teenagers to be her foot soldiers for the event.

"No, it's not about Thanksgiving," Cara said as she plopped herself into a chair. Maggie stayed standing, looking unusually nervous.

It occurred to Maya that they looked like sisters; both different shades of blond, both wearing Lost Harbor High hoodies, so comfortable with each other that they could be family.

An even more alarming thought struck Maya. "Is this about—"

"No, not that." Cara spoke quickly before Maya could finish

the sentence. Maya knew that she hated talking about the stalker. She just wanted to live her life, and who could blame her for that? "It's about Maggie."

"What's up?" Maya directed her question to Maggie. "Is everything okay at home?"

"Yes, but—" Maggie looked to Cara, who urged her on. "When can I meet my mother?" she blurted. "I really want to see her."

Maya's heart sank. She saw the longing in the girl's pale eyes, the frustration of finally knowing who her mother was, but still being kept apart from her. "It's not up to me, Maggie. Your mother doesn't think it's safe."

"But why is she so afraid?" Maggie demanded. Her nervousness was gone now that she'd spoken up. "The evil man who kidnapped me is gone."

"Yes, but we think he was working with someone, or being controlled by someone. Until we know who and why, it's not safe for you."

"So why can't you find out!"

Maya jumped at the girl's passionate outburst.

"Yeah, isn't there an investigation or something?" Cara chimed in. "Isn't someone doing something?"

"I'm sorry. They weren't getting anywhere so they ended it." Maya winced as she delivered that news, which was probably twice as frustrating for Maggie as it was for her.

"So...no one's doing anything?" Two spots of color burned in Maggie's cheeks. "Not even you?"

"It's not my jurisdiction. I'm in charge of Lost Harbor, not the wilderness. That's federal and state territory out there." Even as she said it, she saw scorn flash in Maggie's eyes. None of that meant anything to a girl who longed to meet her mother. "I'm sorry."

God, that sounded pathetic.

Maggie dropped her head and stared at the floor, her shoulders slumping. Cara grabbed her friend's hand and looked back and forth between the two of them. "I bet there's something you can do, Maya."

The faith that shone in the girl's sea-green eyes, so much like Rune's, made Maya feel even worse.

She didn't answer. Agent Clement had warned her about torpedoing her career in Lost Souls, and she knew he was absolutely right. But where did that leave Maggie?

And what was the point of her career if she couldn't help someone as vulnerable as Maggie?

She cleared her throat, but even so her voice came out huskier than usual. "Is there anything else, girls? I don't want to miss my yoga class."

"Yes." Cara raised her hand. "I just wanted to say that I'm really glad you and Rune are dating. He seems so much happier."

Maya opened her mouth to clarify that they weren't really *dating*, then closed it again. As far as Cara knew, they were. And more and more, it was hard to find that line between fake dating and real dating. The energy between them kept shifting into something heated and exciting. Something that kept her up at night. But they still hadn't lost that original "friend" connection. The combination was incredibly seductive.

She blinked away those distracting thoughts. "Is there anything that's more of a police matter?"

This time Maggie answered, lifting her gaze from the floor. She still looked upset, but she'd gotten ahold of herself. She'd survived being raised by a fugitive trapper, she would survive this disappointment. But that didn't make Maya feel any better. "Have you found Mrs. Holt's yak yet?" she asked.

"No. Do you know something?"

"I don't know anything, but I could spread the word."

"I think we've done a good job of that already, between the

flyers and reward. We've been mentioning it on the radio and on the Bush Lines."

"No, not with people. With the animals." Maggie's wide gray eyes lit up with eagerness. "They're all very busy right now getting ready for winter, but I can try."

"Okay. Sure. Give it a try." Why not? They weren't getting anywhere with the search so far. At least she could give Maggie that—a chance to be helpful.

Cara's phone beeped and she shot to her feet. "Rune's here to pick us up. Bye Maya, thank you!"

A thrill traveled through her. Damn, if even hearing Rune's name got her excited, she might have a problem.

"When you talk to those animals, make sure you tell them about the reward," she called as the girls left her office. "We can pay it in birdseed or something." They waved, not really listening.

If only Rune was there to get her joke. She could always count on him to appreciate her sense of humor.

As she gathered her things, Maggie's stricken expression refused to leave her. The poor kid had gone through so much. All she wanted was to see her mother. That didn't seem like too much to ask, especially during the holidays.

The holidays.

Slowly, an idea formed. Maybe there was a way to pursue the Lost Souls investigation *and* give Maggie what she wanted.

Maybe she could make the holiday season work in her favor here.

She checked the time. She still had a few minutes before she had to run off for yoga.

As always, it took a while for the call to connect, the sound traveling through underwater cables to reach the wilderness, and to get through Kelsey's multiple layers of security. "Aurora Lodge, Kelsey here."

"Hi Kelsey, it's Maya Badger from Lost Harbor."

"Police Chief Badger? Is everything okay? How's Maggie?" Tension vibrated through the woman's voice.

"She's fine. Sorry, I should have said that right away. She's doing great. In fact she was just here with her new best friend."

"She was?" Now Maya heard longing instead of fear. "I'm glad you're keeping an eye on her. I can't tell you what a relief that is."

"We're all doing that. Count on it." That was one thing about living in a tiny town on the edge of wilderness. No matter their differences in other areas of life—like religion or politics—most people genuinely did look out for each other. "I'm calling because Maggie's pushing hard to be able to see you."

Kelsey sighed. "I know she is. She mentions it whenever we talk. I keep telling her it's not possible—"

"I had an idea about that. What if a group of us booked the lodge for a holiday event? She could blend in with the rest of us. Her new friend looks a lot like her. We can make it seem that they're sisters."

A short pause followed her suggestion. "You want to book the entire lodge?"

"That would be the safest, so we don't have bystanders wandering around. I have no idea what that would cost."

"A fortune."

"Right." She didn't have a fortune, and this wasn't anything she could charge to the Lost Harbor police department. So much for that idea. "Well, I had to suggest it." She hesitated, then decided to apply just a teensy bit more pressure.

"Maggie was crushed when I told her there wasn't anything I could do. I'm worried she might hop in a boat and find you herself."

"She can't do that." The fear was back in Kelsey's voice.

"Maya, please make sure she doesn't. Let me look at the calendar. Hang on."

Maya heard the clicking of computer keys.

"There's only one way this would work," she finally said. "But not until Christmas. The owners always close the lodge for that week. I could request to keep the lodge open for a special event, but I can't keep the staff here."

"We can do our own cooking and cleaning and whatever else is needed," Maya said quickly. "We don't need any staff. Just you," she added. "Since that's the whole point. Did you have other plans already?"

Kelsey gave a shaky laugh. "As if any plans would be more important than seeing Maggie. No, I plan to be here. Let me clear it with the owners. Since there will be no staff, maybe I can comp you the rooms."

"That would be very helpful, since I'd rather not mortgage my house for a party."

"This would be amazing," Kelsey said. Hope radiated through all those underwater cables. "Christmas with my daughter? It's almost too much to hope for."

"One step at a time. Let me know what the owners say."

"I will. Thank you, Maya. Thank you so much."

And that was the rest of her plan. With Kelsey in a happy holiday mood, and reunited with her long-lost daughter, maybe she'd finally be willing to talk. Which meant she could get something concrete for the FBI.

She ended the call and began mentally composing a guest list as she closed up her office. She needed some backup out there, of the first responder variety. Darius, Ethan. Maybe Rune.

And just like that, sunshine spread through her heart. With Rune with her, this holiday party/investigation would actually be fun. She'd have an ally, someone who always made her feel beautiful and...singular. As if there was no one else like her in the world.

The same went for him. Who else was that perfect Rune combo of openhearted fun and rock-like strength? No one. That was who.

She sighed and slipped into the bathroom to change into her yoga clothes.

CHAPTER SIXTEEN

After Rune dropped off Maggie, he parked at Harris' house for one last home nurse visit before Thanksgiving. Cara skipped down to the fish house to study for a makeup calculus exam.

As he attached the pulse ox to Harris' index finger, Rune grinned at the older man. "You've done it, my friend. Recovery from heart surgery can be a haul, but you've made it to the other side. Congratulations."

"Thanks go to you, kid. You're a fine nurse."

"Nah. You did this. Give yourself credit. You're a tough old sailor."

Harris chuckled as Rune marked down his vitals. "Runs in the family."

"Says the father of the police chief."

Harris put a hand on his shoulder, making Rune look up in surprise. "She's not as tough as she seems, though," he said. "So watch how you handle things."

Okay, then. This was *that* kind of conversation. Under normal circumstances it would be awkward, but given the confusing state of things between him and Maya, it was a thousand times more so.

"To be honest, she's in charge," he said with a laugh. *Keep it light.* That was the way to handle this.

"Maybe." Harris gave him a shrewd look from deep brown eyes that seemed to see right through him. "But she doesn't show everything she's feeling."

Rune took out a stethoscope from his bag and draped it over his neck. "Mind if I check your heart?"

"Mind if I check yours?" Harris shot back.

Rune laughed ruefully. "Touché." He set the sensor on Harris' chest. "Look, you don't have to worry about me and Maya. We're friends, we're always going to be friends. I'm...here for her, that's it."

"Jerome is here."

The abrupt change of subject made him jolt. "He is?"

"Yeah. He and Leanne are having Thanksgiving with her family. Maya didn't tell you?"

"I haven't seen her in a few days. I've been working shifts at the fire department."

"It's going to be tough for Maya. He hasn't been back since he embarrassed her in front of the town."

Rune held up his finger for a moment of silence so he could listen to Harris' heartbeat. Steady, no hint of a murmur. Excellent.

"Your heart sounds great," he told Harris.

"That's good, but unless I know Maya's going to be okay, my heart's not the most important. Hers is. So what's your plan, Rune?"

"My plan? Like I said, my plan is to let Maya lead the way."

"You sure that's the best plan? Maya doesn't always know what she wants. She thought she wanted Jerome, and that boy wasn't worth the toilet paper on her shoe."

Rune hid a smile as he put away the stethoscope. He didn't mind hearing that about Jerome. Not at all. "It's not like that with me and Maya."

He straightened up, flexing the muscles that had gotten cramped while he'd been crouching next to Harris. The man gazed up at him as if Rune was disappointing him greatly.

"Do you know that at first I didn't like you and Maya being friends in Hawaii?"

Rune absorbed that information without much surprise. He'd picked up on the man's disapproval. "I think I knew that."

"I didn't have a lot of trust in white boys. Hurtful things can be said, whether you mean to or not. But I can't keep her in a cocoon. So I let her keep playing with you and I kept a close eye. A very close eye."

"No wonder I got nervous every time I went to your house." Rune managed a smile. He'd always tried to behave well around Harris. He'd looked up to him. A steady, caring father figure wasn't something he was used to.

"I put the fear of God into you, didn't I?" Harris chuckled. "That was on purpose. I'm a peaceful man, until someone messes with my Maya."

"So how come you never kicked me out? I could be such a little shit sometimes."

"Yes, you could. I saw it. But I saw Maya stand up and speak on it too. Like the time you said she didn't need sunscreen because her skin was already dark, and she gave you a lecture on melanin right then and there. She schooled you about how black people get sunburn like anyone else. And you listened to her. You always listened to her."

"Of course I did. She was a lot smarter than I was." He chuckled as he stowed away his stethoscope. "Not that I was dumb, but I didn't always do the smart thing."

"Maya chooses her friends very carefully. She chose well with you. I didn't see it at first, but eventually I did."

Rune turned his attention to packing up his medical bag, partly to hide the emotion that suddenly closed up his throat. Praise from Harris Badger wasn't just an ordinary compliment. Coming from a man he admired, who also happened to be Maya's father...that was pretty special. "Thank you," he said finally. "I'm glad you didn't kick me to the curb."

"I might now though."

He turned back with a frown. "Excuse me?"

"If you let Maya call all the shots, this thing ain't never going to get anywhere. She's too gun-shy. It's up to you, kid."

"But I told you, it's not like that with me and—"

Harris waved both hands in the air. "Don't waste a heart patient's time. I have eyes. I know Maya. I know you pretty well, too, after all that close attention I paid when you were nine. It *is* like that. But it won't be unless you do something soon."

Was there anything more embarrassing than getting lectured about your love life by the father of the girl you were involved with? "I...uh..." He rubbed a hand across the back of his neck. His respect for Harris Badger ran deep. He owed the man some honesty.

"There's a situation," he finally said. "Cara and I, we may have to leave Lost Harbor soon."

Harris frowned and cocked his head at him. "Is it the job? Travel nurse?"

"Not exactly."

Taking a deep breath, he explained about Cara's stalker. Then he had to explain why he and Maya had delayed telling Harris about it.

"If you're worried about this creep showing up here, we can clear out in a flash. We're used to it," he added.

Harris kept shaking his head as he absorbed the news. "Nah, he'd best stay far away from me or he'll regret it. Why do you want to leave? To my mind, you're in the best place you could be. Small town, police chief right down the road. You gotta take a stand somewhere."

"Maybe." He shrugged. "But I can't take chances with Cara's safety."

Harris' eyebrows quirked. "I see that. There's some other chances you're not taking either."

Rune closed his bag and got to his feet. A sadness came over him, a sense of a missed opportunity, a life he could have lived if it weren't for the stalker. "You can't always do everything that you want."

A short silence followed, then Harris said, "Well, you think hard about what I'm saying."

"I will, Mr. Badger. I always listen to what you say. Learned that lesson early."

Harris chuckled.

"And I'll send a final report to Dr. Morrison. She'll be handling your case from here on out." With a last smile, he headed for the door.

"Listen to your heart," Harris called after him.

"See you at Thanksgiving tomorrow."

Outside, the frosty air held the scent of spruce and fog. A storm was in the forecast for Thanksgiving, but tonight, an eerie mist was filtering onshore from the lake.

Listen to your heart.

If only he could do that. His heart had all kinds of things to say about Maya. That she grounded him, that she sent his pulse into overdrive, that he wished there was a holiday party every night just so he could hold her hand.

For a moment he let himself dream. What if he could stay here and pursue Maya and win her heart without fear of having to leave? What if the two of them could just...be together? No fake dating. No hiding his real feelings.

That would be heaven. Pure heaven.

He got into his car—and just like that, the dream shattered.

On the passenger seat sat a letter with no postage and block letter handwriting. It was addressed to Cara.

He jumped out of the car and scanned the immediate area. He hadn't been inside Harris' house for much more than half an hour. But the driveway dissolved in a blur of fog. Whoever had been here was nowhere to be seen.

Pulling out his phone, he ducked back into his car.

"Cara, you okay?" he asked as soon as his sister answered.

"You mean because my brain might explode from these calculations? No. I'm not. I need a freaking hot fudge sundae."

He relaxed as he steered the car down the slope to the fish house. At least the creep hadn't gotten close to her yet.

He dialed Maya next. "How far away are you? Can you come over? It's an emergency."

"I'm on my way home from yoga. What happened?"

"I found a letter in my car. Like the kind we used to get—"

"I'll be right there. *Don't* touch it."

"I won't."

He parked outside the fish house and jumped out of the car. Even though he'd just spoken to Cara, he had to check on her. Thick mist hovered over the ocean and the little dock disappeared into a foggy limbo. The temperature hovered around freezing. Each particle of mist that landed on his face left a prickle of cold.

He locked the car door, then hurried into the house. Cara sat on the sofa with a crocheted blanket on her lap, glaring at her algebra book. "I hate math," she announced.

"Okay." God, he hated to insert darkness into her oh-so-normal teenage moment. The sound of a car engine caught his attention. Maya was coming. Reinforcements. Something he hadn't really had up to now.

"Listen, Cara. There's a letter in the car addressed to you. Maya's on her way to check it out."

"*What?*" She shoved aside her math book and jumped to her feet.

"Have you noticed anything suspicious? Anything at all?"

"No!" All the color left her face, leaving her eyes burning blue against her pale skin. "I thought we were safe here. I was so sure of it."

He heard a car door slam outside. "Come on. Maya's here."

"I just have to grab a coat."

He didn't wait for her, but went outside to join Maya. She wore a dark parka over her yoga clothes, along with Sorel boots and a burnt orange bandanna tied around her hair.

She was pulling on a pair of examination gloves as he came around to the passenger side and clicked the key fob. "Where did this happen?" she asked, without any preliminaries such as greetings. Police Maya—that was how she rolled.

"At your dad's place." He gestured to the top of the mist-shrouded property. "It was there when I came out. I looked around but didn't see any sign of an intruder."

"I'll do an extra sweep when I'm done here." She shook open a plastic evidence bag and reached for the envelope with her gloved hand. "You didn't open it, right?"

"You said not to touch it."

She slid the envelope into the plastic bag, where it lurked like poison about to destroy his world. He wasn't ready to leave Lost Harbor. He didn't want to start all over again somewhere else. He didn't want to leave *Maya*.

The thought wrenched at his heart.

Stop whining, he told himself. *It is what it is.*

Light splashed across the snowy yard as the fish house door

opened. Cara trudged over to them in unfastened snow boots. "Can I see it?"

Rune gave Maya a nod. She clicked on a pen light and played it over the envelope so Cara could get a look at it.

Unexpectedly, she turned beet red.

"That's...that's for me."

"Obviously," Rune said. "It says right there—"

"No, I mean, it's not from the stalker. It's from a...friend. He... ugh. Can I just see what it says inside?"

Maya's eyebrows lifted. "You know who left this for you? Why didn't he just give it to you?"

"I don't know. He's shy."

"These are block letters, Cara. You can't possibly recognize that handwriting. You don't know for sure—"

"Yes, I do. He uses Sharpies for his artwork. He's a really talented artist. You should see some of the drawings he does. Those aren't just any old block letters. See how he blended the different colors? It's amazing how he can do that with nothing but Sharpies. Just—give it to me." Her face was still flushed; Rune's heart went out to her. Nothing like getting busted on your first crush.

Maya turned to Rune. "What do you think? Does the block writing look like our guy?"

He bent down to examine it more closely. Now that he did, it clearly was the work of someone younger and more artistic than Stalker Chad. "Not really," he admitted. "Sorry for the false alarm."

"Hey, don't even worry about that. Better safe than sorry." She handed the envelope to Cara. "Go ahead, open it. But if there's anything in there that doesn't look right to you, I need to examine it."

"Okay." Cara hesitated as the two of them watched her. "A little privacy, please?"

With a roll of his eyes, Rune took Maya by the elbow and walked her a few steps away. "I'm sorry. You were all Zen-ed out from yoga and I dragged you down here for nothing. How can I make it up to you?"

Her forehead crinkled. "It's my job. You don't have to make up anything."

"Hot fudge sundae? The perfect post-yoga treat? I was going to make one for Cara to get her through her algebra. I can make one for you too."

Her deep honey eyes glowed against the drifting mist. "I haven't even had dinner yet."

"Neither have I. Cara's probably been munching Cheetos. I'll make us some fish tacos."

Harris had told him to make a move, after all. Fish tacos counted, right?

"Okay," she finally said. "I don't have anything at home except leftover takeout from lunch two days ago."

He shook his head, frowning. "As a medical professional, I have to point out that you should be taking much better care of yourself."

"Noted. You aren't taking away my hot fudge sundae, are you?"

"Of course not. That would be cruel." He glanced over his shoulder at Cara, who was still completely wrapped up in her love note. How long could the thing possibly be? "This is bad," he said mostly to himself.

"It's normal. She's a teenager."

"She's a teenager who might have to pick up and leave at any moment. That part's not normal."

Her expression sobered as she took in Cara's rapt expression. "Poor kid. What are you going to tell her?"

Tiny icy droplets landed on his face as he thought about it. They felt like frozen tears. "I can't tell her to stop liking him.

That ain't gonna happen. So I guess I'll tell her to just be real and get to know him as best she can during whatever time she has here."

Her gaze held his for a long moment. "That sounds like good advice," she said softly.

Everything seemed to still around them. He heard the soft whisper of mist landing on the snow and the crinkle of Cara's envelope. Something was happening here. She was sending him a message. He didn't want to miss it.

He replayed his own words. My God—of course the same advice could apply to them. *Just be real. Enjoy the time you have.*

But what about the risk of hurting Maya when he left?

"Do you think it's good advice?" he asked cautiously. "Because I could say something else. 'Don't get close, it'll be too painful,' that sort of thing."

He watched her closely, wondering if she'd understand that he was referring to them, not just Cara. Of course she did; Maya didn't miss things like that.

"That's true. And it's definitely worth thinking hard about. But nothing in life is ever a guarantee, is it? You have to consider all angles and then make a choice. There's always risks, whatever you do."

Energy pulsed between them. Her lips parted; he loved her lips, their full curves and satiny texture. He drew closer, as if she was a magnet and he was a helpless...paper clip or something.

Just then, Cara spoke behind them. "All clear on the letter. It's definitely not from the stalker."

Rune straightened up, startled out of his Maya-induced trance. He held her gaze as he answered Cara. "Good to know. I guess we can stay a little longer then."

"Maybe a *lot* longer. Maybe we found the place he'll never find. Lost Harbor is named after being lost, after all. You guys coming?"

Maya answered. "Your brother promised me tacos and a hot fudge sundae. You bet I'm coming."

"Oh good! Party!" Cara scampered toward the door, as much as she could while dragging heavy winter boots through the snow.

"After your algebra," Rune called to her.

He ushered Maya inside with a hand on the small of her back. Happiness flowed through him like the mist blowing in from the lake. "How's your algebra?"

"My algebra lives in my phone in a little app known as a calculator."

He laughed, already feeling the joy her company always brought him.

"I need some help too," she told him.

"Name it." Maybe it would involve kissing, or necking down on the dock, or snuggling in his loft...

"I have to decide what to bring for Thanksgiving tomorrow."

Another dream crushed. Rune mentally laughed at his overeager fantasy life. "On it. You know I'm here for you, babe. We'll figure it out."

CHAPTER SEVENTEEN

Thanksgiving

THE NEXT AFTERNOON, Rune swung by Maya's house to pick her up for Thanksgiving dinner. She lived about a mile down the road from her dad, close enough to be able to run over if he needed something, but not in the same space, where they might drive each other crazy.

Her house was a two-bedroom cedar-shingled piece of heaven. She'd decorated it meticulously, with mostly muted tones along with splashes of tomato red. She only allowed comfortable pieces of furniture in her house. But the best part was the custom bathtub where she liked to soak after a long day at work. Candles, bubbles, a glass of wine, the works. She had a whole collection of bath salts and oils, along with lotions to smooth into her skin afterwards.

Only her girlfriends knew about this side of her. They all knew they couldn't go wrong with a good bath bomb for her birthday.

As she let Rune into her house for the first time, she was torn between watching his reaction to her personal space and admiring the way he filled out the hand-knit sweater he wore.

And his tight black jeans.

"Which little old lady knit you that sweater?" she asked him as she grabbed her wool overcoat. She'd spent some time picking out her outfit—a form-fitting brown suede skirt and shiny claret patent-leather boots. A scoop-necked top showed off her favorite necklace—a whimsical abstract gazelle one of her aunts had sent her from Ghana.

"I don't kiss and tell," Rune said gravely.

"So that's how it is? I see where I stand." She shrugged on her coat and picked up the sweet potato casserole she'd made from her grandmother's recipe. In the end, she'd gone for the tried-and-true. Everyone in town had tried her casserole at some point, but it still got her compliments.

"You stand wherever you want to stand." Rune took her free hand and drew her toward him. "Right about here works for me. Or maybe a little closer."

The heat in his eyes made desire flare in her belly. He looked as if he wanted to toss aside the sweet potatoes and eat her up instead. Last night, over tacos and hot fudge sundaes, he'd shot her so many secret hot looks that she'd needed that ice cream just to cool down.

Now he was doing it again.

"Stop looking at me like that. We're late."

"We could skip Thanksgiving and hang out here. I never vibed with the pilgrims anyway. Those weird shoes and those funky black hats."

"We're not skipping Thanksgiving." She sent him a severe look, even though she wouldn't *mind* ripping that sweater off his body and seeing how those muscles looked without clothes. "I worked too hard on this dish."

"Fine, be that way," he grumbled. "I suppose Cara would be worried. She's already at the bakery helping Jessica set up. How's Harris getting there?"

"Vicki." She made a face. She still couldn't say that name with anything resembling a smile. "She's driving him in her fancy red Jeep that she finally put snow tires on after I threw several fits."

"Then we don't have to pick up anyone else? It's just you and me? I can hold your hand while we drive?"

"No, you can keep your hands where they belong. Ten and two."

"You take all the zing out of Thanksgiving," he complained, as if that made any sense.

They got into his car and drove down the road that would take them past Harris' place, along the mudflats, past the Lost Harbor airport and eventually to Seafarers Beach, where the bakery was located.

"There's so much to catch you up on," she told him as he drove. "I didn't want to say anything last night with Cara around, but I have an idea about Christmas."

"Already thinking about the next holiday party?"

"Oh, there's plenty more between now and then. But I might cut back because—" She bit her lip. That was another thing she hadn't wanted to mention last night; that Jerome was in town. She still didn't particularly want to talk about it.

"Because of Jerome?" he asked gently.

She swung her head around in surprise.

"Harris told me. I think he's worried about you."

"He always worries about me. Honestly, though, it's fine. I haven't run into Jerome yet. Maybe I won't. If I do, I do."

"That's right. You got this. With any luck, you can give him a ticket for something when you do."

She laughed. "Can't say I haven't thought about that myself."

A sense of real contentment came over her as they reached the mudflats. Silvery shadows on the mud reflected the low heavy clouds overhead. A light sleet began to fall, but the two of them were cozy inside the shelter of the car.

Being with Rune was so satisfying that she could barely remember the time before he came. He pleased her on so many levels—his sense of humor, his kindness to his patients, his competence in his field. The way he'd dropped everything to take care of Cara gave her a deep respect for his fundamental character. And that, she knew, was one of the most important things to her—respect. She needed it, and she needed to give it, too.

A flash of red in a snowbank up ahead interrupted her reverie. "What's that? On the right."

Rune clicked on the windshield wipers. "Looks like a car went off the road."

A red car? Stark terror seized her. That red was the same color as Vicki's damn Jeep.

"We have to stop," she told Rune in a tight voice.

"Of course." He leaned forward to peer through the sleet. This part of the road had no streetlights. The only illumination came from the periodic blink of the warning lights at the nearby airport. "It's definitely a Jeep," he said in a tense voice.

She could make out the tracks of the vehicle now—it had fishtailed on the slippery sleet. Vicki had veered right, then left, then right again and finally hurtled off the side of the road and down into a drainage ditch.

Please don't be hurt, please don't be hurt, she repeated like an incantation under her breath.

Along with the fear came fury. She was going to throttle Vicki. No, she'd throw her in jail for endangering an...elder. So what if that wasn't a thing? She'd make it a damn thing.

Rune pulled over as close to the Jeep as he could get and put on his hazards. Both of them jumped out of his car and hurried toward the accident. She slipped on the slick road and would have fallen if Rune hadn't grabbed her arm. Right—she was dressed for Thanksgiving dinner, not a car accident. She'd completely forgotten.

Rune kept a grip on her arm while they covered the last few feet to the Jeep. Amazingly, the police part of her mind kept operating even while panic raced through her. The Jeep was precariously perched on its passenger-side wheels, jammed up against a pile of snow left by a snow plow. That was good; snow was a more forgiving obstacle than a tree.

Harris was in the passenger seat so he would have borne the brunt of the crash. Still, the Jeep had only traveled a few yards before coming to a rest in the snow bank. There was a good chance that neither of them had been injured too badly.

Even so, this was *all* Vicki's fault.

As soon as they were close enough, Maya furiously tugged her arm out of Rune's grasp and dashed the rest of the way to the driver's side window. "Vicki, I'm going to—"

The window rolled down and a familiar face emerged. Familiar—but not Vicki's. "Maya? Is that you?"

She skidded to a stop and nearly toppled over backwards on her damn patent leather boots. The wall of Rune's body served as a backstop, but she barely noticed.

"*Jerome?*"

"Yeah, I thought this rental had snow tires but I should have checked." He flashed her his million-dollar grin, the one that had lured investors into that failed geothermal project. "My bad."

"My bad?" she repeated. "Okay. How's—" She gestured with her head toward his passenger. She couldn't make out much about her, but guessed it was Leanne.

"I'm mostly okay," came a trembling female voice from the other seat. "I think I might have a cut. Something's dripping on me."

Rune trudged through the snow to her side of the Jeep, and bent over to look inside. He used his phone flashlight to assess the damage. Which meant that he was thinking much quicker than she was.

"I do see some blood on the side of her head," he said quietly to Maya. "And she's probably in shock too. We need to get them to the emergency room."

She nodded and pulled out her phone. "I'll call the station."

But when she got ahold of the dispatcher, she learned that accidents were happening all over Lost Harbor due to the sleet, and that it would be at least half an hour before anyone could get to them.

"Sorry, Rune, we're going to have to make a detour," she told him quietly.

He nodded without any hint of worry. She could see why he made a good paramedic; he was coolheaded in a crisis. "I'll work on getting the driver out first. Why don't you call your dad and make sure they made it safely."

Would anyone else have thought of that? Jerome sure wouldn't have.

"Make sure the car is stable first," she told him.

"Of course. Paramedic, remember? I got this. Check on Harris so you don't worry."

She stepped aside and clicked her father's number on her phone.

"Baby? Where are you? Everyone's waiting on you here," he answered.

"You're at Jessica's?"

"Got here fifteen minutes ago. There's a whole feast spread out here. I can hardly talk for how much my mouth is watering. You coming?"

"We ran across a car off the road. We need to get them to the emergency room. You all go on ahead, just save us some leftovers."

She heard noises in the background, then Harris must have handed the phone to Jessica, because the next voice was hers. "What happened, Maya?"

She covered her mouth so the sound wouldn't travel. "You're not going to believe it, but we're in the midst of a vehicular extraction. Jerome and Leanne skidded off the road. We have to get to them to the ER."

"My gosh, are they okay?"

"Both conscious and alert. They'll be fine."

"Oh good, that means I can enjoy the fact that I can't imagine a more satisfying first encounter than that, can you? Is there any way you can put him in jail? That would be the best."

Maya bit her lip to hold back her own urge to laugh. "You're terrible."

"When it comes to my friends, my pettiness knows no bounds. Don't worry about us. You go take care of business, we'll see you when you get here."

She stuck her phone back into her coat pocket and stepped back to the rescue operation. Rune was bracing the Jeep door open while Jerome fought against gravity to climb out of the driver's seat.

Rune kept a tight grip on Jerome's arm as he staggered into the snow. He slipped and wound up on one knee. Not so cocky now, was he?

Maya shoved aside the ungracious thought. She was better than this. She didn't need any kind of revenge for how Jerome had treated her.

Then again, it wasn't as if she'd personally shoved him into the snow the way she'd imagined so many times. He'd gotten there on his own.

Rune dragged Jerome upright and kept a hold on him until he'd gotten his balance. "Do you have any pain anywhere?"

"Everywhere," he complained. "Damn, I forgot how freaking cold and dank it is here. I'm Jerome Morris." He stuck out his hand for Rune to shake.

"Rune Larsen. Want to go warm up in the car? We'll get your friend out."

"My wife. Leanne. Maya knows her." Jerome dropped his hand and limped toward Rune's car. "Good to see ya, Maya," he said in a lower voice as he passed her.

She ignored him and moved to Rune's side to help him with Leanne. Getting her out was much more challenging. The windshield had gotten caved in by a branch; the shattered tempered glass was only an inch away from her face. It probably accounted for the cut on her head.

Rune took the lead by calmly directing the shivering girl, step by step. He reached in and unfastened her seat belt. "We can't open the passenger-side door, so you'll have to climb across the gear shift. This'll be a lot easier if you can back your seat up. There's not a lot of room in these Jeeps, but see what you can do. Even a little bit helps. Do you remember how to do that? Okay, great. Fantastic. Now scoot to the left, closer to me. Great, you're doing great. Perfect. You're brilliant. Now reach toward me. I'm going to put my hands under your armpits and pull you out. Got it?"

It was part extraction, part pep talk—but it worked. Leanne found enough composure to do what Rune said, until he was able to gently maneuver her across the driver's seat and out the door.

Maya was there to receive her. "I got you, Leanne. You made it."

The girl gasped as the icy sleet hit her. Her slight frame trembled in Maya's hold. Still blond and tiny, just the way Maya remembered her. "Where's Jerome?"

"He's warming up in the car."

Trust Jerome to take care of himself above all else. Leanne shuddered as blood ran down her face. "I feel so weird. Like, I know I'm bleeding but I can't tell where it comes from."

"It's okay. The doctors will figure that out."

Rune shone his light across her face. "This isn't the best in terms of flashlights, but can you follow the light?"

She had trouble focusing her gaze and instead looked toward the Toyota. "Where's Jerome?"she asked again.

Rune met Maya's gaze, concern in his eyes. Probably a concussion, she'd guess. "Let's take you over to him," she told the girl.

Rune opened his medical bag and took out a towel. "Press this to your head until we get you to the ER. Can you do that?"

She nodded with an expression like a child's, almost adoring, then took the towel in her hand. He guided it to the bloody side of her head.

"Ready?" Maya asked. "Here we go. We got you." With her on one side and Rune on the other, the two of them helped Leanne across the snow to the idling Toyota. Her high heels were even less snow-worthy than Maya's.

When they reached the car, Jerome reached across the back-seat and opened the door for them. "Come on, baby. Come warm up next to me."

With a sob, she dropped onto the seat beside him and burst into tears. He gathered her against him and met Maya's gaze.

"She gets a little emotional sometimes."

"Yeah, well, this would be a good time to get emotional," Maya said sharply. "She might have a concussion."

He snapped his mouth shut and sat in silence while Rune drove through the eerie, empty streets of Lost Harbor to the ER. Sheets of sleet swept from the bay right across the town, the streetlights creating a red glow in the condensation.

She got on the phone to dispatch and let them know that two injured parties were being taken to the Emergency Room. She noted the location of the accident so that no one would feel obliged to check out the abandoned Jeep.

In a low voice, Rune murmured, "Tell them to meet us at the ambulance entrance. She's disoriented, with altered mental status."

"Right." She relayed those instructions to the dispatcher. "We'll be there in five."

"On it. Be safe, Chief Badger."

When they reached the ambulance entrance, a team ran outside with a gurney, their PPE whipping in the wind. Rune rattled off Leanne's vitals—at some point he'd checked her pulse, but Maya had missed that.

Rune and Maya stepped back while they transferred Leanne to the gurney. Jerome hovered behind, looking almost bewildered, his usual slick confidence nowhere to be seen. "Can I go with her?"

"Possible shock here too," Rune told the ER doctors. "No visible external injuries. Can someone help him out?"

One of the doctors came to his side and shepherded Jerome toward the entry. Stumbling, he looked back over his shoulder at Maya. "Good running into you, Maya. Maybe we can all get together after Thanksgiving. Call me."

Maya waved as he disappeared into the hospital. "He's acting like we just ran into each other at cocktail hour."

"People can be really strange after an accident. They want to go on as if everything is normal. I once assisted a woman in Hawaii who'd accidentally chopped her finger off with a machete. She collected the finger and started walking down the road toward the nearest hospital. She got a hundred yards before she fainted and someone called 911."

Maya shivered as the wind pushed a wave of sleet against her face. "You're right. Also, he's always like that. He's very smooth. I can't believe I fell for his act. I used to think he was so charming and magnetic. Especially compared to me."

"Excuse me?" Rune put his arm around her and steered her back to the car. "You lost me on that one."

"You know I'm more of an introvert," she said when they were both safely inside the warm car. "Jerome's the opposite. He knows how to win people over."

"Maya, you have it all wrong. When you speak, people listen. When that dude speaks, I tune it out because I know it's mostly bullshit."

She let out a gurgle of laughter. "You got that right. I wish you'd been around back then to warn me off."

"I wish I had too." He started the car and swiftly backed out of the ER entrance, as if he'd done so many times. He probably had, at other hospitals, other emergency rooms. This one too, during his volunteer shifts.

He was an excellent EMT.

"You did really well out there," she told him.

"Thanks. It's my job. Or my old job, anyway."

She remembered how Leanne had looked at him with that expression of adoration. She knew exactly how the girl felt. There was nothing quite as sexy as a first responder in a crisis.

Oh, who was she kidding? She knew plenty of first responders and had never wanted to swoon over any of them.

It was Rune she found so sexy. That was all. End of story.

CHAPTER EIGHTEEN

Rune's pulse was still racing when they reached the Sweet Harbor Bakery. Not just from the adrenaline of the rescue, but from the way Maya kept looking at him, with that soft light in her eyes.

It made wild thoughts cartwheel through his brain and lust flood into his veins.

The bakery was located only a few hundred yards from one of Lost Harbor's most famous beaches. Lanterns in the shape of stars lit the windows of the bakery. The warm lights glowed like a beacon in the dark sleet-filled night. He could see movement inside; people laughing and getting up to help themselves to more food.

Beyond the bakery, the road continued for a short distance and dead-ended at a parking lot at the beach. It made for a great view spot to take in the surf along the shoreline and the majestic mountains in the distance.

He'd gone running along the beach a few times, going as far as he could before the incoming tide met the bluffs and he had to turn back.

He didn't mind at all when Maya said softly, "Keep going," as they reached the bakery's driveway. After the intensity of a rescue—even one with light injuries—he too could use a little time to decompress before facing all the people waiting for them in the bakery. All the questions, the curiosity—he wasn't ready for any of that.

Long driftwood logs separated the parking lot from the beach. Usually the spaces were filled with the vehicles of dog-walkers, beach-strollers, hikers. Tonight, they were the only ones present to witness the storm riling up the ocean into foaming surf that flung itself onto the shore.

The roar of the waves fought the sound of his engine for dominance—and won as soon as he turned off the car.

For a moment, they sat in silence as they absorbed the spectacle before them. Turbulent gray clouds drove waves of sleet onto the beach. It whipped against the car, which shook with each gust of wind. He hoped that no one was out on the water tonight. It felt almost as if they were on a boat themselves, alone in a tiny bubble sheltered from the forces of nature raging around them.

The only sound from inside the car was that of their breathing. Maya stared out the window, just as riveted by the storm as he was. He remembered a trick he'd heard; if you want someone to connect with you, sync your breathing to theirs. But his and Maya's breathing were already in tune, as if rising and falling on the same churning surf.

"That was—" he began at the same time she spoke.

"I was so scared it was—"

"Your father. I know. That red Jeep."

"Everyone loves renting red Jeeps." She gave a shaky laugh. "I should have figured. Vicki was raised in Bethel, she's a lifelong Alaskan. She knows how to drive in the snow." She rubbed her hands down the front of her thighs.

Her suede skirt was speckled with darker spots left by the precipitation.

He covered her hand with his. "Of course you were worried about them."

She turned her hand over so their fingers interlaced. "Yeah, but I was ready to rip Vicki's head off as soon as that window came down. Jerome's actually lucky I recognized him in time. Not that he doesn't also deserve a good head-ripping," she added.

He wondered if it had been tough for her, seeing him again, but didn't really want to talk about the dude. He'd been completely unimpressed by him and would never have approved of him for Maya if she'd asked.

"His wife seems sweet," he said instead.

Which was apparently *not* the right thing to say. Maya drew her hand from under his and wiped a hole in the condensation forming on the window.

"You would think so," she said pointedly. "You are a man, after all." Facing him again, she went on, the hurt clear in her voice. "All the guys love Leanne and always have. She's tiny and blond and smiles a lot and—"

He stopped her flow of thought by snatching her against him. "No."

"No?" She blinked up at him.

"No," he repeated firmly. "I don't care how much she smiles, she's not you."

Her lips parted. The next thing he knew, they were kissing. A fierce, passionate, no-denying-it kiss. Pressing his mouth to hers, all the adrenaline and urgency inside him pouring into her. All the feelings he'd been stopping up and shoving aside.

"She's not you," he muttered against her mouth. "That's the only thing I noticed. She's not you."

Did she understand?

She must have, because she returned his kiss with the same

kind of fire that burned inside of him. Her lips parted for him and he feasted on that rich flavor that was pure Maya. He caught her fast breaths in his mouth, along with her sighs. He wanted it all, every throb and pulse and heartbeat.

They clutched at each other, straining against their seat belts. He cradled her head in his hand, savoring the texture of her skin, the soft spring of her hair. She'd left it unpinned for the night, which was unusual for her. Didn't matter; however she wore her hair, he found her beautiful.

When they were gasping for breath, they pulled apart. He ran his thumb across her lower lip, feeling its swollen warmth. Her eyes gleamed in the darkness, wide and soft. Wind jostled the car.

"Maya, I—" He struggled with the words. "I think I..."

"Wh-what?" She breathed rapidly. Her tongue slid across her lips, where his mouth had been. Where he wanted it to be now, except that he had to say this first.

"I think I'm...falling in love with you."

Her lips parted again, a look of shock shivering across her face. "What?"

"Yeah. I know. It's...nuts. I know we're friends, and I'm your holiday date, but I can't help how I feel."

"And you..." She seemed too stunned to finish her sentence.

"I'm in love with you. I thought you should know. I'm not good at hiding my feelings."

She scanned his face, confusion in her eyes. "I—I don't know what to say."

Ouch. That was very far from what he'd been hoping for. He drew in a breath. He couldn't *make* her feel the same way he did. All he could do was say how he felt. "I get it—"

"You're my friend," she interrupted. "But we've been flirting and kissing, inching toward something else. I want the something else. But I didn't know—" She broke off, tugging her lower lip between her teeth.

"I sprung it on you, I know. I'm sorry. I just need to be completely honest with you. Our friendship deserves that much." He gave a laugh that he hoped didn't sound too awkward.

"I—thank you." She looked away, glanced at him again, then looked back, as if still trying to put all the pieces together.

"I don't want things to get weird," he said, more lightly. "Nothing's changed. I'm still Rune, you're still Maya."

"Technically, you're Jay-Jay."

"I'm still *me*." He picked up her hand and placed it on his chest. "I'll always be your friend. I don't want this to change anything. If you want to dump me as your fake holiday boyfriend, I understand. I didn't mean to ruin everything by falling for you. It just...happened."

It was so quiet inside the car that he could hear his heart beating. Or maybe it was hers. Or the wind buffeting the car. Or the time running out on their relationship. Would things ever be the same?

A smiled tugged at the corners of her mouth. By now, she didn't look quite so shocked. "You didn't ruin anything," she said softly. "I just don't—"

He flung up a hand, not wanting to hear the words straight out. "You don't feel the same way. I get it."

She shook her head quickly. "It's just a lot to take in, that's all. I've been trying to ignore all that," she waved a hand at his torso, "and everything else too. Just stick to the friendship, with some flirting. Now I'm confused. I mean—" She snapped her mouth shut.

"What? What are you confused about?"

"Does this mean you don't want to sleep together?" she blurted. "Because I thought that's where this was going."

Inwardly, he cursed himself up one side and down the other.

If he'd kept his mouth shut, they might be dry humping in the car right now. Or racing back to her place and tumbling into a bed.

"I...wouldn't mind," he said—which was so awkward that he dropped his forehead onto the steering wheel and bonked himself a few times. "Can we rewind and try this again?"

She laughed softly. "You're pretty cute right now, you know that?"

He lifted his head off the wheel and glanced her way. That smile playing across her lips, the light in her eyes, the teasing expression—he would have thrown himself in front of a car for her.

"That doesn't sound like a good thing. I'm a man, not a kitten."

"Yeah, I've noticed." Again, her glance flitted across his body. It acted like gasoline on a fire. His cock pulsed hard.

He cleared his throat. "So, you know where I stand. Ready for action. All in, baby. Fired up and ready to go. It's all on you now."

Her phone rang, making both of them jump. His head actually hit the roof of the car. She looked at the number.

"It's Dad. I'm sure they're wondering where we are."

He gestured for her to answer, which she did. "Hi Dad. Yeah, we're on our way. It took a little longer at the ER than I expected. Yup, almost there. We're right around the corner. Don't worry, we'll drive safe. Yes, Rune's right here next to me." She mouthed something to him that he couldn't make out, but was probably naughty.

He made goofy gestures in response, as if they were playing a game of charades. She smiled at his clowning. Good—maybe his surprise announcement wouldn't throw things off between them too much.

"Yes, I have the sweet potato casserole with me. Dad, I have to hang up now. Rune is trying to say something to me."

Finally, she ended the call. "We have to get our asses over to that dinner or my dad's going to need more heart surgery. Can we maybe come back to this?"

"I'm here. Not going anywhere." He winced, since that wasn't completely true. He *would* be going somewhere. It was just a matter of time, unless Stalker Chad got lost in the mists of the bay. "You know what I mean."

"I do." She scanned his face. "You mean you're here for me."

"Exactly. That's exactly it. I'm here for you. Whatever that looks like."

Somehow, it felt like a promise.

CHAPTER NINETEEN

The rest of Thanksgiving might as well have been a third-grade reenactment of the landing of the Pilgrims; it was all a blur to Maya.

Rune was *in love* with her? And he'd come right out and said so, on the very night that she'd seen Jerome for the first time since he'd incinerated her heart?

It was too much to take in.

The Sweet Harbor Bakery was toasty warm, filled with the aromas of roast turkey and sage. The only sign of the storm outside was the occasional burst of sleet pattering against the windows. All the Café tables had been pushed together to form one long banquet table. Everyone else had finished eating and had pushed back their chairs to relax.

Her father and Darius were getting their instruments tuned up; fiddle and standing bass, respectively. After Harris waved a greeting to Maya and Rune, he launched into "The Wreck of the Edmund Fitzgerald," which felt very appropriate on this stormy night.

All of the dishes were laid out on the bakery counter. As the mournful chords and murmurs of conversation swirled around them, Maya and Rune filled their plates with turkey and ham and green beans and collard greens.

It felt almost surreal to Maya, as if the storm had shifted the entire night into an alternate reality. Or maybe it had blown away the fog so she could see more clearly the man at her side. Rune wasn't just her fun best buddy from Hawaii. Not just a strong and caring (still fun) nurse. He'd just opened a door for her—for them. Beyond that door...

She shivered with excitement at the thought.

As they sat down at the banquet table, Vicki jumped up and brought them both glasses filled with something bright and scarlet.

"It's cranberry wine," she whispered over the plaintive sounds of the music. "I make it every year. It's a bit tart."

Maya felt so bad about how she'd blamed Vicki for the crash that she gave her an especially beaming smile. Vicki nearly dropped the glasses in shock.

Quite possibly, she'd been a little too hard on Vicki. She had to admit, her father seemed happy. If he didn't mind Vicki's occasional ditziness, why should she? Maybe Rune was right and she needed to let go.

"Can't wait to try it," she said politely.

Rune gave her an approving wink.

She made a little face at him, just to prove she wasn't completely giving up her potential objections to Vicki. She'd still be keeping an eye on her, especially since the wine puckered her mouth and brought tears to her eyes.

"That's...good," she managed to gasp.

Rune surreptitiously slid her a glass of water.

Everyone wanted to know about the incident that had delayed them. Maya and Rune took turns telling the story through bites of food. Even that felt different. Usually during the holidays she felt lonely in the midst of a crowd. That was the hardest part. That was what she'd wanted so desperately to avoid.

Thanks to Rune, she hadn't felt that way once this year.

As she filled her plate with seconds, Jessica joined her at the bakery counter. "So..." she asked in a low voice, away from the others. "What's the *real* Jerome report? How was it seeing him? Was it difficult? I have a tub of fresh-made caramel sauce that I can pour over ice cream for you. I made it for the apple pie, but your mental health is more important."

"I'm fine. I have no need for stress eating."

"No twinges? No sparks? No tears?"

"Not a peep." Maya shrugged as she popped another clover-leaf roll onto her plate. Jessica added a big dollop of butter next to it. "Five years did the trick, I guess."

"I don't think it was the five years." Jessica shot a glance back at the table, where Rune was listening to Ethan tell a story about his trip to Lost Souls Wilderness. The easy lines of Rune's big body projected calm, but also alertness, as if he was ready to leap into action if need be.

He would do exactly that, Maya knew. He'd done it for Cara, he'd do it for Maya's ex-boyfriend or any random stranger. And he'd do it for Maya.

When Rune said he was there for someone, he meant it.

The tight band around her heart loosened another notch.

"I need some advice, Jess," Maya whispered to her.

Jessica looked almost shocked. "You do? You're usually the one handing out advice."

"Yes, but that's about other people's lives. This is about mine."

"Come here." Jessica tugged her back around the counter to the kitchen area, which featured a tiled stonework oven that radiated heat. "No one can hear us back here. What's up?"

"So you know how we always joke about being either Team Sex or Team Romance."

"Of course. You never really picked a team. Keeping your options open?"

"No, it's more like I got kicked off of Team Romance so I played on Team Sex. Mostly in Anchorage so I didn't get people talking down here. But now..." She worried at the inside of her cheek. How much should she reveal to Jess? Jessica was very good at keeping secrets, but would she be betraying Rune's confidence?

"You're not sure where Rune falls?"

Trust Jessica's famous intuition to help her out. "*I'm* not sure. But Rune is. Let's just say that he's on Team Romance and he's very open to Team Sex. But if he's Team Romance and I'm not sure if I am, wouldn't Team Sex be the wrong move?"

Jessica's amber eyes filled with laughter. "I'm not sure why you're dancing around this. He has feelings for you and wants to sleep together, and you're not sure if that's a good idea."

Maya leveled a stern glare at her. "I was trying to keep his feelings private."

"If he wanted to keep them private, he wouldn't keep looking at you as if you were Thanksgiving and Christmas all rolled into one. Are you worried about it? Everyone already knows you're dating."

"I don't want to hurt him. I know how it feels to get your heart decimated. I don't want to do that to someone I care about."

Jessica touched her arm sympathetically. "Understandable. You say you care about him, but is it just as a friend or is there more?"

"I told you, I'm not sure."

"Well, you can't think your way out of that one. You can't investigate it like a case. You have to let yourself feel whatever you feel."

"Let myself? What does that mean?"

"You know what I'm talking about." She glanced back at the table, where Rune was now laughing at something Vicki was saying. "Honestly, I don't know how you can resist. That man is like a bowl of whipped cream spiked with cognac. If I wasn't madly in love with Ethan, I'd be questioning my commitment to Team Romance."

"Maybe those teams should be disbanded."

"Probably. One more thing, Maya. You don't need to over-think this. You deserve some happiness and joy. It's the holidays, after all. Maybe Rune is like an irresistible gift-wrapped second chance dropped into your life by destiny."

Now *that* was an interesting point. "This is definitely the best holiday season I've had in years."

"You deserve it. And more." Jessica winked at her.

As Maya carried her plate back to the table, Rune caught her eye and gave her such a tender, wicked smile that she tripped over an invisible crack in the floor. Even though she caught herself in time, everyone looked her way. "My boots got wet in the snow, and..."

She trailed off as Rune rose to his feet to take her plate and pull out her chair for her.

"Now that was hot," he whispered as she sat down.

"What was? Nearly falling on my face?" She plucked her roll off her plate and and bit into it.

"No. Just existing. That was the hot part."

Oh good God. How was she supposed to resist this man?

She couldn't. She didn't want to. She wasn't going to. "Want to come over tonight?" she murmured.

His eyes darkened to a smoky jade. "That would be a hell yes."

CHAPTER TWENTY

But first there were pies. Then there were goodbyes.

Her father always took forever to leave a party, and it turned out Vicki did too. They had that in common. Maya offered to help with dishes, but Jessica told her that was what her commercial-grade dishwasher was for.

Then she had to check in with the station about the twelve accident calls that had come in that night.

All the while, the secret electricity between her and Rune kept ramping up. Light touches in passing as they helped clear the table. Their eyes meeting at unexpected moments. The constant pull of awareness, as if they were connected by an invisible golden tether. A murmured word in her ear during the lengthy process of goodbye. *Tonight. Tonight.* The word drummed through her veins and simmered in her blood.

And then, at the last moment, as they were standing in the Sweet Harbor parking lot, shivering in the frigid aftermath of the storm, Cara asked if she and Maggie could have a sleepover that night. Maya almost panicked. Did that mean Rune would have to supervise? That he wouldn't be able to duck out?

But after extended negotiations between the three of them, it turned out to be a good thing. It meant that Rune wouldn't have to leave Cara alone.

"You two can take the loft, there's more space," he told them.

"What about you?"

"I'll be in and out," he said vaguely. "I have some patients to check on."

"On Thanksgiving?"

"Holidays can be difficult."

Maya pressed her lips together to stop her laughter. The girls didn't ask any more questions about the arrangements, just chattered away during the drive along the mudflats.

"Drop me off first, okay?" Maya murmured. "I left my place kind of a mess."

"I don't mind mess."

"No, it's bad. Seriously. I couldn't decide what to wear."

"Fine, but I'm coming back as fast as I can. I don't want you changing your mind."

Another thrill traveled through her. With her heart already racing and heat pulsing in her belly, there was no chance she was going to change her mind.

After he dropped her off, she raced into her bedroom and plucked all her discarded outfits off the floor. Tossing everything into the closet, she shoved the door shut so it wouldn't all fall out. Then she realized she hadn't taken off her boots and had left a trail of damp boot prints across her floor.

She'd just unzipped one boot and hauled it off when a knock came at the door. Hopping on one foot, she made her way to the door. Even though it had only been a few minutes since she'd seen Rune, the sight of him at her door sent a rocket flare of lust through her. The snug fit of his pants, the breadth of his shoulders, the wicked shine of his eyes...the pure physical pleasure of seeing him did something primal to her.

She saw the same deep heat in his eyes as he came toward her. Almost prowling.

"That took forever," she told him.

"Don't I know it. Quickest perimeter check I ever did." He gestured at the boot still in her hand. "Are you going somewhere or about to get naked?"

With a laugh, she tossed the boot aside. It landed with a clunk on the floor. "Door number two."

His eyes darkened as he pulled her against the hard length of his body. Pure muscles and heat pressed against her. Firm hands gripped her hips. His body heat surrounded her and the residual scent of wine and pecan pie made her head swim.

"Rune," she whispered.

"Mmm?"

"I want you."

He slid his hands under her ass and hoisted her off the floor, making her suede skirt ride up. Underneath, she wore a pair of leggings that she wanted off her body, like *now*.

"I'm damn glad to hear that. Because if I don't have you soon I'm going to cry like a baby. Where am I going?"

She flung an arm in the direction of her bedroom. "Promise you'll ignore the mess."

He walked toward her bedroom as she clung to his shoulders. "All I can see is you. That beautiful face of yours, your eyes like wild honey, that body that haunts me every time I close my eyes. Why'd you have to grow up to be such a damn goddess? I didn't see that coming."

His compliments were like a shower of sweetness raining from the sky. She wanted to close her eyes and soak them in. "Same, kid. Same. Some day you better tell me how you put on all that muscle."

"Turns out my dad was a boxer. It came with the genes. Hit a certain age and wham."

"That explains why you got into so many fights."

"That's the old me. I choose my fights now."

He turned sideways to maneuver through the bedroom door —then stopped dead. "You have a princess bed. Holy shit. The police chief has a princess bed."

She giggled. "Don't tell anyone. It's a closely guarded secret. It's the bed my dad made for me when I was sixteen. It's ridiculous, I know."

Ridiculous, but she loved it. The entire bed was draped with gauzy curtains, so when she closed herself in at night, she felt like she was in a magical fairy tent.

"Harris made that bed?"

"He's pretty good with carpentry. It took him a while. He had to read some do-it-yourself books and consult with some professionals. But yeah, he pulled it off."

"He really loved his little girl."

She didn't answer, because she really didn't feel like talking about her father right now. She had no idea if he'd approve of her getting this close to Rune. When they were kids, he hadn't been Jay-Jay's biggest fan, except for the fact that he'd saved her from the rogue wave.

Now another rogue wave—a stalker—had brought Rune back to her life and all the way to her bed.

Rune paused outside the closed curtains around her bed. "So my master plan of tossing you onto the bed like a caveman has been foiled. I don't want to rip down your pretty curtains. They look fragile. How do you get in there?"

With a laugh, she slid down his body, lingering at the hard bulge she encountered on the way. Excitement shot through her.

"You have to be invited." Giving him a seductive look, she parted the two lengths of fabric that formed the opening. Beyond it lay her bed, complete with fluffy pillows, a fuzzy stuffed panda, and the softest, downiest comforter known to womankind. Everything was in a shade of pale lilac, which had been her favorite color when she was sixteen.

He whistled softly as he took in the whole picture. "You have a serious hidden girlie side, don't you?"

"I don't know about 'hidden.' It's just private. When I come home from work I like to indulge myself."

He interlaced his hands and flexed them. "I'd like a crack at that job, if you don't mind."

"Indulging me?"

A smile hovered around his lips. "Sit down. You're still wearing one of your boots."

Ha! She'd forgotten about that. Her desire for Rune had scrambled her brains.

Her breath skipped and she plopped down on the edge of her bed. He kneeled in front of her and put both hands on her knee, just above the edge of her boot. The warmth of his touch penetrated through her legging and brought a sigh to her lips. He unzipped her boot and tugged it off, then gently rubbed the arch of her foot. As if he knew those boots were just a little bit tight, right there.

She moaned and leaned back on her elbows as he set her foot on top of his thigh and massaged it. Pure heaven. Pleasure skittered up her nerve endings and her eyes closed halfway. After a luxuriously long time, he switched to the other foot. He took just as long with this one, until she started to drift into a happy trance. He seemed so unhurried, as if he'd be perfectly content with just massaging her feet all night.

Maybe not *just* her feet, because next he turned his attention to her calves. He ran his thumbs along the swell of her muscles, easing tension and releasing happy endorphins into her bloodstream.

"You must have done well in anatomy," she murmured. "You know right where all those tendons and shit are."

"This is a muscle. The tendon's here." He touched her Achilles tendon, making her jump. "Ligaments here." He pressed the backs of her knees, creating another deep thrill of pleasure. "And yeah, knowing anatomy is helpful in my work." He dropped his voice to a low growl. "Even more helpful in bed."

Her mouth went dry. "Huh," was all she could manage as he glided his fingers up the insides of her thighs.

He moved his hands under her skirt to the waistband of her leggings, which now felt intolerably itchy and unwanted. She lifted her butt so he could strip them off her. Goose bumps rose on her legs as her skin was exposed to the air. He took care of that immediately by running his warm hands all over her.

Well, not all over her, because he was avoiding her skirt and everything that lay under it. He seemed to want to lavish all kinds of attention on the backs of her thighs, the inner skin of her calves, her sore feet. Every touch sent her into a deeper state of pure pleasure.

When his lips touched the tender inner skin of her thigh, just above her knee, she nearly leaped off the bed. A jolt shot through her that felt almost orgasmic. It shocked her. How could he have such a powerful effect on her?

"What? Too much?" he asked.

"No." Her voice strained, she sat up and pushed him away. "It's not too much. It feels great. But—" She looked down at her legs, radiant brown against the paler skin of his hands. "We're in this together, right?"

He looked at her alertly. He probably didn't understand what was stopping her—she wasn't sure herself—but he went along with it anyway.

Maybe it had something to do with her being all exposed while he was still fully dressed. It felt like too many walls coming down at once.

She reached behind him for the hem of his sweater and

tugged it over his head. The movement mussed his hair, leaving a tuft of tawny brown sticking straight up. Just the way it used to do when skinny Jay-Jay used to skateboard onto her driveway.

And suddenly she wasn't worried any more about being exposed. This was Rune. He'd told her that he loved her. She had nothing to fear from him. She could allow herself to enjoy this without any worries or caution.

Under his sweater, he wore a clean white t-shirt. The smell of laundry soap drifted toward her. She breathed in the scent of his skin—a little bit sweat, a little bit fresh air.

She put her hand under the hem of his t-shirt to touch his stomach. How she'd been dreaming about this moment—while also thinking it might never actually happen. Hard to believe he was here, now, right in front of her, his lake-green eyes full of desire and his muscles bunched with tension.

Tugging the t-shirt up, she feasted her eyes on the ridges of muscle she revealed. Was that really all genes? With some spearfishing and skateboarding thrown in?

Didn't matter where it came from, it was Rune that made it work. If that same body belonged to someone else—someone more cocky, more like Jerome—she would have found it a total turn-off.

Once she'd gotten his t-shirt mostly off his body, he took care of the rest. He dropped it onto the corner of her bed and stood before her—a gloriously half-naked man, the clear lines of an erection pressed against his pants.

Oh man. It was almost too much. Her heart hammered. She felt light-headed. Giddy.

"Do you still have that scar from when you fell on the lava?" she asked him.

"You mean when I fell on my ass and had to get ten stitches in my right buttock?"

"Yeah. That time." She pressed the ball of her foot against his thigh. "Just worried about my old buddy, that's all."

"Oh really?" he said dryly. "Happy to show you my scar. But I've been wondering about that bee sting you got. Remember when a honeybee got trapped in your bikini top?"

She shuddered. "I'll never forget that. You were very cool headed. You untied my bikini with a quickness."

"Already training to be a paramedic," he said virtuously. "Lucky for you. Then I remembered the thing about baking soda and begged some from a food truck at the beach."

"That's right. I was crying so hard I didn't know what was happening until you came back. As a matter of fact, you did such a good job that I don't even have a scar."

"That's impossible. You'd better go ahead and show me."

She tugged her lower lip between her teeth. All this teasing, and the way he was standing there bare-chested, looking at her with those hot eyes, was getting her stirred up beyond bearing.

"Fine." She sat up and pulled up her sweater to reveal the side of her bra-encased breast. "It was about there, I think."

"Oh no. It was more like here." He touched the underside of her breast. A shudder of pleasure trickled through her. "Yes, this feels familiar. Or maybe it was the other one." His voice roughened as he slid his hand under her top and cupped her other breast though the black silk of her bra.

Which he could see for himself when he eased her top all the way off her body. She got the sense that he was gobbling her up with his eyes as he devoured the sight of her in nothing but a bra and that miniskirt.

"God, you're fucking beautiful," he muttered. He slid his finger along the edge of her bra, dipping down to the valley between her breasts and then back up. That light touch sent starbursts of heat along her skin. She arched her back to make access even easier.

The next time, he slid under the fabric and found her nipples, first one, then the other. A gentle touch, then a squeeze had her biting her lip hard at the fierce sensation. She dropped her head back, savoring each caress.

With a groan, he abandoned the soft approach and filled both hands with her breasts. "I don't remember all this from that bee sting," he murmured. "I probably would have fallen off my feet."

"I was pretty flat then. But I was still embarrassed, when I stopped writhing in pain."

He snuck one hand behind her back and unsnapped her bra. Quick work—one-handed too. The man had skills. "I intend to have you writhing again, just so you know. Not from agony though."

She sighed. He sure was off to a good start. The bra fell away from her body and he bent his mouth to the aching tip of her breast. The instant his tongue touched it, sharp pleasure ran like a zip line from the nipple to her sex. She let out a sound that would have made her laugh if she hadn't been too swept up in the sensations.

She propped her hands behind her on the bed and abandoned herself to the magical effect of his tongue and lips on her nipples. His hair, so tawny and tousled, brushed softly against her chest with each movement of his head. She loved the delicious contrast with the bronze-brown of her skin. Like a piece of artwork done in different shades of deepest sepia.

He planted his hands on the bed, on either side of her, and eased her farther back, until her head rested on her plush comforter. His torso was all muscles and straining tendons and golden skin. He was beautiful, this man who used to be her skinny little friend.

He lifted his head from her breasts, allowing air to flow against her sensitized nipples. "You doing okay?" he asked in a rough voice.

"Yeah. Are you?"

"Oh man. I'm so okay right now." He tilted his hips so his erection slid against her upper thigh. It was hard and throbbing, even through his pants.

"Take those damn things off," she ordered him in her best voice of authority—which was pretty damn good, by all accounts.

He just smiled. "Make me."

"Oh, so that's how you want to play it?"

She used a wrestling move to flip him over onto his back. It wasn't easy, since he was so big and strong, and if he'd resisted at all she wouldn't have been able to do it.

She straddled his hips and unsnapped his fly.

That's when she noticed that he was grinning widely. "This is like the ultimate fantasy right now." He planted his hands on her breasts and flicked her nipples with his thumbs. She bit her lip to keep from crying out from pleasure.

"You planned this?"

"More like I willed it into existence. I want Maya sitting naked on my lap. Repeat it enough times, and now here you are."

While he talked, he played with her nipples, until her breath came in hard gasps and sweat beaded her forehead. She tugged down the zipper of his pants. Navy-blue boxer briefs peeked from under his fly, and beyond them, hard glorious flesh strained against the fabric. She outlined it with her palm, her mouth going dry as she mapped its length and girth through his briefs.

When she slid her hand underneath and wrapped it around his shaft, he gritted his teeth and closed his eyes.

"I can't look at you right now or I'll come," he ground out. "This is—I've thought about—your hands on me. So much better. Imagined." His words came in short bursts, apparently all he could manage through his clenched teeth.

The fact that he found her so desirable was very, very satisfying. Especially after—

Don't think about that now.

She eased up his body, closer to his groin, and rotated her hips against the ever-hardening bulge of his cock. Her skirt was all the way around her waist now, with nothing between her and Rune except for her favorite burgundy silk panties. She'd always liked the way their jewel color looked against her skin.

He obviously agreed, because when he finally opened his eyes again and craned his neck to watch what she was doing, he groaned out loud. "Damn, Maya. Just...damn."

After that, things shifted and started moving fast. He used her own wrestling move and flipped her over, onto her back. In seconds, her skirt was off her body and somewhere on the other side of her princess bed veils. His pants were gone too, vanished into the same oblivion. As if everything outside the bed was a blank.

"Underwear next," she told him, just in case he had any doubts.

"Yes ma'am."

Hers went first, as he tugged the burgundy silk down her thighs. "Sweet mama," he murmured. He brushed his hand across the soft hair guarding the vee between her legs. He slid a finger along her already slick folds and found the aching nub of her clit. Pleasure arrowed through her when he touched the beating heart of her arousal.

"God, Rune," she gasped as she arched upwards. "Don't stop." She needed more, craved more. The way he handled her with his strong, skilled fingers made heat surge deep in her core. Her hips moved restlessly, seeking more of the friction he generated with his thumbs and his tongue and his knowledge. Pleasure zapped across her nerve endings, building, speeding, chasing...

She slipped into an orgasm as if he'd pushed her down a water slide. It exploded so naturally and beautifully, like the perfect union of two opposing chemicals. Her climax pulsed through her body in long, sweet, endless arcs. Release and joy, pleasure and oblivion chased through her being. And the whole time, Rune was there, his hand right where she needed it, not moving an inch, no matter how she arched and writhed.

Just like he'd promised. *I'm here for you.*

CHAPTER TWENTY-ONE

At first Rune thought Maya had fallen asleep. *Deal with it. Let her be.* He'd have to deal with his own ferocious arousal. Maybe later, back home.

But he was wrong. Maya opened her eyes, which were lit with such soft satisfaction that he could have beaten his chest in triumph. "I have condoms in that top drawer over there." She gestured at the bureau outside the curtains of the princess bed. "Want to grab them?"

"Hell yes." He lifted himself away from her, taking a moment to feast his eyes on her limp and boneless form, radiant as precious bronze. His cock pulsed hard under his briefs.

"Hey, weren't you supposed to take those off?" Maya complained. "You know, so I can see your scar?"

Oh lord. This was going to be interesting. That scar had never healed right because he'd refused to stay still.

"I'll show you my scar. No mocking, though."

"I'd never."

He slid to the end of the bed and stood up, his back brushing against the filmy curtains. First he had to pull the tented cotton away from his erection—hoping he didn't spontaneously climax in the process. Then he pushed his underwear down his thighs and turned his back to her.

His plan had been to flash her for a brief moment, then duck out to find the condoms. But instead, the damn princess veils got in his way. He was still clawing his way out of them, trying to find the opening, when he heard her burst of laughter.

"Hey, I said no mockery."

"That was before I *saw* it. I mean, it's a happy face. How am I not supposed to laugh?"

"Fine, laugh your ass off."

"*Laugh your ass off.*" His little joke just made her laugh harder. "You know I'm not laughing *at* you, right?"

"You're not?" He swatted at the netting around him.

"No. I'm laughing at your ass."

He grumbled through his smile. "Can you take a break from your hilarious laughter to tell me how to get the hell out of here?"

Still giggling, she crawled naked across the bed and found the gap. "There you go. Mind if I watch you walk over there? I want to see if your happy face smiles when you clench."

"You're a child," he said with as much dignity as a guy with a happy face scar on his ass could manage. He stalked across her room toward the chest of drawers she'd directed him to. Conscious of her gaze, he made sure to flex his muscles as much as humanly possible. His scar might have drawn her attention, but maybe his ocean-honed muscles would get her hot again.

It must have worked, because by the time he got back with the condom, she was kneeling on the bed, her lower lip between her teeth, a dark flush on her cheeks. He shoved the princess fabric out of his way and stood before her, bracing his legs apart, his erection rearing between them.

She touched him lightly, her lips parting as she gazed at his shaft. He knew that if she so much as touched her mouth to the tip of his cock, he'd explode. More than anything, he wanted to be inside her. So when she swayed toward him, he put a hand on her shoulder to keep her where she was.

"I need to be in you," he muttered. "Just hang on a second."

He ripped open the foil and rolled the condom onto his penis. Safely covered, he strode forward until their bodies met. When they were pressed against each other in this position, his erection was at the level of her lower belly and her breasts were squashed against his abdomen.

Which was nice and all, but not what he was after right now.

He edged her backwards so he too could kneel on the bed. His cock slid between them and he nudged her legs farther apart. Slid his fingers between them to play in the slippery heat of her sex, until her sighs grew urgent.

He moved his hands around to her ass to lift her a few inches higher, just enough to poise his tip right at her entrance.

There, he paused to gauge whether she was ready. *My heart is yours*, he wanted to say. *This is it for me. You're the one. The only one.*

But he held his tongue, because he hadn't forgotten how she'd reacted to his first declaration—with total confusion. He didn't need to confuse things further right now. They were fucking and enjoying every second of it and he'd take it.

She reached around him and clamped both hands onto his ass. A shudder passed through him as she urged him closer. God, it felt incredible. *She* felt incredible. Slick and hot, her channel gripped his penis. He flexed his hips and pushed into her. His own hand was still on her ass, where he could rotate and move her just where he wanted. He tilted her so he could penetrate deep, deeper, right there. He slipped one hand between them to stimulate her clit, then plunged again, and again, deep, powerful, fast, hard, *again*, until her breath came in urgent gasps and her body clenched around him and everything exploded into a blinding orgasm that had him collapsing onto the bed, wrapped in her arms.

Still joined together, he convulsed inside her for long, exquisite moments of sheer pleasure and release. All the buildup of holiday parties and boat trips and conversations and just *being around her* detonated into a full-body experience that he wouldn't even limit by calling it a climax. It was more than that. It was a...revelation.

You're the one. The only one.

Slowly, he came down from that high-as-a-kite peak and opened his eyes to find her watching him with a soft smile.

"You okay there?" She sounded almost amused by how hard he'd come.

"Oh yeah. Doing fine. You?"

"Still good." She brought her hand to his face and fixed a lock of his hair that had fallen in his eyes. "Very very good. Your hair is doing that thing it used to do."

"Mmmm." Sleepy, content, he let her mess with his hair.

"Did you ever think we'd end up here, like this?" she whispered.

"Did you forget the time I said we should get married someday?"

Her eyes lit with laughter. "Right after we kissed behind the lifeguard stand. I remember now. I threw sand at you."

"Such a romantic moment."

He drifted a bit after that. The princess curtains gave him the sense that they were floating together out on the ocean. It was a wonderful feeling that he knew wouldn't last—too many dangers were lurking out there under the surface—so he wanted to enjoy it as long as possible.

She was still stroking his hair with gentle fingers. In his half-sleeping state, it brought him back to childhood, to the time when his mother had had her shit together. When she'd tucked him into bed and whispered stories to him so he'd sleep. Stories about knights and dragons and castles and moats. "You'll be a hero one day," she'd whispered. "Never doubt that. Shoot for the moon and even if you miss you'll land among the stars." Quoted from a magnet on their refrigerator.

What kind of hero wandered from state to state, simply trying to keep his sister away from a stalker? The only kind of hero he could be. And somehow, magically, that journey had brought him here.

Where would it take him next? He didn't want to think about that. Not now, when he was right where he wanted to be.

———

HIS SLEEPY REVERIE was interrupted by the sound of a phone ringing. "Station calling?" he murmured. Who else would call her phone this late?

Maya rolled over and stretched out on her stomach to reach her phone, which had somehow ended up on the floor.

"It's Cara," she said, with a glance back over her smooth brown shoulder at him. "Why's she calling me?"

He went instantly alert. "Maybe my phone died."

"But how would she know we're together?"

"I *am* your fake holiday boyfriend," he pointed out. "It's not much of a stretch."

"Right." She shook her head, the light finding deep copper glints in her hair. "It's getting hard to keep track of it all." She answered her phone. "Maya here."

"Maya, have you seen my brother?" Cara's panicked voice carried into the room. "He's not answering his phone."

"What's wrong?"

"There was a noise outside and we thought it was just an animal or something, but it keeps happening and I'm scared."

"I'll be right there." Maya's calm tone was exactly what Cara needed. "Lock the door, stay inside. I'll just be a few minutes."

"Can you find Rune too?" The anxious waver in her voice made Rune's heart clench. He nodded at Maya and slid off the bed.

"Yes," Maya said, leaving it that. "Do you want to stay on the phone while I head over there? Will it help?"

"No, that's okay. We're up in the loft right now and piled up some stuff like a fort. Maggie has her knife, too. She says she can hit a squirrel at two hundred feet."

Maya made a face. "On my way." She ended the call and swung her feet off the side of the bed. Rune was already peeling off his condom. "We need to get there before Maggie knifes a squirrel."

"Bathroom?" he asked, holding up the condom. She waved at the corner of the bedroom, where a door stood open. He ran over to it and found the wastebasket, taking note of the profusion of bath salts and lotions and creams everywhere—and the deluxe two-person tub taking up half the room.

He could think of a few things to do in that tub.

Later.

If there was a later.

He rushed back to the bed to find Maya already dressed in sweats and a hoodie. She handed him his clothes, which he yanked on in record time.

This could be it. Their last time together. He knew it, but he could tell that it hadn't sunk in for Maya yet. She was simply responding to a call for help. Doing her job. She wasn't gaming out the scenario to its logical conclusion.

If the stalker had arrived, he and Cara would be leaving.

How could fate be so cruel, to rip them apart just when they'd found each other?

So he took a moment, even in their hurry to get to Cara, to cup both his hands around Maya's face and give her a deeply passionate kiss. *My heart is yours. You're the one. The only one. Don't forget me.*

And then the two of them dashed for the door.

CHAPTER TWENTY-TWO

Maya could still feel the effects of that kiss as she raced toward her car. It had made her head spin and her knees wobble. But she pushed all that aside. Time for Police Chief Badger to take charge.

"I'm driving this rig," she called to Rune. "You can drive yours if you want, but I need this one in case there's an arrest."

He slid in next to her. "I'm coming with you. You might need backup."

She didn't argue, since backup was always a good idea, and Rune had proved his abilities earlier that night with the rescue of Jerome and Leeann.

It felt like a month ago since they'd spotted that red Jeep, instead of hours. So much had happened since then. Rune had told her he was in love with her. They'd had sex. Now they were racing toward the moment that might end it all.

It felt as if their entire relationship had gone into fast-forward mode.

It took only a few minutes to reach Harris' property. She turned off the headlights as they passed his house. The last thing she wanted was for her father to put himself in the line of fire—which he would, in a heartbeat.

She noticed that Vicki's Jeep was parked in the drive. For the first time, that didn't bother her. Maybe that cranberry wine had cast a spell on her, but she was glad her dad had company. Vicki would keep him occupied and safely inside.

After they'd passed the house, she turned the headlights back on so she could see where she was going. "See if you can spot anything unusual," she told Rune. Luckily, the storm clouds had cleared and sleet was no longer pouring from the sky. A quarter moon had risen, though it had to fight through patches of racing dark clouds to be seen. Even so, visibility was much better than when they'd parked down at the beach.

When he'd told her he loved her.

Don't think about that now. Deal with the emergency.

"There's something back in those woods to the right," Rune said in a low voice.

"A person?"

"I can't tell what it is. I caught movement, that's it."

"Okay. Let's park and see if binoculars help."

She brought the car to a stop next to the old fish house and reached into the backseat for the case that held her binocs.

"I'm going inside to check on Cara," Rune told her.

"No, I'll go. You stay in the car with the binoculars. You're the one who saw something, you can locate it better." Before he could object, she swung out of the car. If someone was going to take a shot at them, it was her job to take the risk.

But nothing happened between the car and the house. She knocked on the door. "It's Maya," she called in a low voice. "Open up."

She heard thumping inside, and then the door opened. Cara hauled her inside. "Oh my God I'm so glad you're here. I'm totally freaking out. Did you see anything outside? Is he out there? Is there a letter or some weird dead flowers or—"

"No no, there's nothing like that," Maya reassured her. Over Cara's shoulder, she saw Maggie, brandishing a hunting knife. "Put that away." Maggie, startled by her police chief voice, stuck it back into the sheath attached to her belt.

"Did you find my brother?"

"Yes, he's outside in the car. Are you both all right? I need to get back out there."

"You mean besides totally freaked out? We're fine."

"Can you say what direction the noise came from?"

"It started on that side—" Cara waved her hand in the direction of the car, where Rune still was.

Maya's stomach twisted. What if an intruder was still out there, and Rune went after him on his own? It was just the sort of reckless thing he used to do.

"But then it came from over there." Cara pointed to the other side of the house, the same direction where Rune had spotted something in the woods. "Then it went away, but it came back again. I thought maybe he was leaving something for me. He's done that before."

"Let's not jump to any conclusions." Maya touched her arm to reassure her, then turned to go. "You girls stay where you are, we got this."

"Be careful. That guy is crazy, you never know what he'll do."

"Do you want my knife?" Maggie asked. "I don't usually lend it to anyone, but you can have it, Maya."

"I appreciate the gesture, but I have my own weapon." She patted the shoulder holster under her jacket. Truthfully, she was rather touched that Maggie trusted her enough to offer up her precious hunting knife.

Back outside, she found Rune safe in the car, peering through the binoculars. "There's definitely something," he murmured. "But I honestly don't think it's a human being."

She shivered at his phrasing. "You think it's something non-human?"

"The fuck if I know what it is. It could be *two* people. It's pretty large. Maybe two kids are making out in the woods and I'm staring at them like a creeper."

"No. I know all the make-out spots, and those woods aren't on the list. We have Harris on this side and a well-armed city council member on the other. Hand me those."

He gave her the binoculars and she focused toward the dark stand of spruce that provided several acres of thickly wooded border between the two properties. It was so dark that she was amazed Rune had been able to distinguish any movement among the trees. Maybe it was just branches moving in the wind. Or a moose who'd missed his dinner. Or even a porcupine; with their quills extended, they could appear much bigger than they actually were. Or—

A cloud drifted out of the moon's way, allowing its pale glow to illuminate the woods and reveal a glimpse of a large, definitely non-human creature. It didn't move like a moose, and it looked bulkier somehow.

"Wait a minute." She dropped the glasses, looked at Rune, then back into the woods. "I think that might be Mrs. Holt's yak."

"*What?*" He snatched the binoculars back and focused on the woods. "I'll be damned. That's what a yak looks like?"

"You didn't see the flyers? We put the damn things everywhere."

"Yes, but it's different in person." He handed the glasses back to her. "What now, Chief?"

"I should call the Fish and Game people, but it's Thanksgiving night. I hate to bother them. Mrs. Holt's probably been asleep for hours. What is it, past three?"

"Three-twenty, last I checked."

If they waited until the light of day, it would be easier to handle the fugitive creature. But she had no idea how fast yaks could travel. Would he still be here in the morning?

"What do yaks like to eat? We can try to lure him closer with sugar cubes or something. Leftover pecan pie might work."

"I don't know what they eat. I can look it up online." Rune pulled out his phone. "I'm texting Cara to let her know she can relax."

He fired off a text, then got an answering ping right away. "They're laughing their asses off," he told her.

A moment later, Cara and Maggie came racing out of the guesthouse. The backseat door opened and the two flushed and giggling girls slipped inside. "I can't believe we were stalked by a yak!" Cara exclaimed. "That's so much cooler than the real kind."

"Keep your voices down," Maya ordered. "We don't want to scare him away."

"Are you trying to catch him?" Maggie asked. "You aren't going to hurt him, are you?"

"Not if we can help it. Maybe we need a fishing net. My dad has some under the fish house." But as soon as she said it, she knew how absurd that sounded. The yak would just wander away draped in the net, most likely. "We have to disable him somehow."

"You *can't* hurt him," Maggie said passionately.

"No way," Cara agreed. "Maggie, can't you talk to him?"

"No, I told you I can only understand animals I grew up around. I've never met a yak. I want to, though. We can't do anything that might hurt him."

"I have an idea," Rune volunteered. "I have some sedatives in my medical supplies. We can try to inject him."

Maya knew that was what the Fish and Game people would

do, but they had experience with such things. "Do you know how much to give a yak?"

"Girls, can one of you look up the average weight of an adult Tibetan yak?"

Cara punched the keys on her phone. "Between about eight hundred and twelve hundred pounds. Wow."

"I probably have enough sedative to knock him out."

Maya eyed the dark figure out there in the woods. "Then what?"

"Hogtie him while he's sleeping and call Fish and Game first thing in the morning?"

It was as good a plan as any. Except— "How do we get the sedative into his system? I don't want anyone getting too close to something that weighs a thousand pounds."

"Well." Rune cleared his throat and glanced into the back-seat. "We happen to have an excellent markswoman here in the car with us. I can rig up a syringe and Maggie can let it fly."

"I can do it," Maggie said instantly. "I can sneak up on him. I'm really good at tracking and being quiet in the woods."

"No. I'm calling Fish and Game."

"But the yak might be gone by the time they get here," Cara cried. "Maggie can do it. I've seen her shoot. She's so accurate."

Oh good God. This was ridiculous. She could think of so many ways this could go wrong. A girl shooting up a yak with a bow and arrow rigged with tranquilizers?

"What if you just make him mad? He could charge you the way a moose would."

"I'll just climb up a tree, the way I did in the wilderness when I couldn't get a moose to listen to reason. Don't worry about me. I'll go get my crossbow. I left it here so Cara could practice." Maggie scrambled out of the car, with Cara right behind her.

Maya chewed at the inside of her cheek, weighing the options and risks. Didn't she always say that being a police chief on the edge of the wilderness required flexibility and creativity?

Rune put a hand on her knee. "I won't make up a syringe without your go-ahead."

"At least someone's listening to me," she grumbled. Then shrugged her shoulders. "What the heck. Just make sure it's not a lethal dose. I don't want Mrs. Holt on my ass."

"I don't even have enough for that."

"Oh, fine." She dropped the binoculars with a sigh. "It's our first sighting in three months. It may be the last. Let's give it a try."

"Operation Yak Attack is a go." He swung out of the car, just as excited as if he was wading into the surf with his spearfishing gear.

"We're not calling it that," she called after him.

Now that she knew the stalker hadn't arrived to steal Rune away, Maya actually enjoyed the rest of Operation Yak *Rescue*.

It took some intense finagling to get the syringe set up in the strings of the crossbow, with a fishing lead against the plunger to provide the force needed to push it into the yak's hide. The plan sounded sketchy as hell to Maya.

"Aim for its rump, that's the biggest target," Rune told her. "The straighter the better."

"And don't shoot until you have an exit strategy," said Maya. "A tree to climb, place to hide, whatever."

Maggie just rolled her eyes. "Don't worry. This is so much easier than math and grammar."

She loped off toward the dark woods, crossbow in hand. Maya kept watch through the binoculars, while Rune and Cara carried on a whispered conversation.

"How's this going to sound in the police blotter?" Rune mused. "*Lost Harbor girl captures runaway yak with a dart in the ass.*"

Cara shot back with, "*Lost Harbor's version of Katniss Everdeen saves the day and wins all the reward money.*"

"What would she spend it on?"

"Christmas presents. Or maybe a plane ride to see her mother."

Uh oh. Maya made a mental note to check in with Kelsey about the trip to Aurora Lodge. "Don't let her do that, Cara. I have some ideas about how to get her and Kelsey together."

"Maggie kind of does what she wants."

"I get it, but will you let me know if she tries? Promise me, Cara."

"Cara?" Rune urged her gently.

"I promise. What's going on, Maya? Can you see anything?"

"The yak hasn't moved. He's just swaying back and forth. I think he might be sleeping. Do yaks sleep on their feet, like cows? I should have done more research. I thought the yak was gone for good. I kept telling Mrs. Holt not to get her hopes up. But she thinks he's her dead husband, so..."

"Did her husband like wandering around in the woods at night?" Cara asked.

"Jack 'Hammer' Holt mostly liked rum," she said wryly. "Rum and playing pranks on other fishermen. He was a pain in the ass for my predecessor."

"And now he's going to get a pain in *his* ass," Rune said gravely.

Cara groaned, but Maya laughed at his goofy joke.

"Don't tell me you like his lame puns, Maya," said Cara. "You must really like my brother."

Yeah. She did. So much. More than she wanted to admit. As if Cupid had hit her in the ass with a dart and sent her thudding to the ground just like that yak.

She squinted through the binoculars as she caught sight of Maggie near the yak. Time for a play-by-play. "Maggie's about twenty yards from the yak. She's putting down the crossbow! She's approaching the yak. Now she's jamming the syringe into the yak's butt. *Ow.* There he goes, he's toppling over. He's on the ground. Not moving."

Cara and Rune erupted into cheers.

Maya set aside her binoculars and the three of them jumped out of the car. They ran toward the woods, Rune carrying a length of rope from the fish house. Racing across the moonlit snow, cold air on her cheeks, Maya experienced a moment of sheer exhilaration. She could have been gliding above the snow on a jetpack.

No stalker was going to take Rune away from her. The wild winds of fate had delivered him here and the joy of being with him again made her laugh out loud.

Maybe the late night and the peekaboo November moon were getting to her. Or the holidays. Right, exactly. She could blame all these wild careening emotions on the holidays.

CHAPTER TWENTY-THREE

Rune decided to avoid mentioning the word "love" when he was with Maya. His feelings hadn't changed. But he had to give Maya a chance to let it all sink in. He knew she was cautious by nature. He also knew she had good reason to guard her heart after getting blindsided by Jerome.

He wanted her whole heart, and he was willing to be patient for as long as it took to win her over. The only wild card was whether Stalker Chad would show up and ruin everything.

The night of the yak capture showed him just how hard it would be to leave. He'd been ready to say goodbye to Lost Harbor, but man...the relief of seeing a yak instead of a creeper made him fucking giddy.

That made two false alarms—the letter and the yak. But that didn't mean he could let down his guard. He just had to take it a day at a time.

Every day they didn't have to leave Lost Harbor was a gift. It was another day he could see Maya. Another day that Cara could have a normal life.

And then there were the nights.

After Maggie proved her warrior skills with Mrs. Holt's yak—who was delivered safely back to her homestead the next morning by Fish and Game—he felt more comfortable stealing away at night to see Maya.

Cara and Maggie kept clamoring for overnights. He would feed them dinner, make sure they got their homework done, then vaguely mention a patient and disappear out the door. He'd race over to Maya's, tap-tap on her door, and spend the next few blissful hours in her bed.

He was ravenous when it came to her. Just the scent of her skin got him turned on. The welcoming curve of her lips as she opened the door brought his cock to immediate attention. He tried to hide it—to ask how her day was—get a preview of the next day's police blotter—see how Harris was doing—find out what the next holiday party would be—get updated on the Lost Souls investigation.

But damn it was hard when all he wanted was to whisk her behind those princess curtains and shut out the rest of the world.

He talked about his day too, of course. Told her funny stories from his patient visits—names redacted. Kept her updated on Cara and all the teenage gossip from the high school.

One night, by the end, he was talking so fast that she burst out laughing. "In a hurry, Rune?"

"Is it that obvious?"

They were cuddled up on her couch. Her feet were tucked under his thigh for warmth, her Lost Souls file on her lap. She wore a snug creamy top that made her rich brown skin look especially radiant. A silk bandanna held her hair away from her face. She was so beautiful and smart and grounded that she took his breath away.

"I am a detective, after all. I notice things."

"Oh good. I was worried you might be so wrapped up in your file that you missed the big white dude on your couch."

She giggled. He could always make her laugh, and it always made him feel good. "Ain't no one going to be missing you, Rune. That would be impossible. For anyone, let alone someone who's seen you bare-ass naked."

He shifted a little on the couch cushions. The word "naked" got him going again. "How much more work do you have to do?"

She sighed. "I don't know. There's something I've been thinking about with this investigation that I'm not even supposed to be involved with anymore."

He wrestled down his arousal. Police Chief Badger was on the job, and he was here for it.

"Want to brainstorm about it?"

She pursed her mouth to one side, thinking it over. "That's probably okay. Just don't tell anyone what we talked about. The FBI closed the case and warned me that I was making a fool of myself over it."

"Got it. It's going into the patient confidentiality vault."

She shuffled through her papers. "The part I keep coming back to is the Berensons. They came to Alaska to adopt a baby—which was Maggie—but the baby was kidnapped by another couple. The Berensons were on their way to pay the ransom, right? They were following the instructions. So why would their plane get shot down? No ransom was delivered because they never made it. It seems counterproductive."

"So you're thinking it was just an accident?"

"No. The NTSB found nothing to indicate a mechanical problem. They believe it was shot down."

"So it was deliberate, just...not connected to the kidnapping?"

"Right. I'm wondering if the ransom demand was a smoke-screen to get rid of the Berensons. Maybe the purpose all along was to get possession of the baby, Maggie."

She tapped a pen against her cheek, deep in thought. He wanted to eat her up, she was so delicious. "But why?"

"Well, one missing piece of information is, who's her father? I always assumed that whoever he was, he was long gone. Kelsey was giving her baby up for adoption because she couldn't raise her on her own. But maybe the father sent the kidnappers to grab her." She frowned and shook her head. "No, that doesn't make sense."

"Why not?"

"They died too. They were drowned by Edgar Murchison, the trapper. If the father had sent them, why wouldn't he have gone looking for her after she disappeared?"

"Maybe he thought she was dead too."

She rubbed at her forehead in frustration. "Maybe. It just seems so strange that two couples lost their lives in this whole thing. It can't possibly be a coincidence. I don't believe in coincidences."

"They do say that strange things happen in Lost Souls Wilderness. Maybe this is one of those things."

She waved her hand in dismissal. "It's definitely strange. But that doesn't mean it doesn't have an explanation. Here's what we know. Someone used Maggie as leverage against Kelsey at Aurora Lodge. They're still watching her, even though Maggie's in Lost Harbor now. They're scaring away intruders. They're protecting something, something criminal. Something lucrative. And it's right across the bay and that scares the shit out of me."

He stroked her bent knee. "But the crash was fifteen years ago. Whatever it is has been going on for a long time. It hasn't spilled over into Lost Harbor, has it? Have you had a big increase in drugs or any other crime?"

"Not really, it's about the same level. Which is more than I wish it was."

"But not *worse*."

"No. For now. But unless I know what it is, how can I protect Lost Harbor?"

He smiled at her earnest passion. She was so devoted to her job. That was one reason why he felt Cara was safer here than in the other places they'd tried. She really was a protector instead of an enforcer.

"Maybe it's no threat to Lost Harbor at all. Maybe it's all about the Aurora Lodge. Rich people stay there, right? I can tell you from living in Hawaii, rich people aren't like you and me. They can twist the world to however they want it to be."

She cocked her head curiously. "How do you mean?"

"As a paramedic I got called to my fair share of vacation mansions of the rich and famous. Mostly overdoses or weird party fiascos. Some people think they can get away with literally anything."

"Hm. But I've pretty much ruled out drugs. That's not what's going on."

"So what's your top theory?"

She hesitated. "I don't want to get locked into a theory. But you have a good point about the lodge. It's obviously a key part of this, or they wouldn't have extorted Kelsey. And now I'm convinced the unnamed father is important too. Which is why..." She leaned forward and wrapped her arms around her knees. "I have something important to ask you."

Her serious expression kept him from making a joke about whether it involved bath bombs or strip poker. "What is it?"

"I just got the go-ahead from Kelsey to have a Christmas party at the lodge. I used the chance to see Maggie as a carrot. Normally they're closed, so there won't be any staff. I want to use the opportunity to question her and poke around out there, but with the cover of a family holiday party to throw off the surveillance. I'd need you and Cara to come. I was thinking I'd ask a few other people I trust too. Darius Boone and Nate Prudhoe and Ethan come to mind. I don't think it would be especially dangerous—I'm not looking for a showdown—but I can't say for sure. What do you think?"

He blew out a breath. "This fake holiday boyfriend gig just got a lot more serious."

She smiled ruefully. "We're way past fake holiday boyfriend territory. I wouldn't ask this if I didn't trust you so much."

He registered the compliment somewhere deep in his heart. "I'd come in a flash, you know me. But why do you need Cara?"

"For Maggie's sake. She and Maggie look like sisters. I'm hoping that will throw off the people who are watching the lodge —if they still are, even in the winter. They'll see two blond sisters instead of one runaway girl. And they'll be bundled up in their winter gear."

"I'd need to tell Cara what's going on."

"Of course." She frowned, looking offended. "Both her and Maggie need to know. Everyone does. I'm not letting anyone go out there blind. The girls will be required to stay inside at all times."

He snorted. "Good luck with that. Two teenage girls in a wilderness lodge at Christmas time? I predict snowmen, snowball fights, snow down each other's backs, whatever they can think of."

"Yeah, I see what you mean. Maybe they can go outside if there are at least two adults with them. And I mean adults who are first responders. I really can't take any chances. The point is for Maggie to see her mother safely. So what do you think?"

He considered it for a while before he answered. That was the difference between the old Jay-Jay and today's version. Before, he never looked before he leaped. "It would make Maggie happy. She talks a lot about wanting to meet her mom. I know Cara would want to help her. She's used to rules about what she can and can't do, thanks to Stalker Chad. I think she'd handle the situation well."

"And you?" Maya asked. "I don't want you to agree just because I'm the one asking. If you don't want to risk it, just say so. I'll still lo—" She shifted gears almost invisibly. "Sleep with you," she finished.

Had she almost said that she'd still love him, but stopped herself just in time? He narrowed his eyes at her. "I heard that."

"Heard what?"

"That you'll still lo—" He broke off just as she had. He repeated it. "*Lo*—"

"Yeah, I was going to say that I'd still lube you."

"You'll still *lube* me?" He took hold of the file on her lap and dropped it onto the floor. Grabbing her bent knees, he tugged her down the sofa and rose over her. "Prove it. Lube me, baby."

"Okay, I didn't mean lube." She laughed up at him. "I meant, I'll still lump you. Like, I'll still lump you in with all the other people I care about."

"Oh, really? You just lump me in with all the others? Do the others do this?" He opened her legs and pressed his hand against the warm place between her thighs. He rotated his palm against her sex, stimulating the clit that hid under the layers of cotton leggings and underwear. All of which had to go, as quickly as possible.

Her lips parted as she watched him, her eyes like liquid dark gold. "Um, not usually..."

"What about this?"

He lifted her butt enough to pull down her leggings, then crouched between her thighs. Her scent drew him closer, his mouth already watering as he kissed those sweet lower lips, already glinting with a touch of moisture. He touched her delicately with his tongue, savoring her flavor. So feminine, so intoxicating, like mulled wine.

She let her legs fall farther open and pushed her sex toward him. *Ah yeah*, finally things were heading in the right direction.

He slid his hands under her ass and squeezed her round cheeks as he licked and tongue-stroked her wet slit. Wild for her, he slashed his tongue across her, seeking that perfect mix of friction and pressure. When she moaned and grabbed at his hair, he knew he'd found it.

Eat her out. Bury his face in her. Lap up every pulse and swell of her little nub. Listen to her pleas for release. Stay with her. Lose himself in the glory of her juicy response. Fill his hands with her ass. Stay with her.

She erupted into a fierce climax—her body in a taut arch—her hands twisting in his hair—her throaty voice at full volume. *Oh yes, oh yes, fucking yes.*

"Lord, Rune," she muttered after she'd come down from that wild peak. "I wasn't ready for that."

He was already undoing his pants. "What about this? Ready for this?"

His erection jumped out, nearly purple from his intense arousal.

"I know *you're* ready" She gave a little laugh as she touched her foot to his thigh. "I didn't even touch you yet."

"It turns me on to taste you. And to watch you come apart. I can't get enough of it. Want to go again?" he joked.

She reached for his erection and circled him with her warm hand. "I have another idea." She kicked off the clothes that he'd merely pushed down her thighs, and climbed onto his lap. Her hot wet sex brushed against his engorged tip.

"Wait," he warned. "Condom. Right pocket."

"I know." He always had a stash in his pockets these days. Just in case. She dug inside his pocket, which was a tease all on its own. Then she brought him to the point of near-madness by bending her head to his cock and swirling her tongue across it.

"Just wanted to say hello before this thing goes on," she murmured. "Hello, you."

He gritted his teeth against the pleasure. He didn't want to release all over her couch. He wanted to draw this out. It was just too good. The chemistry they generated together was epic. Better than any bonfire they'd danced around.

She took her time, using long loving strokes of her mouth up and down his cock. Each one sent a new rush of sensation to the pleasure center of his brain. Everything else got chased away until all that was left was her. Her warm mouth, her silky-rough tongue, her sensual movements.

He made a warning noise in his throat when he didn't think he could hold off any longer.

She understood immediately and withdrew her mouth. The sound of the foil tearing came next, then the slow slide of her fingers along his cock, unrolling the condom.

He lifted her up and set her onto his erection. With a slow surge, he impaled her from below. She bit her lip and flung her head back. Flexing his hips, he went deep, thrusting up into her warm weight. But he wanted to go even deeper, harder, so he wrapped his arms around her and swung her over to the couch, onto her back. Her eyes went wide with surprise, dark pools drawing him in.

"I want to fuck you like this," he said roughly. "Been dreaming about you splayed out under me." He moved inside her, not just aiming for a destination, but savoring each inch of progress along the way. Her channel clung to him with a slick juicy grip. She'd already come once, and he could feel the effects of that. He aimed to make her come again. Slow friction to start, then picking up the pace as her body reacted. Faster, harder, deeper. His cock seemed to swell bigger with each stroke, until he was sure he would explode.

But he wanted her to come again first, so he slipped a hand between them, to the clit he'd so thoroughly tongue-lashed before. It didn't take but a touch for her to buck in response. A climax flowed through her body like a roller coming in off the ocean. She called out his name—Rune—his good luck middle name—and he let the leash off his need.

With a harsh growl, he exploded into her. The orgasm blotted out everything else—the room, the couch, the night, his own fricking name. Head over heels he went, as if tumbled by the ocean, tugged under by the force of the water, then lifted to the surface by pure joy.

Making love to Maya blew his world apart. Every single time.

CHAPTER TWENTY-FOUR

About a week after Thanksgiving, Jerome knocked on the door of Maya's office.

"Check the fancy nameplate. I guess it's real, then, that's why they put it in fake gold letters on some fake-ass wood-looking plastic." His cocky smile assumed she would find him amusing.

She didn't. Not anymore.

"How can I help you, former citizen of Lost Harbor who is no longer my responsibility?"

Not, strictly speaking, true. Everyone was her responsibility when they were on this side of the town borders.

"Just saying goodbye. Me and Leanne are about to head out."

"Happy holidays to you both."

For once, it had been a happy holiday for her, at least so far. Thanks to one person, and one person only.

"You've changed, you know that? You're a real hard-ass now. Did I really hurt you that bad?"

Oooh, just as arrogant as ever. "Don't worry about me. Worry about your own actions. Be good to Leanne. She's a sweet girl."

"You think I don't know that?"

His sincerity actually caught her by surprise. She'd never understood their relationship, but maybe he genuinely loved Leanne. "Well. Good."

"How about you? Is it true that you're fucking that paramedic you were with that night?"

A little shock ran through her at his blunt tone. He had no right to ask her anything like that. And she didn't like him putting his grubby hands on the connection that existed between her and Rune. "It's a lot more than that. Better go, Jerome. There's a storm coming and you have a long drive."

"A lot more? Like what? You're serious about that guy? I heard he's a nurse."

"Go on." She flicked her fingers toward the door. "Don't you worry about what he is or isn't."

But he refused to leave. "Must not be smart enough to go for a real medical degree. Nurses don't make much money, do they? I still care about you, Maya. I don't want to see you lower yourself. Just because it didn't work out with us doesn't mean you have to settle."

Rage shot through her. Forgetting everything except the smug man in front of her and the beautiful one taking care of patients somewhere, she planted her hands on her desk and surged to her feet. "Rune Larsen is *one hundred times* the man you are. He's kind, caring, strong, smart, and he fucks like a superstar. He makes me come every single time we're together. Before I was with Rune, I had no idea how good things could be with a man. I thought they were all cocky and selfish like you. So I suggest you take your arrogant ass out there to your stupid not-fit-for-Alaska rental car and hit the road."

Beyond him, she caught sight of heads turning in the bullpen. *Ooops.* Sergeant Hollister's mouth was open in an "O" shape. Mrs. Holt, who had an appointment to see Maya, stood a few feet away from her office door, blinking rapidly.

At least Lucy the reporter wasn't around at the moment. But it hardly mattered; this would be all over town in a flash.

Jerome pressed his lips together. "You act like it's my fault I fell in love with someone else."

Her mouth dropped open. Did Jerome have a point? He hadn't set out to hurt her. He'd just...fallen for Leanne.

"What's your fault is that you didn't tell me what was going on! You acted like everything was fine up until Christmas Eve."

"You didn't want to go to all those damn parties alone, did you?"

She blinked at him, with no clue how to answer something so idiotic.

When she stayed silent, he spun around on his heel. He pushed past Mrs. Holt and in a second was gone. Out of her life, her head, her heart—but most especially, her damn office.

Maya let out a long breath and beckoned to Mrs. Holt. "Come on in, Janet. What can I do for you, and more importantly, how can I get you to forget what you just saw?"

"Well, that's not going to happen because it was just too juicy." Janet Holt flicked her long gray braid over her shoulder. Every stitch of her clothing had been made by her own hands. She was a master crafter who attended stitch-and-bitch with Harris. No doubt her little outburst would be topic number one at the next meeting.

But then Mrs. Holt surprised her. "Good for you, Maya Badger. Good for you. And that Rune...well, I can't say I'm surprised."

Maya closed her eyes briefly. She could practically see the gossip already making its way around town. Everyone jabbering and yakking...

Speaking of yakking... "How's your yak doing?"

"He's happy to be home. He probably just needed a little space. Jack used to do the same thing. He'd disappear onto his boat for days. But that's not why I'm here. I think someone's been sleeping in my barn."

"Oh yeah?" The Holt homestead was a sprawling spread of several acres, home to the accumulated junk of a lifetime of roughing it. Not junk—"resources" as Alaskans preferred to say. "Have you spotted someone?"

"No, but I found a beer can in there. *Not* Jack's brand. And the barn had a different smell than usual."

A different smell. Now there was a solid clue to follow up on. "It's probably just teenagers sneaking a beer. Has anything gone missing?"

"I have no idea. Jack left so much stuff behind, it's impossible to say."

"So you're worried because...?"

"Well, it's trespassing, isn't it? I didn't invite anyone onto my property to drink beer or neck or anything else. I've a mind to sit out there with my shotgun and put a scare into them."

"Don't shoot anyone," Maya told her sternly. "We don't want a repeat of the Valentine's Day incident."

A few years ago, Janet Holt had actually shot her husband in the big toe when they'd gotten into an argument over how much salt went into the salmon chowder. February could be a tough month around here; by then, everyone was sick of the cold and the darkness.

Maya relied on bubble baths to get her through it. But this year...

A pang went through her as she realized there was a good chance Rune and Cara would be gone by February. Come to think of it, was there a chance the barn squatter could be Cara's stalker?

Janet Holt was now talking about setting up some kind of surveillance.

"Good plan," Maya told her. "You can also make it look like

there's an active camera without actually recording. That's a little cheaper to install."

"Oh no, I want to know exactly who's sneaking into my barn. Unless the police department can send someone over to stake it out, that's what I'm gonna do."

Yeah, there was no way she was going to set up a stakeout at Mrs. Holt's barn. "Let me know what you find out. I'll come check it out as soon as I can. And if you get any hint that something nefarious or dangerous is going on, call me right away."

"I will."

Mrs. Holt paused on her way out the door. "How's Harris doing? We hardly see him at stitch-and-bitch these days."

"He's doing well. He's spending lots of time with his new girlfriend."

"Harris and Vicki, who would have thought? People are saying we might be hearing wedding bells soon."

Maya's stomach gave a hard twist. "I don't know about that," she managed.

"Sometimes the family's the last to know. I just learned that Lucas and Megan are having a baby, and she's already three months along."

"Megan's pregnant?"

"Where have you been? It's all over town. I guess you've been distracted." She winked broadly and hurried out of Maya's office.

She wasn't wrong about that.

Maya gave herself a moment to collect her thoughts. She hadn't been spending as much time with her father as usual. But he would have let her know if things were getting *that* serious. Chalk it up to the town gossip mill going overboard. Speaking of which...

She marched into the bullpen area, which was basically a bunch of old metal desks crammed together with barely room to walk between them.

"Anyone discovered to be repeating anything that I said in the privacy of my own office—no matter how loudly—will be on my shit list."

She couldn't technically reprimand anyone for that, but she could try to scare them.

The two officers who were present—Sergeants Hollister and Chen—looked at her with expressions of utmost innocence. She turned on her heel and spun back toward her office, almost missing Hollister's cough and the "superstar" buried inside it.

Oh God. She was never going to live this down, was she?

CHAPTER TWENTY-FIVE

As soon as the holiday season hit, lights sprang up all around Lost Harbor. Twinkle lights, snowflake lights, lights with colors ranging from vivid purple to holly red. Strings of lights outlined buildings in the historic downtown area. A few especially magnificent spruce trees were draped in twinkling lights.

Rune's favorite was a classic old Chevy pickup on the way past the mudflats. Lights ran the length of the open bed and framed the windshield. A close second was the old-school bear cache adorned with brilliant white lights. Many of the boats in the harbor got into the spirit too. Lights hung from masts and lit up cozy little wheelhouses.

Anything to brighten up the long winter nights; that was how the farmer Max Bruner explained it to him. He'd even decorated his chicken coop with lights, and his pet goat wore a jingle collar that made a festive sound with every step it took.

Rune could brighten his winter nights just fine without lights. All he needed was to walk through Maya's door and everything lit up along with her intimate smile of greeting. As soon as he set eyes on her, all the cold and darkness and "wintry mix" of snow faded away. Like magic.

Rune had gotten into the habit of checking in on Harris whenever he came home from a shift. He'd pop in just a few seconds on his way past and make sure the man didn't need anything.

He rarely did, thanks to Vicki. They were spending more and more time together, almost as much as he and Maya were. He wasn't sure if Maya realized how much; she rarely talked about Vicki anymore. Hopefully that meant she'd come to accept her father's new lady love.

Soon after Thanksgiving, he got a call from Harris asking him to swing by Vicki's salon and pick up some vitamins Vicki had ordered online.

Beauty By Vicki was located close to the high school, so he was able to stop by the cute little shingled building on his way to pick up Cara.

As soon as he walked into the fragrant warmth of the salon, a hush fell across the women in the barber chairs. As if they'd been talking about something they didn't want him to hear.

Fair enough.

He held up his hands. "Not trying to interrupt anything, ladies. Just stopping by to pick up something from Vicki."

A giggle spurted from under a hair dryer.

At a loss, he caught Vicki's eye and lifted his shoulders in a shrug. She too looked like she might burst out laughing, but she put down her scissors and came toward him with a brown paper bag. She wore hoop earrings with little Santa's elves dangling in the middle.

"Here ya go, sweetie. Tell Harris to take one right away, and that I'll see him later."

"Will do. Thank you. Nice earrings." As he took the paper bag, he noticed more jewelry—a ring on a dainty chain around her neck. A pretty gold one, with a tiny sapphire sparkling against her smock.

He lifted his eyebrows in curiosity. With a panicked look, she tucked it out of sight. "Don't say anything," she whispered. "Harris wants to tell Maya himself."

"I won't, but you know how this town is. Better hurry."

"Oh, I know. By the way," she lowered her voice even more, "you're hot topic number one right now. Just thought you should know."

"Me?" He hadn't done anything scandalous, as far as he knew. He and Maya were old news; at least they ought to be, after five hundred and twenty-two holiday parties. "Thanks for the heads up."

Shrugging, he headed for the door. He didn't much care if people talked about him, but it might matter to Maya. He'd better warn her as well.

As he pushed open the door, a blast of wintry wind swirled past him. Someone was calling after him, but the gust whisked it away before he could make it out. All he caught was the word "superstar."

Huh.

He heard the same word when he stopped at the grocery store to grab some potatoes for dinner. He didn't quite catch who said it, but someone definitely did. *Superstar.*

Even Cara was acting weird. She stayed buried in her phone the entire drive home, with none of her usual chatter about her friends or her classes. As they reached Harris' house, he spotted Maya's car parked outside. Now he had two reasons to stop in.

"I'm going to drop off these vitamins for Harris. Want to come in or wait in the car?"

Cara leaped out of the car as if she'd just gotten sprung from prison. "I'll walk the rest of the way."

He hesitated, since it was the kind of thing that would have worried him earlier on. It would only take her five minutes to walk the rest of the way, but what if Stalker Chad had found a way inside the fish house? What if he was lurking under the dock? What if he was—

"That's fine," he told her. "Just keep your eyes open."

If that didn't prove that he'd relaxed here in Lost Harbor, he didn't know what would.

She hopped through the snow in her red boots, her blond head bright against the twilight sky, and he felt a moment of deep hope that they'd be able to stay here.

Hope could be a tricky mother-effer, so he pushed it aside.

He knocked on Harris' front door, found it open, and strolled inside—into a brewing storm.

Maya had her fists planted on her hips as she faced off with her father, who was walking back and forth across the kitchen as he dried and put away dishes.

"You're just telling me *now*?" Maya demanded.

"She just said 'yes.' I'm sorry you're upset, honey." He wiped the inside of a mug with a dish towel with an embroidered badger on it. Badgers were a theme in his house, from salt shakers to "Badger of Honor" throw pillows. "Hi there, Rune. Come on in, if you dare."

Rune stepped far enough into the kitchen to drop the brown paper bag on the counter. "Is everything okay in here?"

"How does it look?" Maya snapped, barely looking his way. "What took her so long to say yes, Dad? She ought to be jumping at the chance. That means she doesn't appreciate you—"

"She was worried about what you would think," Harris said, his grizzled eyebrows pulling together. "You got her terrified with all your scowls. I had to convince her you weren't going to throw her in jail if she said 'yes.'"

"Throw her in—Dad, come on—" She swung around to face

Rune. "Rune, tell him that's ridiculous. I've been so nice to her. I drank her vile cranberry wine."

Rune wanted to back right out of this situation while he still could. He had no right to get in the middle of Maya and her father's fight. But now both of them were giving him pleading glances. Too late for an escape.

"Of course Vicki's nervous about what you'll think, Maya. That's normal. She knows how much you love your father."

Her glare relaxed a tiny bit.

Harris shot him a grateful look. "That's right. Listen to the man, Maya."

"Listen to the—" Maya spluttered indignantly, causing Rune to step in again.

"Maya, as your dad's nurse—"

"*Former* nurse."

Wow, she really was on edge. "*Former* nurse, I'd like to turn down the temperature here. We don't want Harris to get too wound up."

"I'm not wound up," Harris declared. "I'm wound just right. I'm getting married, and I'm sorry if that's hard for you to get used to, Maya. But maybe it's time. You won't have to worry about me so much anymore."

"I don't mind worrying about you! Don't do anything until I run a—"

"*Maya*," Rune interjected before she went too far with her accusations against Vicki. He put one arm around her shoulders. "How about we talk about this outside?"

"This is between me and my dad!" Her eyes were bright with tears, dark with emotion. They blazed with a fire that he knew wasn't really anger.

"Go talk to him, honey," said Harris. "Hear what he has to say." He shot another pleading glance Rune's way. The poor man could obviously use some help here. Rune sympathized with him, but also with Maya. It was disorienting when your parent decided to take a new partner. He'd been there.

Maya shrugged his arm off her shoulders. "I don't want to talk to Rune. He's going to want me to be calm and reasonable and I—I—"

Rune took her hand and steered her toward the door. "Come on. I promise you don't have to be calm. You can yell and scream if you want. Let's give your dad some space."

She pulled away and stormed ahead of him through the living room and the arctic entry—grabbing her coat on the way— then out the door.

Outside on the snowy front yard, she stopped. Steam practically rose from her bare head.

He stepped toward her, trying to figure out the best thing to do next. Stay here? Drive somewhere? Go home?

She gave him a helpless glance that made his heart twist. She didn't know what to do with herself.

"Come on." He took her by the hand and pulled her toward his car. Maya didn't argue. She seemed to be struggling to hold back tears. She got into the passenger seat, and he took his place behind the wheel.

He backed out of the driveway, skidding a bit on the slick gravel. He pulled onto the road and headed toward town. With night closing in, all the color leached from the world, painting everything in shades of black and silver.

"Where are we going?" she asked after a few moments.

"Just driving."

She didn't answer, either to agree or to object. He didn't push her to say anything. If she was upset, she was upset. He had no answers to give her. Sometimes you just needed time to adjust to a shift in your reality. He knew what that felt like.

"What does he *see* in her?" she finally burst out. "No, don't answer that. I know she's nice. She's nice, right? She'll be good to him?"

"I think so. But it's not up to me."

"It's up to him. I get it. I know that. But he went and *proposed* to her. Without even telling me first. Or asking for my advice. Why didn't he ask me for advice? Everyone asks me for advice. Freaking Jessica asks me which boots she should buy. My own father just goes and gets engaged without a blip?"

"Crazy kids," he murmured.

"Don't try to make me laugh! It's not going to work. I'm still going to be upset."

They reached the end of the mudflats and he turned in the direction of the boardwalk. Everything out there was closed in the winter, except for the Olde Salt Saloon and the Eagle's Nest Resort, but it still made for a beautiful, blustery drive. A nearly constant wind cut across the bay, churning up water and sending surf crashing onto the stilts that held up some of the boardwalk storefronts.

With all the stores and restaurants closed, the only light aside from the streetlights came from the boats in the harbor and the stars in the sky. The Olde Salt provided a dim ember of a glow in the heart of the boardwalk. All the way at the tip of the board-walk, the lights of the Eagle's Nest glimmered against the dark backdrop of the mountains.

As they drove down the empty boardwalk road, wind howled at the windows of his car like hyenas trying to claw their way in. The glass rattled.

"Are you coming to Lost Souls?" Maya asked abruptly. "Did you decide?"

"We're in." He'd talked it over with Cara, who didn't like the restrictions but was very excited about the trip. "When do you want to go?"

"A few days before Christmas. I'm pulling in some favors from friends with planes."

"Friends with planes. Wish I had a few of those."

"*Don't* try to make me laugh."

"I'm not. I swear." He cast around for something non-funny to talk about. "Hey, I have a mystery for you. Something to wrap your detective brain around."

She brightened, turning to him with an expression of relief. "Good. I need a change of topic. What is it?"

"For some reason, every time I turned around today, I heard the word 'superstar.' Vicki warned me I was a hot topic, but she didn't say why. Do you have any clue what that's all about? Superstar?"

For a moment, she just stared at him with an expression somewhere between shock and horror. Then she laughed. And kept laughing. Big heaves of laughter that had tears rolling down her cheeks. "I—I'm so—sorry," she gasped.

"You're laughing. I wasn't even trying, I swear. What'd I do?"

That question triggered a new round of hysterical peals of laughter. Jesus. He had no idea what this was about, but Maya was fricking losing it. He turned off the road into the parking lot of the deep-water section of the harbor. No one would be coming and going from here after dark.

The only other vehicle in the lot was a truck hooked to a trailer carrying a battered fishing boat. Ahead of them, a retaining wall protected the lot from the rise of the tides. Dark water lay beyond. On this lee side of the boardwalk, the water was almost unruffled by the wind.

Maya laughed and laughed until finally she blotted her eyes and blinked at him. "Wow. I guess I did need to laugh after all. Thank you."

"For what? You'd better let me in on the big joke." If he was going to be a laughingstock, he wanted to know why.

"It's my fault. Jerome came to my office today and got under my skin. I yelled at him and one of the things I said—very loudly —was that you fuck like a superstar." She screwed up her face as the words left her mouth. "I'm really sorry. It was very inappropriate and I feel terrible about it. I did what I could to keep it from leaving the office, but apparently that didn't work. They're always trying to get into my personal business. This time I just put it on blast." She let out a sob-giggle. "I don't even know why I'm laughing. It's wrong. So wrong. Are you mad? Of course you're mad."

A long moment passed while he tried to get his head around the entire town calling him "superstar." Good God, the women in the salon? Random people at the grocery?

Maya cleared her throat. "How mad?"

CHAPTER TWENTY-SIX

Maya stole a glance at his shadowed face. It was a given that he would be furious. She would be, if he'd blabbed around town about their sex life. But he wasn't saying anything. Why wasn't he saying anything?

"Rune?" she tried. "How can I make this up to you?"

"What makes you think I'm upset? Fuck like a superstar. That's not exactly an insult."

But she could hear in his voice that it bothered him. "It's private. It's between us. It's not anyone's business, especially Jerome's."

Still he was quiet. "Why'd you say that to him?"

"He said something dismissive and it pissed me off. I was...I don't know. Defending you."

"I didn't know I needed defending."

"You don't. He got under my skin."

A shadow passed across his face, but she couldn't tell what it meant.

"Did it work? Did you shut him up?"

"Mostly. Rune, I was angry. I was lashing out at Jerome. Our relationship is a lot more than just fucking."

He slanted a glance at her. "Is it? I don't know what it is, really." He shook his head roughly, as if ridding himself of whatever thoughts were dogging him. "You know my situation. Fucking ain't so bad. I'll take it." He turned to her and she caught her breath at the look in his eyes. Dark and intent. Hot and dangerous. "I'll fuck you right now. Put your seat back and let's do it."

The brusque order made her breath come fast and furious in her chest. In her daily life she gave the orders. And she didn't like them coming from men, generally. But Rune was different because she knew him so well. This was a mood, a dark ride he was inviting her on. She could say no. He wouldn't argue if she asked him to take her home.

But she didn't want to say no.

She clicked the passenger seat back. Heat already pulsed between her legs. A gust of wind made the car rock from side to side. Outside, utter darkness pushed at the windows.

He angled his body over her and unzipped her pants. He shoved his hand under the tight cloth of her black jeans, more roughly than he normally would. It didn't bother her, the roughness. It felt like exactly what she needed right now. She was craving a hard smash, a harsh release, and somehow he knew it.

He buried his hand in the damp nest of her sex. She arched against him and widened her legs even farther. His strong body hunched over her as he focused one hundred percent on his task. He dragged his hand through the slippery softness of her pussy. Used the heel to grind against her clit until it throbbed with fierce pulsing need.

She groaned out loud. "Rune..."

"You want to come, don't you? I want you to come. I want to feel you gush into my hand."

She heard another zipper sound, and then he grabbed her hand and pulled it inside his pants. He wrapped it around his cock, which was already hard to the touch. It burned against her palm.

"Wait," he muttered.

He pulled her hand out of his pants and slid it into her own, replacing his. He rubbed it up and down until her own juices covered it. Then he switched their hands again so her now-slick palm wrapped around his erection. And his rough calloused skin was once again working her clit.

They didn't say any more words. Nothing but harsh grunts filled the air, mingling with the whine of the wind battering the car from outside. The energy of that wind seemed to travel right through the metal into the two of them. Maya felt electrified with the same wild feeling that comes before a storm. *Tear it apart. Blow it open. Fuck me hard.*

The only reason they weren't joined together, with him buried inside her, was that he was just too big for the small space. But they were as close as two humans sharing the front seat of a car could be. Hands down each other's pants. Hot breath in each other's ears.

He tugged on her earlobe with his teeth. She gasped and bit the tendon straining along his neck. He growled and pinched her clit between two fingers. She fingered the tip of his cock with her thumb. He lowered his head to her closest nipple and bit her through her top. She squeezed her legs tighter, clamping his hand harder against her sex.

Move, countermove...action, response...give, take...battle, retreat.

And then, surrender to the most glorious grind-it-out orgasm she'd ever experienced. The rough pad of his fingertip working her clit against her own folds took her to a delirious screaming peak. Rune came too, jets of liquid spilling onto her hand. His cock pulsed against her palm in time to his husky groans. "Oh yeah. Oh fuck yeah."

And then it was done and he collapsed back into the driver's seat. A sense of... emptiness stole over her. Everything had drained out, leaving her empty of the fear and hurt she'd felt at her father's announcement. Empty of anything except amazement that she was here, right now, with Rune.

She didn't want to be anywhere else.

For a long moment the two of them just breathed together as their heart rates slowly went back to normal. He reached for the backseat and found a towel in his medical bag. He used it to gently wipe off her hand.

She let out a long, heaving sigh.

"Feel better?" he asked.

"Yeah. I really do. Thanks, I guess I needed that." Was it weird to thank him? She didn't care. "I didn't know I had so much emotion all worked up inside me."

"No surprise there. I never really got used to my stepfather. Cara's dad. But you and Harris are still going to be close. I don't think you have to worry."

"Rune, about what happened with Jerome..." She wanted to say so much more. She wanted to tell him how important he'd become to her. How happy their relationship made her. How much she cared for him. How for the first time since her heartbreak, her walls weren't going back up. How he made her feel adored, safe, sexy, hopeful.

But the words didn't want to come out. They clogged in her throat and the next thing she knew, someone was tapping at the window.

She startled and quickly zipped up her jeans. Next to her, Rune did the same. Good thing the dome light wasn't on and that they'd managed to steam up the windows. If one of her own sergeants was out there, she'd really never hear the end of it.

Composing her face into stern police chief mode, she rolled down the window. Not a sergeant, thank God. Boris Clancy stood astride his bike, the wind whipping his yellow oilskin jacket against his body. A chicken wrapped in a sweater huddled in his front basket. She had no idea how he handled the cold on a bicycle, but even on the iciest days he made his regular rounds.

"No one's supposed to be here," he began, before he saw that it was her. "Oh. Sorry, Chief. It's you. And—" he peered past her. "And him. The superstar."

Oh good lord. If the gossip had spread all the way to Boris, that meant the Olde Salt crew and all the "harbor rats" were in on it too.

"His name is Rune, and we're just having a quiet conversation while enjoying the view."

She waved at the cranes and piles of compressed metal that made up the industrial landscape of the deepwater harbor.

"You aren't doing surveillance?"

"No. Not right now."

Boris picked at something in his beard. He seemed disturbed by her response.

Her detective instincts pinged, a little tap on her shoulder.

"Is there something I should be surveilling?" she asked. "Have you noticed something?"

"No," he said quickly, almost fearfully. "No. I didn't say that. You should go away. I have to go now."

He hopped on his bike and pedaled hard toward the main road.

Maya shared a glance with Rune. "That was weird. He seemed scared of something."

Rune nodded, watching him go in the rearview mirror. "Want to follow him?"

"No, that would send him into a meltdown. He gets paranoid pretty easily. We probably wouldn't learn anything that way."

"Maybe he's acting scared *because* he's paranoid and sliding into a mental break."

"That's possible. Or he's genuinely frightened. Maybe he saw something, or maybe someone's threatening him."

"Do you think it could be related to the Lost Souls situation?"

"I'm not speculating on that. I'll have to pry it out of him some other time." She shivered. Now that the heat they'd generated was wearing off, the cold was stealing in.

He started up the car and turned on the heat. "Home?"

"Yes please." She hesitated, not wanting this time together to end. With Rune, she didn't have to be so guarded. The responsibility she felt as Lost Harbor's police chief faded, and she just felt like... herself. He seemed to care about *her*. Her feelings, her mood, her wishes. Just *her*. It was such a relaxing feeling. It made her want to cuddle up next to him and let the rest of the world vanish.

Of course as soon as they drove up Harris' driveway, where she'd left her car, it all came back. Because Vicki's red Jeep was there, and her father was getting married and that meant the one person who had always been there for her one hundred percent was going to have different priorities now.

And she'd just have to get used to it.

"Want to come back for a hot bath?" she asked Rune as she was getting out of his car. "Bubbles and everything?"

"Rain check," he told her. "I want to make sure Cara's okay. She was a little weird on the drive from school."

"I can explain that one for you."

His eyes glinted green in the light from his dashboard. "Oh yeah?"

"One word. Superstar."

He groaned and dropped his head onto his steering wheel. "Fuck me."

"I'll find a way to make it up to you, Rune, I swear. Think about that bathtub."

"Oh, I'll be thinking about it, you don't have to worry about that."

CHAPTER TWENTY-SEVEN

Maya swung by the Holt homestead to check out the barn. Besides the beer can, she found the discarded wrapper of a vending machine snack pack. Lost Harbor had very few vending machines; only the hospital and the gas station came to mind. She left behind a flyer for the local homeless shelter.

Not that she thought anything nefarious was going on in Mrs. Holt's barn, but her complaint, especially combined with Boris Clancy's strange behavior, equalled a red flag.

Then she drove back to town and stopped in at Gretel's Café. Gretel was a newcomer to town, the sister of Dr. Bethany Morrison. A reformed party girl, she'd set herself the challenge of surviving an Alaska winter and in the process, fallen in love with her next door neighbor, Zander Ross.

"Are you ready for winter number two?" Maya asked her as she ordered her favorite hazelnut latte.

"Is anyone ever really ready for an Alaskan winter?" she said with an impish smile. Gretel was a tiny and free-spirited blond who always made Maya feel kind of earthbound.

"Good point." She accepted her to-go cup and offered

payment, which Gretel waved off, as always. Maya stuffed the five dollar bill in the tip jar instead. "It's a shock every year." She stirred an extra dose of sugar into the cup and shot a quick glance behind her to make sure no one was close enough to hear. "Gretel, can I ask you a couple of questions?"

Gretel's turquoise eyes widened in alarm. "Did my license lapse? Did the last open mic night get too loud? Old Crow really got into that sea shanty he was singing. I knew a drum circle would be a bad idea. It won't happen again."

"No no, nothing like that. Although now that you mention it, the drum circle would be much better on the beach."

"I totally agree. My ears are still ringing. So what's it about?"

"You get a lot of teenagers in here."

"I get *all* the teenagers." Gretel rolled her eyes. "And they all run tabs, and I'm too much of a wuss to say anything."

"Want me to talk to them?"

"No, I just have to ovary up." A twinkling smile lit up her face. "The bright side is I get to eavesdrop on some juicy teenage drama."

"Which is exactly why I came to you. Have you heard anything about a new hangout place? Or a make-out spot? Some place where the kids secretly get together?"

"All I hear about is bonfires on the beach. I haven't heard about anything else. Why?"

Maya shrugged and tested her coffee. "Just ruling out possibilities. What about Boris Clancy? Have you seen much of him lately?"

Gretel's fine eyebrows came together in a frown. "As a matter of fact, no. Is he okay? I've been saving food scraps for his chicken."

So something was going on with Boris. He relied on his routine, and for him to miss his weekly trip to Gretel's Café was a very loud alarm bell.

"I'm not sure what's going on with Boris, but if you see him, give me a call. I want to talk to him in a relaxed environment."

"I will," Gretel promised. "And if I hear anything about teenage miscreants, I'll let you know. They tend to forget that I'm not their age, so I hear a few things."

"Consider yourself an unofficial undercover officer." Maya toasted her with her coffee cup. "Lord knows none of them are going to talk to me."

Gretel smiled and waved goodbye, turning her attention to her next customer. Who—Maya realized with a shock—was Alastair Dougal, the man who'd gone to Lost Souls Wilderness to investigate his sister's plane crash. Wasn't he supposed to be in New York?

"Chief Badger." Alastair addressed her with a formal nod of his head. "They told me I'd find you here."

"Alastair Dougal. I heard you went back to New York."

"I just got back," he said in his soft Scottish brogue. "Can we talk for a few minutes?"

She glanced around the Café, which was still mostly empty except for two Coasties warming up with hot coffee in the corner. "Sure." She beckoned toward the most private table available.

"How've you been doing?" she asked, warming her hands on her mug.

"It's been a bit of a roller coaster. Seeing the wreckage of my sister's plane for myself was...tough. But I was finally able to hold a proper burial. That was helpful. Then I was informed the FBI dropped the investigation. Rather infuriating."

"I know. I'm sorry."

"Lack of evidence, they say."

The doubt in his voice made her jump to the FBI's defense. "That, and there's two feet of snow out there now. It's hard to investigate anything in the wilderness in the winter."

He ran a hand through his thick black hair. "I'm not here to push for anything. I'll go out there myself. I did it before and I can do it again. I'm not giving up."

Watching him, sympathizing with his frustration, she took a sip of her coffee. "What else are you planning? All the official reports are in. There's nothing to pursue."

"So you're ready to give up as well? When there's clearly something fishy going on out there?" His voice rose in frustration.

"Mr. Dougal—"

"Alastair."

"Alastair, what do you want from me?" She set her mug down with a click. "Lost Souls Wilderness isn't my jurisdiction."

"So you're giving up." He shoved his chair back, ready to go. "Good to know."

"Hey, hey." If nothing else, Maya wanted to know what had brought him back here in the middle of winter. "I haven't closed the file. You must have something to tell me, so why don't you and we'll go from there?"

He sat back down and scanned her face for a long moment, then seemed to come to a decision.

"I'm betting that you want to crack this case as much as I do." He pulled out his phone and shoved it across the table at her. "Right after I got back to New York, I got this text."

She scanned the message. It said, *Half mil delivered. Don't come back.*

"Half mil? As in dollars?"

"Yes."

"Someone sent you half a million dollars?"

"They did. It's in my account. I tried to figure out where it came from but I couldn't. I don't know what the hell to do with it, but I'm not touching it."

"You need to report it."

"That's what I'm doing right now. I'm reporting it to you. My local authorities know nothing about the investigation, but you do. Also..." He hesitated, worry in his eyes. "If someone is sophisticated enough to transfer that much money to me, what else can they falsify? It's a bit unnerving to say the least."

She nodded slowly. "You think they're trying to set you up somehow?"

"To keep me in line, yes. So I don't push this investigation any further. That's my theory."

"I'm no forensic accountant," she told him. "That's who you'd need to figure out who sent that money. It's most likely a series of shell companies and LLCs, possibly registered in other countries. It's obviously not my area of expertise."

"I realize that. That's not why I'm here."

She cocked her head, waiting.

"It's just information I think you should have. You seem like a dedicated officer who won't just take the easy way out."

Inwardly, she flinched. Was that really true? Agent Clement had warned her to stand down, and she had. Mostly.

"Whoever the people are who shot down Caroline's plane, they have lots of money. And they're not just backwoods folks protecting their territory. To pull off a secret anonymous transfer of that much money, that takes a high degree of sophistication and funding."

Very true. And very alarming.

"Whoever sent you the money, they don't want you to go back to Lost Souls," she said. "And yet you're here. Why?"

"I don't like anonymous threats, even when they're accompanied with half a million dollars."

"So you're willing to defy this extortion attempt."

His expression brightened. "You sound like you have an idea. Whatever it is, count me in, Chief."

Maya drew in a breath. Alastair was right about her, damn him. She didn't want to give up on the case, even if the Feds had. The huge sum of money connected the dots to Aurora Lodge.

What had Rune said? *Rich people aren't like you and me. They can twist the world to however they want it to be.*

She thought about the last time she'd been in Lost Souls, when she'd hitched a ride on a Forest Service helicopter to pick up Jessica and Ethan at the Aurora Lodge. As she'd chatted with Jessica, she'd noticed someone watching them from the forest through binoculars. They'd seen her. But had they identified her? She hadn't been wearing her uniform. Maybe they'd seen a random black girl and decided she had no significant role to play.

That could be a plus for the trip out there.

"As a matter of fact, I do. But not as police chief. I'm planning a trip to Aurora Lodge just before Christmas. It's cover for doing some more digging. You can join us if you like."

"Aurora Lodge? How'd you swing that?"

"We're bringing Kelsey Lewis' daughter with us. It's a chance for them to see each other."

An odd expression flitted across his face. "You mean the baby my sister was planning to adopt."

"That's right."

"I'd like to meet her myself," Alastair said softly. "In another world, I'd be her uncle now. I'd probably spoil her silly with gifts from all the airports I travel through."

"So you're in?"

"Bloody right I am."

She finished her coffee and got ready to go. "I can't guarantee any answers. The Feds already think I've wasted their time. I'm risking my reputation, to be honest."

He tilted his head in acknowledgement. "Some risks are worth it. Thanks for taking this on."

CHAPTER TWENTY-EIGHT

"I invited someone else on our Aurora Lodge Christmas trip."

Maya relayed this information from the other end of the bathtub. He could barely see her through the billowing piles of fragrant bubbles. Her hair was piled on top of her head, with a silk bandanna protecting it from the water. Candlelight flickered over the skin of her face and shoulders, giving it a rich burnished bronze glow.

"Someone safe and definitely not Cara's stalker?"

"I already ran a background check. He's clear."

"This is shaping up to be the ultimate holiday party of the season."

"Yes, it is. Jessica's already got all the menus planned out. She's packing up boxes of ingredients. I scheduled my time off from the station, I'm good to go."

"Same."

Under the soapy surface, Rune tangled his legs with hers. He wasn't generally speaking a hot bath kind of person. They were suited more for Alaska than Hawaii. And he didn't really fit into this tub, its oversize dimensions notwithstanding. While she was mostly immersed in the water, he could only get some of himself underwater at a time.

Even so, he loved this bathtub. Some of their best conversations took place here.

In the relaxing warmth of the scented water, Maya gradually opened up about her life. She told him all about Jerome, and her high school boyfriend, Lucas Holt, and how at her first dinner with his family, old Jack Hammer had made a racial comment that he'd never apologized for. Lucas finally had, years later.

In that same vein, she told him about the many times strangers to town had looked right past her, assuming Hollister or Chen was the chief. And the time the school librarian, an amateur genealogist, got angry when Maya pointed out that her family had been in America longer than most people's. She didn't believe it, so Maya brought in a family tree that went back to the 1600s.

On the lighter side, she talked about summers spent with Kate and Jessica, Toni and another girl who'd left Lost Harbor—Chrissie. They'd spend sunny days sunbathing on the deck of Jessica's stepfather's boat. As teenagers, they worked scooping ice cream or frying shrimp or guiding tourists in kayaks.

They also did things like sneak into the Olde Salt Saloon and flirt with tourists. Keeping Kate Robinson out of trouble was often Maya's primary mission.

"Did you and Harris ever think about coming back to Hawaii?" he'd asked at one point. "I always thought you would, but you never did."

"Not really. My dad didn't really like it. He prefers the cold. Says he can breathe here. He doesn't like humidity."

"Excuse me, the weather is always perfect in Hawaii."

She'd giggled. "I bet you'll be happy when you can go home again."

Yes and no. Yes because it was home. No because it didn't have Maya.

Right now, in the luxurious two-person tub, Maya's foot was sliding along the inside of his thigh.

"Do you think we should give each other presents?" she asked, her breath stirring the soap bubbles.

"I vote yes. Cara says it's hard to buy presents for me, so I'll give you a hint."

"Okay, what?" Her dark honey eyes shone at him over the froth.

"As long as you give it to me naked, it can be anything."

"Ha ha." She lifted her foot and flicked soap suds in his face. He snagged her ankle and kept it lifted above the water.

"Hand me that pumice." She had an adorable little pumice stone shaped like a sea horse. He knew this because she'd actually given him a tour of her bathroom and all her guilty pleasures.

She handed it to him and he rubbed it across the rougher skin of her heel. She sighed and relaxed into the tub again, her eyes closing.

"Did you learn how to do that in paramedic school or with a surfing babe?" she asked.

"Paramedic school," he said seriously. "We had to practice on each other. The pedicures were the hardest part."

"Funny."

"You think I'm joking. Hand me the nail trimmers. Let me work my magic." Actually, he knew nothing about such things. He was just going on instinct here.

"When did you lose your virginity?"

That was the thing about their bathtub conversations. All kinds of questions surfaced. "Where'd that question come from?"

"I'm just curious. The way you touch me, it always feels like you *know* things."

"Know things, huh?"

"About women. All women, not just me."

"You make me sound like a man whore." Even though he made the comment lightly, he wasn't entirely joking.

"No no no." She touched his other foot, which was nestled snug against her hip. "I really don't mean it like that. Really really. I just mean that I love how you touch me."

"Well, I do fuck like a superstar, never forget," he joked.

"How could I when you remind me almost every night?"

"Boom!" He flicked soap suds at her as she laughed. "Okay, you win an answer. I lost my virginity to an older woman. I was seventeen and she was twenty-one and worked as a lifeguard at the beach. She always told me to come see her when I turned eighteen. But I couldn't wait that long, so I fudged it a little." He grinned. "Boy was she mad when she found out. But by then we'd been boning like bunnies for months."

"Was she Hawaiian or white?"

The question caught him off guard. "She was biracial. Her father was white and her mother was from Thailand."

"And now you're with a black girl. So what...you don't see color, is that it?" Even though she was smiling, he caught a shimmer of something else in her expression.

"I see color. I see *you,* Maya Badger. And your color. And everything else that makes you, you."

How else could he tell her that he adored everything about her? She was quiet, watching him through the soap suds. Should he say again that he loved her? It was almost three weeks since he'd bared his heart at the beach lot in the storm. She still hadn't said anything about her feelings for him. In fact, he wasn't completely sure how she felt about him. Maybe "conflicted" would be in there somewhere. He knew she loved spending time with him, in and out of bed. And bath.

"Sometimes I think people here forget I'm not white, because there's not a lot of black people here," she finally said. "But I never do. I'd never want to."

"It's pretty white here, except for the Native population. So different from Hawaii. Does it bother you?"

"I'm used to it. It's home. Once in a while I have to check someone who says something dumb."

"I know the feeling." He grinned at her ruefully. "You've called me out plenty of times."

"The thing with you is, you always listen to me. That goes a long way."

"Count on it. Whatever you want to say, I'm here for it." He hesitated, then plunged onward. "Hypothetically, if I was more than a fake holiday boyfriend, would your family have a problem with me being a white dude?"

She flicked some soap suds at him. "Hypothetically? You know my dad doesn't, but that's because he knows you. Maybe some others." She shrugged, her bare shoulders rising through the suds. "How about your family?"

He laughed. "My mom would pop open the Lambrusco. Then again, she does that every day anyway. She always loved you because you kept me out of trouble."

"Tried," she corrected. "So what happened with your lifeguard girlfriend?"

Abrupt change of subject. He went along with it. "She ended it and broke my heart." He shrugged ruefully. "I was just a kid, after all. She moved on. I think she's married now."

"I'm sorry your heart was broken."

"Hey, I'll never regret it. She was a dream come true for my horny teenage ass. She was an incredible surfer. That's how I knew her first, from the water."

"Did you know that people surf here too?"

He put the pumice stone back on the edge of the bathtub,

next to one of the candles in its glass stand. "You're kidding. In full dry suits or do they just skip right to the hospital gown?"

She smiled. "Dry suits. You should try it sometime. People say it's amazing with the views of the mountains and so forth."

"Maybe. When it's eighty degrees and sunny, with a five-foot swell."

She was quiet for a bit as she piled soap suds under her chin.

He loved this girlie side of her, the part that indulged herself in long hot baths. Of course, he loved all the other sides of her too.

Even the cautious, reserved side that refused to think about how she felt about him. He could be patient—until the day he had to leave. Which might come at any time.

But just lately, he'd come to the conclusion that he and Cara were safe until next year. Stalker Chad probably had some form of family somewhere. The holidays would throw a wrench in his stalking plans. And with Lost Harbor empty of tourists, it would be harder for a creepy stranger to sneak into town.

At least that was his deepest wish and hope, for himself and for Cara. Cara and Maggie were so excited about the Christmas trip to Lost Souls that it was all they could talk about. At least let Cara experience the wonderful winter holiday she'd always dreamed of.

"Rune?"

He startled at the sound of Maya's drowsy voice. "Yeah?"

"In case I don't tell you enough, I'm really glad you're here."

He smiled to himself as he picked up her other foot and applied the pumice sea horse. He was wearing her down, he knew it. "Because I take such good care of your heels?"

"Yeah. It's all about the heels." She sounded as if she was falling asleep in the clouds of steam. "Head over heels."

Head over heels? That meant...his hands paused on her foot. Did she mean it the way he thought?

A soft snore came from the other end of the tub. He chuckled darkly. He wouldn't be surprised if she was faking it because she'd realized what she'd just said.

No matter. The holidays weren't over yet. Miracles could happen.

CHAPTER TWENTY-NINE

A few days before Christmas...

AN OLD COAST GUARD buddy of Harris Badger's offered up his Piper Cub for their journey to Aurora Lodge.

The Piper Cub only held four people, including the pilot, so Ben would have to make several trips in order to ferry them all across. Maya insisted on covering the cost of the fuel, though she had to insist hard.

"I hate taking money from the Badger family," he rumbled. "Between your dad saving my ass in the Aleutians, and you catching that burglar, I owe you Badgers."

"You're a good man, Ben. But I'm paying for the fuel, and that's that."

After all, it was going to take him half the day to make all the necessary trips. Their group included Maya and Rune, Alastair Dougal, Jessica and Ethan, Maggie and Cara, Darius, Kate, and Darius' son Dylan—awkward, because Dylan and Maggie were "taking a break," whatever that meant.

Sadly, Nate and Bethany weren't able to come. The Morrisons were holding a command performance Christmas party back in Connecticut, so they and Gretel and Zander and the boys had flown there a few days ago. Toni was throwing her usual Christmas party at the Olde Salt for the fishermen without families.

That left a core group of Maya, who of course had brought her firearm, along with four people she'd trust in a crisis, two question marks (Alastair and Jessica) and three teenagers.

Then again, neither Maggie nor Cara were ordinary girls. Maggie probably belonged in the category of people she'd trust in a fight, and Cara could go into the "unknown" category. She'd taken self-defense classes after that first attempted kidnapping, but Maya had never seen her in action.

Still, she felt fairly comfortable with that pared-down group.

A group that didn't include her father.

For the first time in her life, she wouldn't be celebrating Christmas with her dad.

"It's too soon for you to travel out there," she'd explained. "It's too unpredictable. I don't know what we'll be facing."

"You do your job, honey. Don't worry about me." But she could tell he was putting on a brave front, and she did worry—until Vicki swooped in with all kinds of plans for the two of them. Caroling with her church, a memorial potlatch for one of her Athabascan uncles, an eggnog party at her salon. A cozy little Christmas morning with just the two of them.

Get used to it, she told herself. *Dad's happier than he's been in a long time. This is a good thing. Don't be such a baby.*

She was still working on that.

The Piper Cub's first flight across the bay included Maya, Rune and Alastair. Maya sat in the front with Ben, while the two men crammed themselves into the backseat.

Flying over the dense snowy forests, it seemed impossible

that they'd be able to spot the tiny airstrip, a mere scratch in the vast blanket of snow. First the lodge came into view, so improbably stately in this wild land. A billionaire had built it in the 1970s as a private retreat, then sold it to a consortium that opened it up for guests.

The suites were absurdly expensive, especially considering that you had to hire a private plane to get there. Maya knew the clientele skewed toward wealthy people who wanted the priceless experience of being catered to in the midst of some of the most magnificent scenery on earth.

But what if there was more to it? There was essentially no oversight in such a remote location. Other than the lodge, only scattered cabins and yurts existed in Lost Souls Wilderness, and those were few and very far between. Between Alastair's strange fund transfer and Kelsey's determined silence, all signs pointed to the lodge.

There was no real law enforcement out there, other than Kelsey herself, who'd been deputized by the sheriff. But since Kelsey had been neutralized by threats against her daughter, there was zero law enforcement.

She thought about the men she'd seen at the cove near Far Point. In her examination of the maps and satellite imagery of Lost Souls, she'd noticed a clearing in the forest not far away. Decades ago, some logging had taken place there, and the forest hadn't recovered. It would be possible for a small plane to land there without anyone noticing.

"Ben, can you take a little detour before we land?" she shouted over the drone of the engine. She pointed toward Far Point and the little cove. He tilted the wings and veered east. They chugged across the frozen landscape of ravines and icebound lakes and glittering cornices on the upper slopes of the mountains. The low midwinter sun had barely risen above the peaks, a sluggish effort, as if all it wanted was to stay in bed.

The shoreline held so many little coves and inlets that it was difficult to spot *the* cove. Her binoculars were in her bag in the cargo section, held back by webbed netting. She should have anticipated better. Not only that, but the glare of the sun across the snow was blinding. She should have brought sunglasses. What was wrong with her? She was distracted, that was it. Distracted by Rune and all the time they'd been spending together in beds and bathtubs and wherever else they could sneak a moment.

"I'll be damned," said Ben, gazing out the window on his side. "Looks like someone's been landing a plane down there. It ain't even plowed."

"Show me."

He performed a maneuver that put the wings at a vertiginous thirty-degree angle. Nausea clawed at her throat, but at least now she could see the mess that a plane's wheels had made in the clearing.

"Is that dangerous?" she asked Ben.

"Hell yes. Must have been an emergency put-down. Don't know why they didn't go back to the lodge."

She knew. They had a mission to complete, no matter how dangerous the landing. She gave Ben a nod and he oriented the plane back toward the lodge.

Rune must be wildly curious about their little side trip. He must recognize the cove he'd taken pictures of. She wasn't sure if she should bring Alastair up to speed; then again, he wasn't the type to sit back and wait for instructions. It would probably be best to loop him in so he didn't go off and do something reckless.

At the airstrip, Kelsey Lewis was waiting for them next to a futuristic-looking four-seater snow machine. Maya had never seen anything like it. As they ducked out of the Piper Cub onto the gritty pavement of the airstrip—this one properly plowed—she waved them over. She wore an anorak in vibrant burnt orange, along with snow pants and a balaclava covering most of her face. With all that winter gear, Maya barely recognized her.

"It gets cold on the snow machine," she told them as they carried their bags across the airstrip. "Better bundle up."

This deep into the wilderness, the air temperature here was a good fifteen degrees colder than Lost Harbor because it didn't have the moderating influence of the ocean.

"I've never seen a snow machine like this," Maya said.

"Four-seater prototype from Canada. We're testing them out here. Nothing but the best for the Aurora Lodge."

With their breaths sending puffs of steam into the cold air, they loaded boxes of food supplies, along with their backpacks of personal items, onto a trailer towed behind the snow machine.

Maya gestured a "thank you" prayer hands to Ben, who waved back from the cockpit as he turned the plane around. She watched the bright little plane lift into the air, then turned back to their task.

She pulled out her phone to text Jessica. *Tell everyone to bring extra winter gear. It's a lot colder here.*

Will do. Is it gorgeous?

She answered yes before she'd even taken a solid look at the surrounding scenery. Of course it was gorgeous, that was a given. Even though she wasn't here for the views, she allowed herself to absorb the breathtaking panoramas on the bone-rattling trip to the lodge. The snow machine seemed to hit every bump and fallen branch on the trail.

Alastair sat in front with Kelsey, while she and Rune huddled behind them. For warmth, of course. Not because she always felt better when she was plastered up against Rune Larsen.

He wrapped an arm around her shoulders and grinned down at her. "Things are never boring around you, you know that?"

She smiled and brushed at the frost forming on the scruff of his beard. His eyes were bright with the excitement of an adventure. Her heart did a slow somersault inside her chest. Why did Rune always make her feel this way, as if the world was filled with joy and the opportunity for fun? But also—which seemed almost contradictory—safe?

The truth had been welling in her heart for days. Weeks. But in this particular moment, with snow-spangled spruce sliding past their vehicle, and the cold making her snuggle against his strong body, she couldn't hold it down any longer.

She loved him.

Once she let that truth come out, it spread through her entire being like a rising sun. It illuminated every corner of her heart and soul. *She loved him.* Without any of the shadows that had marked her feelings for Jerome. No doubt, no insecurity, no anxiety. Just pure joy to be with him, for however long that lasted.

He must have seen the change in her expression, because his eyes darkened and his face hovered closer to hers. She felt his warm breath against her chilled skin and saw his lips part.

Just then the snow machine came to a jerking stop outside the service entrance of the lodge. Back to business. She climbed off the rig and looked around the property, automatically scanning for anything out of the normal.

The deep forest surrounding the lodge was filled with shadows and snow, but she caught no glint of binoculars or weapons. Good.

The machine had kicked up a swirl of snow crystals, which were now descending through the air in a glorious fall of glitter. She held out her gloves to catch a handful, the way she had as a kid. Maybe that was the Rune effect; he brought back that carefree time in her life.

The four of them ferried the boxes of supplies into the kitchen. Maya got the sense that while she and Rune had been mooning at each other in the backseat, Kelsey and Alastair had argued about something. Interesting.

When they were done unloading, Kelsey told them to pick whichever suites they wanted.

"The lodge is at your disposal. Maya, can I have a minute?"

She pulled Maya into the walk-in pantry, which was about the size of Harris' entire fish house. Out here, stocking up for the winter was serious business. Cases of canned tomatoes filled the shelves, along with pallets of pasta and commercial-size containers of cooking oil. Half of Costco seemed to be in here.

"I'm nervous about this meeting with Maggie." Kelsey twisted her hands together. Behind her horn-rimmed glasses, her vivid blue eyes were wide and anxious. Her dark red hair was twisted into an over-the-shoulder braid. "How do you...what do you...how should I..."

Maya put a comforting hand on her arm. "You don't have to worry. Maggie is as straightforward as they come. She's excited to see you."

"She's not angry with me because I didn't rescue her from that crazy trapper?"

"Of course not. She doesn't blame you for anything. Maggie deals with what's right in front of her. She doesn't overthink things. She doesn't get distracted. I've learned a lot from her, to tell you the truth. She's quite a girl."

Kelsey chewed at her lower lip. "Will you come with me to pick her up?"

Maggie and Cara were coming on the Piper Cub's next trip, along with Ethan.

"How will we all fit on the four-wheeler?"

"We'll take two. You can drive one. Please, Maya."

Kelsey, who had always seemed to be a fiercely capable person, looked so rattled that Maya agreed.

"Of course. But at the airstrip, it's best to greet Maggie like any other guest. We don't want to tip off anyone who might be watching."

"Yes. Of course," she said, sounding a little distracted.

Maya eyed the manager, wondering if it was the right moment to ask the question she most wanted the answer to.

Then again, she might not have a better chance—alone in a pantry surrounded by reassuring stacks of food stores.

"There's a question I need to ask you, regarding Maggie."

Kelsey's expression shifted to one of wariness. "I'll answer if I can."

"You'll probably get this question from Maggie too, so you might as well be prepared. Who is her father?"

If Maya wasn't a detective, she might have missed the quick flash of fear in Kelsey's eyes, so quickly did she mask it.

"He's not in the picture."

Which didn't answer the question. *Ding ding.* Maya knew she'd been right about the father. He was connected to this somehow.

"Is he a threat to Maggie? Is he involved with whatever's going on out here?"

"*He's not in the picture.*" Kelsey's forcefulness just added to Maya's conviction that she was right. "Maggie will be safe here, but we have to keep her inside."

She tried to push past Maya, to leave the pantry, but Maya didn't budge. "Can you at least tell me if you were pregnant before you came to the lodge? Or did you get pregnant here?"

Kelsey stared at her, a muscle ticking in her cheek. "I got pregnant here," she finally said, reluctantly. "It was a fling. I was young and I lost my head."

"A fling with a guest?"

"Yes. That's why he's not in the picture. He's long gone."

Maya knew she was lying. She knew the signs.

"Gone where? Gone from Lost Souls? Gone from Alaska?"

"All of the above. And more."

And *more*? That was a strange way to put it. Maybe he was

gone from the country. She thought about Maggie's pale gray eyes and light coloring. She didn't look much like Kelsey, who had dark red hair and blue eyes. Maggie looked more like the Old Believer Russians who lived in the tiny villages in the hills around Lost Harbor.

Was her father *Russian*? Not just a Russian living in Alaska, but a Russian national? If so, the residual fear in Kelsey's eyes could mean that the criminal acts going on in Lost Souls had a transnational component. A cross-border Alaska-Russia connection.

Other parts of Alaska were much closer to Russia than Lost Souls Wilderness was, but maybe this area was simply more useful for whatever they were doing.

Because of the lodge?

Maya's gears were turning. Maybe the Aurora Lodge offered the perfect combination of remoteness, luxury, and accessibility. But for who? And what?

Kelsey's lips were pressed into a tight pale line; Maya knew she wasn't getting any more out of her today.

"You might want to flesh that story out a little for Maggie," she said wryly. "She'll have just as many questions as I do. And she isn't shy about asking them."

Kelsey gave a tight nod and pushed past Maya into the kitchen. "I'll get the other snow machine ready."

Back in the kitchen, Maya met Rune's curious glance. He and Alastair were guzzling glasses of water next to the sink. The door to the mud room was just swinging closed; Kelsey must have run out of there as if her hair was on fire.

"I'm going to take a second snow machine out to meet Maggie and Cara," she told Rune. "Want to come with me?"

"Absolutely. This is the big reunion, right?"

Maya nodded. "Kelsey's a little nervous about it. Alastair, are you cool here on your own?"

"First pick of rooms. No complaints." He gave them a little salute and wandered out of the kitchen.

"I asked Kelsey who Maggie's father is and she freaked out. Not a normal freak-out, more of the she's-too-terrified-to-say kind," Maya whispered to Rune as they put their boots back on in the mudroom.

"Sounds like you're onto something."

"I think so. But she's really scared. It's a good thing Jessica's bringing eggnog supplies and lots of rum."

"That's your plan? Get her buzzed and interrogate her?"

"I have no shame. At least the holidays are good for something, right?"

He looked up from his boots with a wicked grin. "I think we've made the holidays good for a lot of things."

As if following the same invisible pull, their lips met in a deep, quick kiss. It didn't last long, but it was enough to make her pulse flutter.

The drone of the arriving plane interrupted them, along with Kelsey's shout for them to hurry.

They smiled at each other, as if the two of them were in on the best secret in the world, one known only to them.

Then they ran out to claim their snow machine.

CHAPTER THIRTY

As soon as the three new arrivals hopped off the plane, Rune beckoned to Cara. He wanted to give Kelsey and Maggie some space for their reunion. She came reluctantly, glancing back at her friend. She and Maggie were all bundled up in nearly identical parkas and snow pants and they really did look like sisters, both with blond braids peeking from under their hats.

"Don't worry, you won't miss anything," he said dryly when she reached them. "We can eavesdrop just fine from here."

"You're no fun," Cara grumbled. She climbed into the backseat of the snow machine while they all tried not to stare at the reunion taking place on the tarmac.

Maggie had stopped a few yards away from Kelsey, who still lingered next to her snow machine, as if the last few steps to see her daughter were simply too difficult to take.

"Crap," Maya murmured. "I warned Kelsey not to do this out in the open."

"Should've warned Maggie too," Rune told her. "Not that it would have stopped her."

"You're right. Jeez, Kelsey looks like she's forgotten how to

breathe. Or move. We'll never get back to the lodge at this rate."
Under her breath, she urged, "Come on, Maggie. Let's get this
moving. It's on you, girl."

Sure enough, it was the girl who broke the ice. After hefting
her backpack onto one shoulder, she marched the rest of the way
toward Kelsey.

"I'm glad that I'm Magpie now," she said, in her direct way.
"But I used to be Spruce Grouse. If a mother Spruce Grouse
thinks someone's threatening her young, she turns her tail
feathers into a fan and struts in the other direction. Is that what
you did?"

Even from their snow machine, Rune could hear the quiver
in Kelsey's voice. "More or less," she managed. "I didn't do much
strutting. But I was trying to protect you."

Maggie nodded, then her usual stoic expression broke. She
darted at Kelsey, who opened her arms wide. The two collided
with an audible sob of joy. Rune couldn't tell who it came from,
but his guess was Kelsey. It had the poignancy of years behind it
—years of stress and worry and now, bone-deep relief.

He caught Maya's gloved hand in his, too overwhelmed with
emotion to witness this moment alone.

Maya smiled, though she still looked nervous. "Okay, you
two. Wrap it up and let's get to the lodge," she called.

Ethan came trudging across the airstrip, loaded up with his
and Maggie's duffel bags, along with a shopping bag filled with
wrapped gifts.

"Hey there, Santa," Rune greeted him. They bumped fists.
Rune gestured with his head towards the mother and daughter
reunion. "Not sure anything in that bag can beat that present."

"Nothing could," Ethan agreed. "Brought a tear to my eye,
and I'm a hard-boiled detective."

Maya snorted. "No one's buying the hard-boiled act anymore,
Ethan."

"And I'm not buying the stern detective bit." He glanced meaningfully at their joined hands. Rune gave hers a squeeze.

"It's Christmas," Maya said with a wink. "Get off my case."

Finally, hand in hand, Kelsey and Maggie came toward them. Both of them looked lit up from inside. In all the time he'd spent with Maggie—all those many sleepovers and rides and so forth— he'd never seen her look so young. As if a few years had just been lifted from her slim shoulders.

"Thank you," Kelsey said fervently. From behind her horn-rimmed glasses, she directed her teary gaze mostly at Maya, but at all of them. "Maya, thanks for making this happen, and to all the rest of you for providing cover. You'll never know what this means to me."

Maya reached a hand to squeeze hers. "I'm glad," she said simply. "But we should get inside as soon as possible."

The flap of a bird caught Kelsey's attention, and she turned to one side with a grin, shading her eyes. "I do believe we have a magpie checking us out. Maggie, do you see—"

The rest of her words were drowned out by the loud drone of the Piper Cub's engine as it took off down the runway. Rune turned to watch it lift into the air.

A moment later, Rune felt a jerk at his side; Maya reacting to something.

"Kelsey?" Maya darted forward. "What's wrong?"

He looked over at Kelsey, who was slumped against Maggie, as if she'd suddenly lost her balance. Maggie was valiantly trying to hold her upright, but she looked completely bewildered.

There'd been a sound buried in that engine noise, he suddenly realized. He'd written it off, unconsciously, as a backfire. But it wasn't.

It was a gunshot.

He sprang forward to help Maya catch Kelsey before her weight grew too much for the slender Maggie.

"She's been shot," he said tightly. "We have to get her back to the lodge. My med bag is there."

Maya threw herself in front of the two girls and drew out her service weapon. "*Sniper*. Maggie, get into the snow machine. *Now*. We're sitting ducks out here."

Maggie ducked behind her as she aimed her gun into the forest.

Another *ping* and a spray of dirt not two yards away from them. The shooter was still active. Jesus.

Maya fired back. No clear target, but at least it might slow down the sniper.

Rune glanced over his shoulder at the girls. Looking shell-shocked, Cara was helping Maggie climb into the snow machine. Rune wanted to push her down into the snow machine but he couldn't leave the wounded woman in his arms.

"Cara!" he yelled at her. "Get down."

Luckily, Maggie still had her wits about her. She pulled Cara into the machine and shoved her down. At least the vehicle would provide some cover.

Still firing her weapon, Maya moved to the other side of the snow machine and took the wheel. "I'll take the girls in this one. Ethan, you take Rune and Kelsey in the other machine. Put them in the back. Give your gun to Rune so he can defend you while you drive."

"Got it."

"Kelsey, can you hear me?" Rune shook her lightly as Ethan came to her other side. Ethan draped her limp arm over his shoulders. "Stay with us. We have to get you to the snow machine."

"Okay," she said faintly. Conscious, but possibly going into shock. "My leg..."

"You've been shot, and they may shoot again. We have to move fast. Let's go." Practically running, carrying her between them, Rune and Ethan hurried toward the idling snow machine.

Maya provided cover for them, firing with one hand while she steered the snow machine with the other. So quick-thinking, so cool under pressure. What a star she was. He'd trust her with his life, and that of his sister, too.

Get in the back, Maya had said. Smart, because he'd be able to triage Kelsey's bleeding back there. Unless he had to fire at some hidden threat in the forest.

After helping the two of them get settled in the backseat, Ethan pressed a Ruger into his hand. He kept his head low as he swung behind the wheel.

The other snow machine was already on the road, waiting for them to go ahead. Maya kept her weapon trained on the forest, but he didn't hear any more gunshots.

Maybe she'd actually hit the shooter?

He could barely make out the two girls. They were using their backpacks as shields, like turtle shells. Only Maya was fully exposed, which would have fucking terrified him if he'd given himself a chance to dwell on it.

Ethan put the snow machine into gear and they leaped forward. Rune felt better now that they were underway. At least they were a moving target now, so it wouldn't be so easy to pick them off.

Rune had never felt so exposed as they rattled at top speed toward the road. Crouching on the floorboards, he aimed the gun into the woods to the right, just to make the point to whoever was out there that he would shoot back.

Kelsey moaned in pain as the snow machine bounced across humped snow and the occasional rock.

After a few minutes, when no more gunshots came, Rune decided he'd be more useful helping Kelsey. Chances were good that they'd raced out of range of the gunman. He put the safety back on the Ruger and set it on the floorboards, then maneuvered himself so he was sitting under Kelsey's stretched-out body. She was very likely going into shock, so the warmer he could keep her, the better.

He huddled his body around her. "We're almost there, Kelsey. You don't know me, but I'm a paramedic and a home health care nurse. I've dealt with quite a few gunshots in my time. You're in good hands."

"I...got...lucky," she managed.

Tough cookie, this one. That didn't surprise him. Anyone who could survive out here, managing a remote wilderness lodge while fending off criminals, had to be pretty freaking tough.

"Tell...Maggie...love her..."

"You're not going to die," he said briskly.

But she didn't seem to believe him. "Maya wanted to know ... Her father...tell Maya...security...transnational ring..."

"You're talking about Maggie's father?"

She gave a nod, almost more of a spasm of her head. Her gaze clung desperately to his.

"He's part of a transnational ring?"

"Head...of security."

"Okay, do I have this right? Maggie's father is the head of security for a transnational crime ring? Is that what you're saying?" He had to make sure he got it correct. Not because he thought she might die of this gunshot wound. He was going to make sure she didn't. But she seemed so desperate to get her message through, and he needed her to relax.

"Russia," she gasped. "He's Russian. Evidence...in office. Tell her...Magpie."

Magpie...now she was back to talking about Maggie.

"I'll tell Maggie you love her, but you can tell her yourself too. You're going to be fine."

Her eyes closed and her muscles went slack. He checked her pulse quickly. Alive but unconscious.

Maybe it was better that she didn't have to experience the rough jolts of the snow machine as they raced back to the lodge.

He looked at the other snow machine just behind them. *Go, Maya, go.* The two most important people in the world to him were in that tiny vehicle.

Everything crystallized for him, just like the frozen ice crystals kicked up by the machine. No matter what happened with the stalker, he was going to fight for his relationship with Maya. He'd make this work. After Cara's safety, nothing was more important to him.

CHAPTER THIRTY-ONE

Ethan pulled up as close as possible to the service door of the lodge. He leaped out and came around to help Rune lift the unconscious Kelsey out of the machine. Together, they carried her into the vast kitchen. A long butcher block worktable filled the center of the room, the kind of counter used for kneading bread and cutting vegetables. Right now, it would be a triage station.

"On the table," he ordered Ethan. The two of them hauled her across the space and settled her onto the table. "Get some towels and put them under her legs. Let's try to minimize the blood stains."

"Already on it." Ethan was opening cabinet doors and drawers in his search for towels.

Rune took off his parka and folded it up as a pillow under Kelsey's neck. She moaned as her head lolled back and forth.

A minute later, Maya and the girls raced into the kitchen. He took a brief moment to look them all over. "Everyone okay?"

"We're good. What do you need? Where's your medical bag?" Maya asked.

"With my other stuff. Cara, can you grab it?"

Cara ran over to the corner where they'd all left their bags.

As she was bringing it to him, Alastair came hurrying into the kitchen. "I saw the snow machines racing back. What's wrong?" He caught sight of the unconscious Kelsey. "What happened?"

"Gunshot."

Ethan popped up with an armload of towels. "You want these under her leg?"

"Gently," Rune instructed. Everyone except the girls crowded close so they could help pad the table with towels.

"Cara and Maggie, we need some hot water," he directed.

"Is she going to be alright?" Maggie asked in a small voice. Rune looked up to catch her gaze. The poor girl's face was completely pale under her knitted hat. She'd just watched her newly discovered mother get shot. He couldn't imagine what she must be feeling right now.

"I'll make sure of it," he assured her. "Now just focus on getting some water boiled."

Maya was hovering over the table. "What do you need from me? I need to call Ben and tell him it's not safe to fly back yet."

"Go."

That's right...they were going to be trapped here until they could make sure they weren't going to get shot trying to get on the plane.

He shoved that thought aside. One thing at a time. He had to stabilize Kelsey and get that bullet out of her leg.

Cara had put his bag on the table above her head. He pulled out some scissors and cut through her snow pants, then her fleece layer, then her long underwear to expose the wound.

It was located on the fleshy part of her calf. Blood streamed from the wound, but not at a pace that would indicate that an artery had been hit. He turned her leg to see the other side and saw what he had hoped to see.

"It's a through and through," he announced with a huge sense of relief. He wouldn't have to pull out the bullet, he could just treat the wound. "That's much easier to deal with."

His bag contained a field tourniquet, which he quickly unwrapped and applied to her leg above the wound.

"How's that water coming?"

"It's ready." Cara and Maggie carried over a tea kettle and a bowl.

"Pour some out while I wash my hands."

They followed his instructions while he stepped over to the sink. He vigorously soaped his hands under the hot running water, then came back to Kelsey's side, his hands dripping. He dipped a towel into the hot water the girls had poured out and gently cleaned away the blood from the entry and exit wounds. With the tourniquet applied, the bleeding had slowed enough for him to be able to sop up the blood.

"There's some antiseptic in the bag, Ethan."

Ethan found the small bottle of antiseptic and handed it to Rune. He squirted it over the wound. Since he didn't know when she'd be able to see a doctor, it was especially important to fend off infection.

The blood was already clotting. He applied a compression bandage and wrapped it tightly around the wound. That would help bring the bleeding to a complete stop.

He felt Kelsey's forehead. Sweat, but no sign of a fever. If anything, she was still chilled. "We need to keep her warm so she doesn't go into shock."

Alastair spoke up. "I've been roaming around this place since you all have been gone. There's a nook in the great room close to the woodstove. It's very cozy and she can stretch out on a sofa. There are blankets and throws everywhere you look. We should have no trouble keeping her warm in there."

Rune nodded. "Sounds like a plan. Mind getting it ready?"

"I'll help you." Maggie skipped to Alastair's side. "I want to make it as comfortable as possible for my mother."

"Let's go," he told her. Cara joined them too—apparently she and Maggie were joined at the hip now—and they all hurried off.

Rune glanced over at Maya, who was just ending her call to the pilot. A frown wrinkled her forehead; she looked like the weight of the world was on her shoulders. "Unless she spikes a fever, I think she'll be okay here. But if she does we'll need to get her to the hospital. Can they send a medevac?"

"They can," she told him. "I called the hospital to alert them to the situation. But I hate to put anyone else at risk until we find that shooter. We'll monitor her and make that call if we have to."

"You think they'd shoot at an air ambulance?"

"I don't know what they'd do. I'm not going to assume they wouldn't. I got ahold of Ben. He's going to stay ready in case we call on him later. Jessica, Kate and Darius are standing by too. But for now, we're on our own."

"Understood."

Maya turned to Ethan and gave him a tired smile. "Sorry you're separated from Jessica for the time being, but I have to say I'm glad you're here. You really came through on that snow machine."

"I'm glad I was here too. But Rune's the one who really saved the day."

The secret, burning glance Maya shot him would keep him going for days.

"She's right, man," he told Ethan. "I couldn't have gotten Kelsey here without you. And Maya, the way you protected the girls, I'm never going to forget that."

"Just doing my job," she said briskly, as if throwing herself in front of a potential bullet was just another day in the life. "By the way, like I told Jess, I'm especially sorry she's not here because that means the rest of us are on cooking duty. She had all the meals planned out."

"Damn." Rune shook his head. A moment of silence followed that sad bit of information.

"We're screwed," said Ethan. "My best dish is microwaved potpie."

"I'm not a *bad* cook," Rune volunteered. "People have said nice things about my fish tacos."

Maya pursed her lips. "Cooking definitely isn't my strong point. But that pantry has enough spaghetti to last a few months. We'll survive."

Maggie and Cara skipped back into the kitchen, followed more slowly by Alastair. "We made a cozy warm nest for her and it's all ready," Maggie announced.

"Wait," said Alastair, scanning their faces. "Is something else wrong? You all look more somber than when we left. Is Kelsey okay?"

"She's doing fine. We're ready to move her into the great room." Rune gestured to Ethan to give him a hand.

"Then why the long faces?"

"We just figured out that our best cook won't be joining us," Rune informed him as he and Ethan got into position next to Kelsey. "We're grieving our lost Christmas dinner."

Alastair planted his hands on his hips. "Well, if that's all it is, you'll probably be happy to learn that I'm a chef back in New York."

"*Really?*" They all gazed at him in astonishment.

"Why so surprised? What did you think I did for a living?"

None of them had an answer for that. Rune, for one, had never met the dude before. But he recognized that Scottish brogue. "Please tell me your specialty isn't haggis."

Ethan snorted, then nodded to Rune that he was ready. The

two of them lifted Kelsey gently off the table. The others hovered alongside, ready to lend a hand, as Alastair launched into a rant.

"No, my specialty isn't haggis, but as a matter of fact it's a very maligned dish that everyone should try at some point in their—"

A chorus of "no thanks" drowned him out, making him shake his head and mutter something about close-minded Americans.

Highly amused, Rune caught Maya's eyes, and they shared a long glance that said so much, without saying a word out loud. *We made it. Thank God you're okay. We'll get through this. I'm glad you're here.*

And, on his end: *I love you.*

Whether she was thinking that too, he couldn't say for sure. But he chose to believe so.

CHAPTER THIRTY-TWO

Maya was sure she'd done the right thing, inviting Alastair, when he used the motley selection of ingredients they'd brought to whip up a feast of the best pasta she'd ever eaten. If they had to survive on all that spaghetti in the pantry, they'd be just fine.

They all sat around the great room with plates on their laps. Maggie didn't want to leave Kelsey alone, and Cara didn't want to leave Maggie alone, and so they just all stayed together, eating quietly in the warmth of the magnificent cast-iron woodstove. Night had fallen early, as it did this time of year, so close to the winter solstice.

It already smelled like Christmas in the lodge. Spruce boughs tied with red velvet bows were draped over doorways, and a pot of spiced apple cider simmered on the woodstove. Kelsey had done a wonderful job decorating for the holidays, but the beauty was lost on Maya.

All she could think about was the fact that Agent Clement had been right. She should have stayed out of this. Instead she'd dragged this group of friends into the wilderness and put them all in danger. It was her fault that Kelsey was unconscious from a gunshot wound. Her fault that they were all trapped here in this lodge.

Not that it was a *bad* place to be trapped. The place was like a fortress. She and Ethan had checked every door and window and found extra security measures and even bulletproof glass.

What the hell was going on out here?

She took a bite of curry, barely tasting the spicy cumin and ginger. When she'd called the hospital about Kelsey, she'd warned them in advance to land on the lodge's front yard instead of the airstrip. That way the bulk of the building would shield the helicopter from the thickest part of the forest, where the gunshots had come from.

But was that enough? The shooter could change locations. There could be more than one shooter. What were they after? Was Kelsey their target? Was that why the gunfire had stopped after they'd whisked her away from the airstrip? All the unknowns made her extremely tense.

As did the phone call she kept putting off.

Finally she put down her food and slipped away from the others to call Agent Clement.

"Let me make sure I'm getting this. You're having a Christmas party out there, but it's not really a party, it's really an opportunity to investigate something that isn't even your jurisdiction and now someone's been shot?"

She clenched her jaw to keep back the angry words that wanted to come out. Based on his scornful tone, if they did, it wouldn't go well for her. "With another shooting, don't you think there's enough to open the case back up?"

"Oh, that's rich. You're trying to turn your mistake into a reason for us to come back down there?"

"But—"

"Take the L, Badger. You're in over your head."

"That's the whole point," she gritted. "This *is* over my head."

"Then why'd you go out there on your own? First you looked like a fool, now you look like a reckless hothead."

Damn it.

A hand settled on her shoulder. Rune. She punched the call to end it and nearly hurled the phone against the wall. Instead she slipped it back into her pocket.

"You okay?" Rune scanned her with concern.

No, she wasn't okay. She was vibrating with frustration. Angry at the agent, angry at herself. Worried about their situation. "I'll be fine. What's up?"

"There's something I need to talk to you about. Privately."

Maya looked around the corridor and noticed a half-open door at the end. Kelsey's office. "Let's go in there."

He followed her down the hall into her office. A window looked out on the forest behind the lodge, but its blinds were closed and she'd already checked that it was locked. A large birchwood desk with a computer perched on it filled the center of the room. The walls were lined with filing cabinets and bankers' boxes.

She closed the door and turned to face Rune. Part of her wanted to just snuggle in his arms and forget all the disasters taking place. But she didn't have time for that, so she just folded her arms across her chest and stood strong.

"Are you sure you're okay?" he asked again.

"I said I'm fine," she snapped. If she actually admitted how the stress was weighing on her, she might collapse. She needed to keep her focus. "Sorry. What do you need?"

Rune gave a brisk nod, as if accepting her all-business approach. "Before she lost consciousness, Kelsey told me to tell you something. I wasn't sure if she wanted the others to hear it."

"What is it?"

"Summarizing, it's this: Maggie's father is the Russian head of security of a transnational crime ring. I repeated it back to her to make sure I got it right."

She blinked once. Then again.

Agent Clement was right. She was out of her league here. She was just a small-town police chief. Not only that, but she'd just alienated the FBI. She was on her own. In over her head.

"Tell me what she said, exactly. Word for word."

He repeated each one of Kelsey's fragmented sentences, ending with, *Evidence...in office...tell her...Magpie.*

"There's evidence here in her office?"

"That was my interpretation."

Maya glanced around at all the boxes and filing cabinets. For the first time since that gunshot, a tiny bit of hope glimmered. If there was evidence in here somewhere, maybe things weren't hopeless. If she actually found something solid, things would be very different. She wouldn't look like a fool, she'd look like a genius.

"Thanks for passing that along, Rune. I'll take it from here. You go check on Kelsey."

He didn't budge. "Kelsey's stable. I can stay and help you search the office."

"No need. I got this." She heard the edge in her voice and knew it came from stress and fatigue. Agent Clement had gotten to her, and now her pride was at stake. She always did her job to the very best of her ability. That was what Maya Badger was all about—no matter what that smug FBI agent believed.

She could still hear that dismissive sneer in his voice, like a taunt. *You're in over your head.*

Rune frowned, his eyes darkening to a smoky green. "What's going on, Maya?"

"Nothing." Why not tell Rune how the agent had talked to her? How he'd shaken her confidence? Pointed out her mistake? Rune would be sympathetic and supportive, like always.

But she couldn't. She was too used to handling all the slings and arrows of her job on her own.

"This is my job," she said stubbornly. "It's my responsibility. I just can't take a chance with this. We're potentially talking about *transnational criminals.* Their lawyers will jump on any little mistake."

"You won't make a mistake."

"I already did. I shouldn't have brought you all out here. Now Kelsey's injured."

She turned away from him to hide how terrible it felt to say that out loud. She *had* made a mistake, and the only way to make up for it was to move the investigation forward.

"Kelsey also got to meet her daughter. I don't think she's complaining."

Maya stood on her tiptoes to reach a box at the top of one of the stacks, then plopped it on the floor. "Listen, I need to get to work. Keep an eye on Kelsey. Let me know if her condition changes."

He was quiet for so long that she glanced over her shoulder at him. From the expression on his face, he saw right through her. He knew exactly what was going on.

"You're shutting me out."

"I'm just trying to do my job."

"So you're shutting me out *and* not admitting it."

She felt her temper rise. "I'm the police chief and I have responsibilities. Just because we slept together doesn't change that. Don't get it all twisted, Rune."

Almost invisibly, he flinched. She hadn't meant to sound so harsh, but those old walls were sliding up and locking into place. Click.

"Got it." His voice tight, his shoulders hunched, he stepped toward the door. "Do you want this open or closed?"

"Closed."

"Of course."

She detected a hint of irony in his voice, but ignored it. She had a room full of files to search through.

At the door, Rune stopped. "You've already proven yourself, Maya. To the town, to everyone who knows you. Was there something in that phone call—"

"I don't want to talk about it, Rune. I'm busy."

She kept her gaze focused on the box, which she'd just opened. File upon file, with color-coded labels, stared back at her.

Tension sang in the air between them. "I guess there's nothing you need, then." He gave one more glance around the office with its piles of boxes. "Good luck with your search. Like Kelsey said, she's quite a magpie."

And then he was gone.

For a while she sorted through the files almost blindly.

Once again, her holiday curse had struck. Not only had this whole trip gone disastrously wrong, but now she'd pushed Rune away. She hadn't meant to.

Or had she?

Her walls had gone up so fast, she hadn't even noticed. But why?

Rune hadn't done anything wrong. Hell, he was a hero. He'd used his own body as a cushion and a shield for Kelsey. Then he'd treated her wound. This wasn't about Rune.

It was about *her*. She'd screwed up and she couldn't live with being bad at her job. She'd let Kelsey down. She'd let *herself* down. Nothing would feel right unless she fixed this.

Focus on your job. She had to find that evidence and save her fricking self-respect.

Rune's last words came filtering back to her. *She said she was a magpie.* That was a weirdly self-deprecating thing to say in a moment of crisis like that. Maybe she'd been referring to Maggie. That made more sense.

Or maybe the "magpie" was a clue.

Slowly she rose to her feet and scanned stacks of boxes. They were all labelled by year. Maybe the year of Maggie's birth was where she'd put the file?

Four boxes fell into that year. She took them down and sorted through them one by one. Receipts, bookings, all the normal workings of the lodge. Nothing more.

When there was only one box left to search, her phone dinged and she answered it. Ethan was on the line. "An air ambulance just landed. They said there's some weather coming in, so they want to go ahead and take Kelsey now, quickly. Do you want to come out?"

"Be right there."

She hurried out to the great room, where she spotted a man in a thick blue canvas flight suit. Dan Stone, one of the most experienced medevac pilots who served the Misty Bay Hospital. Kelsey was already on a gurney, and had woken up enough to whisper something to Rune, who was covering her with a blanket. Maggie hovered nearby, looking anxious, while Cara stayed close to her for support.

Dan straightened up to greet Maya.

"Hi Dan. Is it just you tonight?" she asked the pilot.

"No, there's two of us. Tom's getting things ready inside the bird. We knew Rune was here to help out."

"Good, I wouldn't want anyone handling a night flight alone. Did you land out front?"

"Yes, we got the word about that."

"Any trouble?"

"All quiet, except for the wind picking up." He turned to Rune. "I got it from here, man. Tom'll help me load her in. You all stay cozy inside. Temperature's dropping with that cold front."

"Fly safe," Maya told him. "Make sure you let us know when you've landed at the hospital."

"Ten-four. Merry Christmas to you all."

Everyone chorused well wishes back to him as he trundled toward the front door with the gurney.

Maya glanced over at Rune, but he didn't look her way. Awkward. Uncomfortable. *Crap*. Some Merry Christmas this was going to be.

Maya decided to go back to her file search. Knowing that Kelsey was on her way to the hospital took a load off her mind. She settled back into the office to look through the last box that was marked with Maggie's year of birth.

Nothing.

Damn it. She sat back on the floor, so frustrated she could scream. Maybe the magpie reference had nothing to do with the files. Maybe it was just Kelsey rambling about her long-lost daughter.

A sudden bird call made her startle, until she realized it came from one of those wall clocks with a different bird for each hour.

"Shh," she told it, irritated. "I've got enough on my mind without any damn bird tweets. Like the fact that I probably ruined my relationship." As she scowled at the clock, she noticed that one of the birds, at three o'clock, was a magpie. Magpies had kind of a *screech* call, so hopefully she'd be done by three.

Wait.

Slowly she stood and walked over to the wall clock. She reached up and eased it away from its mount. And there, taped to the back of the clock, was a small thumb drive.

Chills swept through her. This had to be it.

Just to confirm, she crossed to Kelsey's computer and turned it on, but discovered that the drive required a password. Magpie? Could it be that easy?

Sure enough, the thumb drive opened. It held a single folder. She clicked on it and a series of files populated the screen. She opened the first one. It contained a list of names and dates. Some of the names were Russian, some were American. She recognized one of them—he was the CEO of a well-known bank.

Holy shit. It was a visitor log of people Kelsey must have deemed suspicious.

Her stomach in knots—she could barely believe this was real —she tucked the drive into her pocket. All these years, Maggie's mother had been a magpie herself, collecting and gathering bits of evidence against a dangerous criminal ring that was personally threatening her. The woman's courage was incredible.

Carefully, she put all the boxes back where they'd been.

Closing the door behind her, she went back to the living room, where Rune was tending to the fire in the woodstove. Maggie and Cara were crouched by a shelf of games, arguing about which one they should play. Alastair and Ethan were nowhere to be seen.

"They both went to bed," Rune explained before she could ask. She checked her phone with a frown. Still no word from the medevac. Maybe the weather had slowed them down.

Cara and Maggie jumped to their feet. She blinked at the two teenagers in their matching Lost Harbor High hoodies. How could they still have so much energy after a day like today?

"Can we make hot fudge sundaes?" Cara asked eagerly. "We waited to ask you, because Rune says you might need a treat."

"Sure, why not? I won't sleep until we hear from the air ambulance anyway."

The two girls skipped off toward the kitchen.

Rune met her gaze, no trace of their argument on his face. "Did you find anything?"

"I did." She showed him the USB file and grinned.

"Nice going." He beamed back at her, pride radiating from him, withholding nothing even though she'd pushed him away.

"It was all Kelsey," she corrected. "I just followed her clues."

"Clues are one thing. Figuring out what they mean is

another. That's all you, babe." A wide smile spread to his eyes. She loved that smile. Basking in its sunshiny warmth, she felt alive and adored. That smile was everything.

And she'd pushed him away. Why had she done that?

"Rune," she began, "about before—"

"It's all right." He raised his hand to stop her. "I know how important your job is to you. I appreciate that. I admire you for it. You're Maya Badass Badger and I'm proud of you."

"Maya Badass Badger?" She wrinkled her forehead.

"Doesn't anyone call you that? They should. I'm going to see about that when we get back."

"You're so silly." A smile quivered on her lips. She hadn't ruined things between them. He was still Rune. He was still here for her, just like he'd said. He wasn't going to be scared away by her walls going up.

And she hadn't even told him that he wasn't all alone on that "I love you" ledge.

Maybe it was time she joined him there. "You were right about me shutting you out. I was doing that, but I don't want to. Rune, the thing is—"

But before she could get another word out, Maggie came racing back into the great room. "He took Cara! She's gone!"

CHAPTER THIRTY-THREE

"Who did? Who?" Rune was already running toward the kitchen. He heard Maya and Maggie keeping pace behind him.

"I don't know. He looked like the other man. From the helicopter."

"Dan Stone?"

"No, it wasn't him."

As they all burst into the kitchen, Maya was already pulling out her phone. Rune ran to the mudroom and saw the taillights of a snow machine disappearing into the dark shadows of the road that led to the airstrip.

He grabbed his parka from the coat pegs. Boots. He needed his boots. "We have to go after them," he said tightly. "It's got to be the stalker."

The bastard had snuck up on them here at the end of nowhere. Had he hijacked the helicopter? How the hell...?

Maya ended her call. "The medevac hasn't made it back to the hospital yet. The only thing I can think is that they put down at the landing strip after they left the lodge, then the other guy—

Tom, isn't that what Dan said? He came back for Cara. We have to go after them."

From the mudroom, he tossed Maya's coat to her, and grabbed Maggie's as well.

As Maya pulled on her parka, she asked Maggie, "What exactly happened? Moment by moment."

"A man knocked on the door of the kitchen. I saw he had on a flight suit just like the pilot so I let him in. I thought maybe he forgot something and had to come back. Then he just grabbed Cara and dragged her out of the kitchen. I didn't have my knife with me. I think it's in my coat." She searched through the pockets of the coat Rune had just thrown to her.

"It's not your fault, Maggie," Maya told her. "Where the hell is Dan Stone?"

"Don't know, but I have a bad feeling. Let's go." Rune slammed his feet into his boots and ran into the biting cold.

Wind whipped him in the face. The storm was still coming on strong. The stalker couldn't be allowed to take off with Cara. Even beyond everything else, it was too dangerous to fly. He spotted a snow machine parked a few yards away and ran toward it.

Beyond the snow machine, in the direction of the front entrance, he spotted a dark lump in the snow. His heart sank. The pilot? He ran over to the figure and sure enough, it was Dan Stone, unconscious and bleeding from the head. Stalker Chad must have knocked him out and stolen the helicopter. Damn it, he should have insisted on helping Stone load the gurney.

"Maya," he shouted. "It's the pilot. Looks bad."

Maya took one look and yanked out her phone again. "Ethan, we need your help right away. Get Alastair too. The medevac pilot's out here in the snow near the front entrance. Cara's been kidnapped and we're heading to the airstrip."

Maya jerked her head at him and they all dashed to the snow

machine. She jumped on and kicked it into gear. Rune swung in next to her. "I should have checked the other guy out," she said tightly.

"*I* should have fucking checked him out. She's my sister." This was his fault. He hadn't given a second thought to the other man in the helicopter because he'd been too preoccupied with Maya's rejection. He'd been busy wrestling his emotions back in line. Lecturing himself for falling so hard for a woman who didn't feel the same.

Face it, he'd let down his guard—and now Cara was in the hands of a madman.

Maggie was barely onboard before Maya opened the throttle and surged forward.

"I already alerted the tower at the Lost Harbor airport," Maya told him over the roar of the machine. "They'll get the word out. I don't think he'll get far."

Rune held on tight as they rattled onto the road that led to the airstrip. At this speed, the headlong trip felt like a fast ride down an icy luge. The wind chill went right through to the bone. The headlights lit up only a hazy slice of the space in front of them. Everything else—the forests, the road, the sky—was dark and ominous.

The stalker must have hiked back to the lodge from the airstrip after he'd landed the helicopter—putting all that rugged military training to use. Then he must have waited until he saw an opportunity to grab Cara.

Up ahead, the little red lights of the snow machine shone like demon eyes. A cold rage filled Rune. His life had been completely disrupted by that demented man. And now he had Cara in his grasp, and Rune had no fucks left to give. He'd tear the man's head off if he got the chance.

Maya must have sensed his state of mind, because she put a hand on his thigh. "Let me handle this, all right?"

He didn't answer.

"Trust me. Promise me you won't do something reckless. Don't make me arrest you. I have a ban on dating people I might have to arrest."

He cast her a sideways glance, because right now, he couldn't guarantee anything. She caught his eye and held it for a moment, even though they were hurtling down the road as fast as the machine would go. Surprisingly, it wasn't the stern police chief expression he saw on her face. Nor was it the hands-off look he'd seen in Kelsey's office.

It was something deeper and more intimate. Rich with secret meaning.

But he couldn't think about that right now. All that mattered was Cara.

"Eyes on the road," he told her gruffly.

As soon as they sped onto the airstrip, he caught sight of the medevac helicopter perched on the runway. Thank God. It was still here. Cara was still here. They still had time. Barely. Maybe.

Yes, there she is.

He spotted a man in a flight suit dragging Cara across the runway from the snow machine he'd ditched.

"Take the wheel," Maya muttered. He leaned across her to grab it, while she pulled out her gun.

"Police!" she shouted as they careened toward the chopper. "Let her go!"

"I have a gun too," he yelled. "Stay back. Stop where you are."

Maya took her foot off the pedal and they slowed to a stop. He and Maya both jumped off the machine. "Stay here, Maggie," Maya told her in a low voice. "Crouch down, don't give him a target."

Still aiming her gun at the stalker, she took a step forward. She'd positioned the snow machine so its headlights illuminated the scene before them; man in coveralls, shivering blonde Cara without a coat, helicopter poised for departure.

So *this* was the stalker. This thirty-something guy with the bleached buzz cut and the manic air about him. Even if Rune had seen him back at the lodge, he wouldn't have recognized him from the single blurry photo he had. Cara had described him as having long brown hair, not a blond buzz cut.

"This won't work," she called to him. "We've already alerted authorities all through Alaska. You won't get far. Let her go."

"Fuck you all. We're meant to be together. It's God's will."

"If it's God's will, why is she fighting so much?" Rune demanded. "She doesn't want this."

"Let me go!" Cara cried. "I don't want to go with you."

"Shut up." He crushed his arm around her windpipe to stop her from talking. "The man decides. The woman does what the man says."

"I'm not even a grown woman! I'm just a teenager."

"That's the right age."

Rune would have been revolted if he wasn't so scared.

Maya switched the direction of her gun hand so she was pointing it at the helicopter's engine. "I can't let you leave with her. I'll put a hole in your tank first."

"Yeah, and risk blowing up your friend on the gurney inside?" He dragged Cara another step forward, even though she was executing her best rag-doll, dig-in-her-heels resistance.

Fuck. *Kelsey.* What was he going to do with her once he'd taken off? Use her as leverage? As a hostage? Dump her overboard? If he was going to dump her, he already would have. She was more useful as a hostage.

An idea formed in his head. If he could just get onto that helicopter...

"You better take me too," he told the stalker. "You're going to need a better hostage. Kelsey's critically injured, and everyone knows you won't hurt my sister."

"Bullshit. It's a through and through."

"I treated her. She has an underlying medical condition that could complicate things. You weren't there for the transfer, but she woke up and told us about it. Me and Dan Stone. But you knocked him out before he could tell you, didn't he?"

"You're lying."

"I'm not. She has a platelet disorder."

Maya was staring at him in astonishment. He hadn't told her about the conversation either; there hadn't been a chance. Kelsey had woken up just briefly and whispered more confessions to him.

He took another step forward, his hands raised in a surrender gesture. "Take me too, man. She's going to need medical help."

"No fucking way."

"If she dies it'll be on you. You're already in deep shit with this kidnapping. You're going to have to offload your hostage at some point. You can leave me with her."

He didn't know if his arguments were working, but at least the bastard wasn't choking Cara quite so hard.

After a long pause, the stalker swung his gun and aimed it right at Rune's heart. "I'll fucking shoot you if you do one thing I didn't tell you to."

"I won't," Rune promised. "You're the boss."

Cara gave a sob of fear through the chokehold on her throat. The stalker gestured with his gun for Rune to step forward.

But as he started to comply, Maya stepped into his path, blocking his way. She planted herself in front of him.

"No," she said firmly, in full badass police chief mode. "No one is getting on that helicopter. Especially not Rune. I need him here."

"Maya," he hissed. "Just let me—"

She lifted her hand to cut him off. "If you want him, you're going to have to shoot the Lost Harbor police chief."

"*You?*" He spat on the ground. "Why shouldn't I just shoot you?"

"You're ex-military, right? Do you really want to put shooting a law enforcement officer on your record?"

"Females shouldn't be cops."

"You're entitled to your opinion. But you're not entitled to shoot me without paying for it. And believe me, you'll pay. I have my phone recording right now. Everything we say is being fed back to the station. They probably have it on blast. The best thing you can do right now is put down your gun and let Cara go. That's your only way out of this."

Her voice was so authoritative, so naturally commanding and full of moral righteousness and good sense, that Rune couldn't imagine anyone not paying attention. Even this demented misogynistic creep was listening.

He gestured at Rune with his weapon. "What do you need him for? Is he your *sex toy*?" He leered, clearly trying to rattle Maya.

"No. As a matter of fact, he's the man I love," she said simply. "Rune is my best friend and the only man I can imagine spending my life with. I love him. And here's the thing about *females*. We fight for the ones we love."

Rune would have thought she was just doing her best to throw the stalker off kilter—except for the ring of deep truth in her words.

She *loved* him. His heart filled up with so much happiness he almost forgot where they were. Maya Badass Badger loved him and was willing to stand between him and a bullet.

Too bad she'd waited until she was facing an armed lunatic to tell him—but he'd take it.

"Took you long enough," he murmured, so low only she could

hear. Her shoulders, squared off and braced for action, quivered slightly. She'd heard him.

"So, what's it going to be?" she called to the stalker. "Time's running out. Tick-tock. I've gotta say, your plan was pretty brilliant. What'd you do, get a job with the medevac crew so you could skulk around town?" For some reason, she'd suddenly gotten chatty. It was very unlike her, but she must have a reason. "You knew Cara was coming out here, didn't you? When you heard about the injury, you saw your opportunity. I'll give you credit for—"

A dark figure ducked under the helicopter and jumped onto the stalker's back.

A knife flashed in the beam of the headlights.

Maggie latched herself to the stalker's back as she plunged the knife into his gun arm.

"Go, Cara!" she screamed.

CHAPTER THIRTY-FOUR

The man howled in pain and shook Maggie off his back, while Cara tore herself away from his chokehold. She ran toward Rune. He caught her against him and held her tight for a brief, powerful moment, then shoved her behind him.

The stalker whirled toward Maggie, who'd landed on her back on the snowy pavement. She was clutching her ankle in pain.

"Touch her and I'll fucking shoot," yelled Maya, leaving no room for doubt that she would. He backed away and transferred his gun into his left hand. Maggie's knife protruded from his right arm, blood seeping into the cloth of his blue coveralls.

The stalker kept his gun trained on Maggie as he used his wounded arm to open the helicopter door and hoist himself onboard. It must have hurt like fire, but he showed no visible sign of it. Military experience, for sure.

With the helicopter in his possession, he had a ride out of here. He was going to disappear, and the whole cycle would start all over again. Rune and Cara would have to leave Lost Harbor, just when Maya had finally confessed that she loved him.

He looked desperately at Maya. Wasn't there something she could do to keep him here?

"You won't get far," Maya called to him confidently. "Everyone's going to be looking for you. You should really stop right there and let us treat that wound."

"And arrest me? Fuck that."

He pulled the hatch closed and a second later the blades stirred into motion. If only Maya could shoot the gas tank. But no way would she do that, not with Kelsey onboard.

As the helicopter lifted into the air, Maya lowered her weapon and ran to Maggie's side. "Are you all right, Maggie? Rune, come look at her ankle."

Cara dashed ahead of him toward her fallen friend. Rune followed at a run.

"He's getting away!" Maggie cried. "He has my mother!"

"Don't worry, wherever he touches down he'll be arrested. I've already called it in," Maya reassured her. "There's nowhere for him to go."

Rune crouched in the snow next to the girl. "Which ankle, Maggie?"

"My right—"

Just then the *crack* of a gunshot from the trees made them all look up. The helicopter was still in its ascent over the forest, like a giant moth heading for the sky. It shuddered, then flames ripped from its belly. It veered to the right, then to the left, then plunged into a spiraling fall toward the trees.

"No!" screamed Maggie. "My mother!'

Maya wrapped her arms around the sobbing girl, while Cara flung herself on Maggie's other side and huddled over her.

Rune watched in stunned awe as the flaming helicopter disappeared into the forest. A second later flames and black smoke rose into the sky.

"It's setting the trees on fire," Rune shouted. "We need to go."

"The fire won't get far," Maya said. "Too much snow." She didn't move from where she was, holding Maggie while she sobbed.

Cara stroked Maggie's arm, tears falling down her cheeks as well. Even though she'd nearly been kidnapped, right now her only concern was Maggie. His little sister was such a sweetheart. She deserved so much better than to be chased around the country by a stalker.

Movement at the edge of the runway caught his attention. Someone was limping out of the woods. Another gunman? He couldn't take a chance on that, so he grabbed Maya's weapon and leaped to his feet.

He marched toward the figure. "Who's there? Drop your weapon."

"It's me," came a female voice, so weak and thready he could barely hear it.

Kelsey.

He put the safety back on the gun and tucked it into his coat pocket, then ran toward her. As soon as he reached her, she collapsed into his arms.

"I got you. You're okay."

Heaving her into a fireman's carry, he headed back toward the others. "It's Kelsey," he called. "She's alive. She wasn't on the chopper."

Maggie scrambled to her feet. "Mother?"

"I'm okay," Kelsey managed as Rune came up alongside them. "I woke up again when the helicopter took off. I was in there alone with him. The pilot was gone. He was ranting about going back for Torrey. I didn't know what he meant, he just sounded nuts. When he landed again, I climbed out and hid in the woods. I would have come to the lodge but I was getting too woozy. I just had to get out of sight. I think I passed out again, until the sound of the helicopter woke me up."

Maggie cuddled her mother's hand against her cheek. "First I thought you were kidnapped. Then I thought you were dead. And that's just today!"

"I'm sorry, Magpie. I'm so sorry. I'm fine." Kelsey stroked the girl's hair as tears froze on her cheeks. "Cold, but fine. We're going to be okay. But we should get back to the lodge. I might be going hypothermic."

"Agree," said Rune. He could feel the tremors still shaking her body. "The sooner the better."

He headed for the closest snow machine, staggering into the wind. Maggie limped alongside him, keeping tabs on Kelsey. Cara kept close to Maggie, while Maya ran toward the snow machine the stalker had driven to the airstrip.

Rune got Kelsey settled into the back of the snow machine. Maggie squeezed in next to her and wrapped her arms around her. Sharing body heat, good.

As he straightened up, Maya came zipping alongside in the other snow machine. Frost clung to her curly eyelashes and the wool of her hat, but she looked exhilarated and just stunningly, heart-stoppingly beautiful.

"Have you noticed that there haven't been anymore gunshots from the woods?" Rune asked. "Any chance whoever shot the helicopter got a taste of instant karma?"

Maya smiled wryly. "Strange things do happen in Lost Souls Wilderness."

"That they do," Kelsey agreed from the back of the snow machine. "The stories I could tell..."

"And I want to hear every single one that relates to this crime ring," Maya said. "Later. Around a fire, with some hot cocoa and a tape recorder. Cara, hop in with me. Rune can take Kelsey and Maggie."

"Can I try driving?" Cara asked her hopefully.

Rune grinned with a kind of full-bodied relief. If she could ask that question, it meant that she was already recovering from nearly getting kidnapped.

Maya caught his eye. In the glow of the snow machine's headlights, their dark honey shine stopped his breath for a moment. "Is this what I have to get used to now? Life with a teenager?"

His heart turned over, then righted itself again. The entire world of cold and windy darkness instantly transformed into pure sunshine and joy. He knew what she was saying: they were going to be together.

"Yup. For better or worse," he said. "Think you can handle it, Chief?"

She revved the snow machine and blew him a kiss. "Watch me."

CHAPTER THIRTY-FIVE

Christmas

MAYA CURLED up with Rune on the loveseat next to the Aurora Lodge's woodstove. A fire crackled cozily behind the smoked glass. The firelight sparked deep garnet glints in her glass of merlot. Outside, the snow fell steadily, as it had been for the past few days, ever since Ben had brought the rest of the group to the lodge.

Their Christmas feast had just ended, and they were all in various stages of food coma. Jessica lay stretched on the thick pile carpet, her back propped between Ethan's knees while he toyed with her coppery hair. Kate sat on the couch with her legs draped across Darius' lap.

Maggie and Cara and Dylan played Uno at one of the inlaid mahogany card tables nearby. Dylan and Maggie had made up enough to carry on a civil conversation, although he kept nervously asking if she'd found her knife yet. It had last been seen in Cara's stalker's arm, before the helicopter crashed.

For the past few days, Maya and a few others had been strapping on snowshoes and skis and searching the crash site for evidence of survivors or victims. They'd found the stalker's remains. Maya had hired Ben to fly the Piper Cub to the Anchorage FBI office with a DNA sample. They'd identified him and notified his next of kin.

His name wasn't Chad after all; it was Dale Nestor. He'd been dishonorably discharged from the Army due to misconduct overseas. After that he'd bounced around from job to job, gotten addicted to meth, gone in and out of rehab, gone through a bitter divorce. At rock bottom, he'd walked into a café in Montana and set eyes on Cara. She'd smiled at him—innocent and kind—and he'd become obsessed. In his delusional state, he saw her as some kind of angel meant only for him.

All of that information had been gleaned from a manifesto that he'd left with Boris Clancy, of all people. Dale Nestor had threatened him *and* his chickens if he said a word to anyone before Dale left Lost Harbor. Clearly, Dale had an abuser's eye for vulnerable people.

When Boris heard about the crash, he brought the manifesto to Sergeant Hollister, who'd scanned it and emailed it to Maya at the lodge. Reading it through, Maya came to the conclusion that he hadn't expected to survive kidnapping Cara—and he intended her to go down with him.

Thank God that hadn't happened. A Christmas miracle.

Unfortunately, instant karma hadn't claimed the sniper after all. But the fire caused by the helicopter crash had helped them discover a hidden bunker in the forest—the hideout for the people surveilling the lodge. Enough evidence had survived the flames to connect it to the transnational ring that Kelsey had told her about.

The ring she'd spent the last few years gathering evidence against. All of it was now in the hands of federal authorities.

Calling Agent Clement about the thumb drive loaded with names and dates and photos had been one of the most satisfying moments of Maya's life.

The investigation had already led to the identification and arrest of the man who'd shot down Alastair's sister's plane. He was cooperating with the FBI; that was how it worked when the rats started fleeing the ship. So was Edgar Murchison, now that the ring was busted. He'd revealed all sorts of information and allowed them to piece together a cohesive timeline regarding Maggie.

Alastair padded in from the kitchen in the cozy slippers Kelsey had lent him. He carried a tray of gooey fudge brownies straight from the oven and a stack of glasses. Close behind him came Kelsey with a pitcher of something steamy and smelling of nutmeg and rum.

Despite her limp, she smiled brightly from behind her horn-rimmed glasses. To Maya, she seemed like a new woman, now that the threat had been lifted. "God, it feels good to be mobile again. Makes me want to celebrate. Who's up for eggnog?"

A general chorus of agreement swept through the drowsy group. Maggie and Cara jumped up to help Kelsey pour out glasses of eggnog and distribute them.

"Yes, you can have some," Rune told Cara before she could even pester him. "We have some toasts to make here, so get ready."

As soon as everyone had a glass in hand, Rune raised his up high. "This is for Maya, who's about to get the biggest freaking commendation the LHPD has ever had. An international money-laundering operation, whew boy. That's a big deal. Apparently the head of the entire FBI is going to call her and personally thank her for her brilliance and hard work."

Everyone raised their glasses, while Maya shook her head, fighting back a smile. "I owe it to Kelsey. She's the one who kept logs of everyone who came through here. With photos and every other detail they need to prosecute."

She lifted her glass to Kelsey, who gave a modest bow. "Yes, but I didn't feel safe enough to do anything with it. But you kept at it. You deserve this, Maya. Congratulations."

"Hear hear." They all drank from their glasses. The rich, creamy drink slid down her throat and warmed her to the core.

Or maybe that was the pride and joy radiating from Rune. He really was the ultimate supportive dude. How had she gotten so lucky?

"So this place was kind of a criminal secret clubhouse, is that it?" Jessica asked from her cozy spot between Ethan's knees.

"More or less. It's remote, but close enough to Russia that it's possible to fly a private plane across the border," Maya explained. "When there was a need for face-to-face meetings between their contacts here, this was the spot they chose. And sometimes cash or documents had to be smuggled out, so they'd use the cove out by Far Point."

"So that's why they shot my float plane?" Jessica asked, just as indignant about that crime as ever.

"The lake you chose to land on was a little too close to their smuggling route."

Ethan lifted his glass. "A moment of silence for Jessica's late lamented plane. A noble death, never to be forgotten."

"She'll live in our hearts forever," Kate murmured as they all drank again.

Ethan continued, turning to Alastair. "Should we toast to you finally getting your answers?"

"I'll take a moment of silence for Caroline and Tony instead. It seems Kelsey's ex—"

"Belnikov, and 'ex' is overstating it," Kelsey cut in. "It was a fling. Apparently the reason he came here fifteen years ago was to scope out the lodge."

"The organization wanted to expand into Alaska, and establish a cell here," Maya explained.

"We had our fling and I got pregnant," said Kelsey. "He went back to Russia, but he'd already recruited spies here. He found out about Maggie and my plans to give her to the Berensons."

Alastair picked up the story. "He was still in Russia, but he wanted his kid, so he paid a couple to kidnap Maggie before my sister could pick her up. The ransom was a smokescreen."

"So they were flying to pay a ransom that wasn't needed?"

"Right. Belnikov didn't want loose ends, so he ordered their plane shot down."

Kelsey dropped her head and stared into her eggnog. "I'm so sorry. I had no idea who Belnikov was and what was going on. I had medical issues and I was a scared kid. I thought I was doing the right thing for my baby *and* for your sister—"

"Good God, it wasn't your fault." Alastair hovered his hand over her, as if he wanted to touch her. But he didn't. "These people are ruthless."

Maggie came over and perched on the arm of Kelsey's chair, listening avidly. She'd heard the story already, but clearly was still fascinated. "Then what happened? After I was kidnapped?"

"Internal power struggle," Maya explained. "It happens a lot in criminal enterprises like this. A rival faction planned to grab you from the couple Belnikov had sent and use you as leverage against him. They sent the trapper, Edgar Murchison, after you. He tracked down the couple, drowned them in a lake, and claimed you. But then he never got any more instructions. By that point, Belnikov had survived the challenge and come out on top. But he didn't know where you were."

"So the trapper just kept me?"

"He just kept you. Belnikov was killed a few years later. He died before he ever found you, I'm sorry to say."

"I'm not sorry," Maggie said flatly. "At least I have one good parent now. I didn't have any before."

She tilted her blond head to rest it on top of Kelsey's dark one. Even though Maggie had her Russian father's coloring, Maya could see the resemblance between her and her mother. Both of them were survivors, tough and direct and blunt.

"Keep going," Jessica urged. "All of that happened fifteen years ago. What about now?"

Maya got up to fill her glass with more eggnog, then settled back under Rune's welcoming arm. "After Belnikov died, the other faction regained power. In the meantime, private air travel across the Alaska-Russia border had been reinstated. That made it even easier to access the lodge. The organization decided to activate Belnikov's original plan. So they came back over the border and contacted Murchison. They discovered that you were alive, Maggie. They decided they could make use of you as a way to gain control of Kelsey, who was now the manager of the lodge. Murchison insisted on keeping you—"

"Because I did all the work," said Maggie.

"Yup." Maya treated herself to another swallow of soothing eggnog. It was so disturbing to think of what had been going on here in this pristine wilderness. "So they came up with the plan to provide photos that would keep Kelsey scared out of her wits for your safety."

"That's so creepy," Cara exclaimed. She and Dylan had abandoned their game and were hanging on every word of this tale.

"Very creepy, but it worked," Kelsey said briskly. "To a point. I turned a blind eye to all the meetings, all the things I overheard. After the sheriff deputized me I was even more useful to them because law enforcement trusted me. But after Maggie ran away to Lost Harbor, things changed. They knew they couldn't control me anymore. That's why they eventually decided to get rid of me."

Maggie went pale as the snow outside. "So it's my fault they shot you?"

"Of course not!" Kelsey exclaimed, throwing her arms around her. "They're criminals. They do criminal things."

"And there's another thing we found out," Maya added. "They had big plans to expand. They were looking into drug trafficking, human trafficking, art smuggling. Maggie, if you hadn't run away when you did, things would have gotten so much worse. It would have spilled over into Lost Harbor. We all owe you a lot —both of you." Maya lifted her glass. "To the intrepid Lewis women."

Cheers rang out as everyone toasted.

After the noise died down, Kelsey settled back in her chair. A bit sadly, she looked over at Alastair. "We still haven't had that moment of silence for Caroline and Anthony Berenson. They were a wonderful couple who wanted the best for Maggie. I hope that wherever they are, they're happy knowing my Magpie is safe and healthy."

Everyone bowed their heads for a moment of silent communion. With her eyes closed, Maya felt Rune settle his warm hand on her thigh. As always, his touch made her heart sing and her blood heat.

How many times had the two of them said "I love you" over the past few days? Over and over again. At random moments. In bed. First thing in the morning. In the middle of the night, as they turned to each other with sleepy desire. While snowshoeing through the woods.

As they all lifted their heads, Darius spoke for the first time. "My turn for a toast." He pulled out his phone and cleared his throat. "Chief, brace yourself."

"Uh oh." Maya took a quick fortifying sip of her eggnog. Rune interlaced his fingers with hers.

"I got a message today from the combined fire and police department. Nate Prudhoe coordinated it."

"Isn't he in Connecticut?"

"He's dedicated. And maybe a little bored. Ready?"

She nodded, and Darius clicked a button on his phone.

Nate's recorded voice carried into the room. "Maya Badger, all of us here in the Lost Harbor law enforcement community would like to say that we're extremely proud of our chief. Not only because you're an outstanding officer and, you know, a *superstar.*"

Oh God. Where was this going? She glanced at Rune and caught the same amused alarm on his face.

Nate went on. "But because you're...well, maybe someone else can put it better." Her own voice took the place of his. Her *recorded* voice. "*Rune is my best friend and the only man I can imagine spending my life with. I love him. And here's the thing about females. We fight for the ones we love.*"

Nate's voice came back. "That's you, Maya. You fight for this town. And now you just gave your department the best Christmas present ever. All this time, they've been nosing into your business and you finally just let it all hang out."

A deep well of laughter bubbled up inside her. So much for walls. Did she mind? It turned out—not really.

"Also, there's no need to be embarrassed. We're all very happy for you and Rune. You deserve it. Oh, one more thing. We've postponed the Winter Parade until you get back. It just wouldn't be the same without you. We already got the plastic snowman out of storage. Merry Christmas, Chief."

Laughing so hard that tears sprang to her eyes, she shook her head at her fellow chief. "I should have known. They're going to pay. Every single damn one of them. Especially Nate."

Darius put away his phone with a grin. "Sorry, Maya. There was no stopping it."

Next to him, Kate's mouth was hanging open, her dark eyes wild with curiosity. "When did you say all that, Maya? It's beautiful! It's so Team Romance, I'm stunned."

"It happened on the airstrip, during that standoff with Cara's stalker. What better moment?"

Rune tightened his arm around her and snuggled her against his side. "Any moment would have been good, but that one was definitely unforgettable." He nuzzled her cheek, making her shiver.

"But how did they hear it?" Kate gestured to Darius' phone. "How did they get it on tape?"

"It's an app on my phone. I have it programmed to transmit to the station if I hit record. I wanted them to know what was going on with the stalker."

"All hail the chief." Kate raised her glass. "Well done."

Of course Maya loved getting props for her work; respect for her abilities had always been her catnip. But it turned out that it felt even better when she was glued to the side of the man she loved.

Rune stirred next to her and lifted his glass of eggnog. "I don't want to toast a death, but I do want to toast the fact that Cara and I can actually choose where we live. We can stay in one place finally. We talked about it and we're making it official. We choose here. Not *here* here, don't worry, Kelsey," he added lightly. "We choose Lost Harbor."

"Amen to that...hear, hear...woohoo!" This toast was the most enthusiastic of all. Glasses chimed against each other, creamy liquid sloshed. The aroma of sugar and rum mingled with the wood smoke and the spruce.

Through her happiness, Maya made a mental note to circle back to Mrs. Holt to explain who had been sleeping in her barn. She and Boris had both encountered Cara's stalker without knowing it, as had Dan Stone and everyone else at the medevac company. For weeks, he'd been infiltrating her town. Infuriating.

Jessica got up to add another piece of wood to the fire. "So, Maya. You solved all these crimes. You captured a nasty stalker, you busted an international crime ring, yada yada yada. But you know what impresses me the most?" She brushed her hands on her purple leggings and dropped into Ethan's lap.

"What's that?"

"That you didn't mind telling the entire Lost Harbor police department how you felt about Rune. That's so—not *un*-Maya, exactly. Just...a really great side of Maya." She blew a kiss at her and Rune.

Maya looked up at Rune, who smiled down at her with that certain look in those smoky eyes that she knew exactly how to interpret. It meant they'd be taking advantage of the lodge's luxurious bedding and outstanding soundproofing later that night.

Goddamn, she loved this man. Her friend, her playmate, her supporter, her lover. Her future.

She turned back to the warm circle of her friends and gave a jaunty shrug. "I guess that's what happens when you..." She paused, drawing it out for drama.

"When you what?"

Maya nestled even more closely into the warm heaven of Rune's embrace. "That's what happens when you fall head over heels."

Jessica clapped her hands. "I called it! Head over heels for the holidays, isn't that what I said?"

Rune laughed, a warm rumble vibrating his body.

"Oh no." Maya corrected. "Not just for the holidays. Head over heels. Period. End of story."

Though she knew, with joy flowing through her heart, that it was just the beginning.

THANK you so much for reading! In the mood for more Lost Harbor holiday romance? Please enjoy a free holiday short called Stormy with a Chance of Christmas.

Join Jennifer's newsletter for an exclusive 'thank you' gift download— and be the first to hear about new books, sales, and VIP giveaways!

For more Lost Harbor romance, find the entire series here.

ABOUT THE AUTHOR

Jennifer Bernard is a *USA Today* bestselling author of contemporary romance. Her books have been called "an irresistible reading experience" full of "quick wit and sizzling love scenes." A graduate of Harvard and former news promo producer, she left big city life in Los Angeles for true love in Alaska, where she now lives with her husband and stepdaughters. She still hasn't adjusted to the cold, so most often she can be found cuddling with her laptop and a cup of tea. No stranger to book success, she also writes erotic novellas under a naughty secret name that she's happy to share with the curious. You can learn more about Jennifer and her books at JenniferBernard.net. Make sure to sign up for her newsletter for new releases, fresh exclusive content, sales alerts and giveaways.

Connect with Jennifer online:
JenniferBernard.net
Jen@JenniferBernard.net

ALSO BY JENNIFER BERNARD

Lost Harbor, Alaska

Mine Until Moonrise

Yours Since Yesterday ~ Book 2

Seduced by Snowfall ~ Book 3

Wicked in Winter ~ Book 4

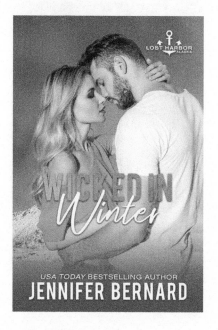

Naughty All Night ~ Book 5

Love at First Light ~ Book 6

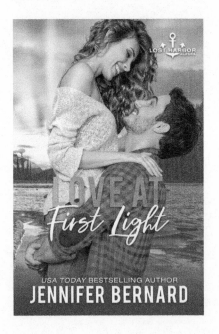

The Rockwell Legacy

The Rebel ~ Book 1

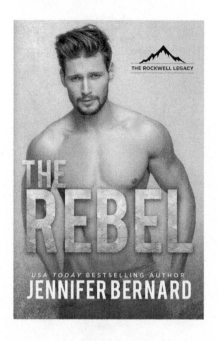

The Rogue ~ Book 2

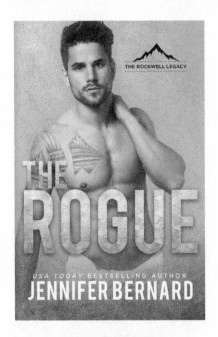

The Renegade ~ Book 3

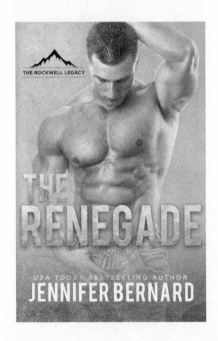

The Runaway ~ Book 4

The Rock ~ Book 5

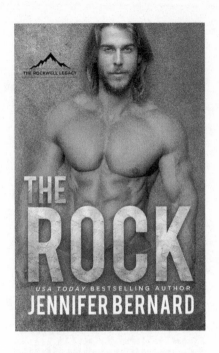

Jupiter Point ~ The Hotshots

Jupiter Point ~ The Knight Brothers

The Bachelor Firemen of San Gabriel Series

Love Between the Bases Series

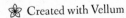